BOOK OF YUGA

Francis Chapman

www.francis-chapman.com

Gilgamesh Publishing, 2020

For Leah, who believed

CHAPTER ONE

Consciousness, that most precious of gifts, returns to me. Dreams of blood-soaked sand recede into beads of perspiration and a hammering heart. I am awake. I feel ancient regret, a truth that I can taste in the back of my throat. A mistake that is my constant companion. My only companion.

I chose one man's suffering over an entire world of souls.

For three decades humanity was my joy, an intoxicating blend of love, imperfection, and introspection. For two millennia, it has been my burden. Regret is a weight on the human soul, and I have broken beneath it.

I swallow the regret, knowing that it will resurface. But for now, I am present.

There is a persistent hum, something mechanical and threatening, though whether it comes from within, or without, I cannot say. My throat is sore, perhaps from the thirst, for they no longer bother to give me drink. My arms and legs are shackled to a steel table, pressed cold and hard against my naked back.

How long has it been?

I... do not know. Being human is so very limiting.

Had I the Kishar Stone...

Futile human thoughts race through the labyrinth of my human mind. I open my eyes.

A young man watches me. I have no idea how long he has been in the room. He dominates the space with his imposing frame. His shiny dark skin is almost onyx, and his eyes are joyless and jaundiced. He wears casual clothes, but the pin on his charcoal grey cardigan, a ruby red eye cast in gold, marks him as one of the Igigi, a soldier of the Annunaki. All who wear the eye have wilfully damaged their soul beyond repair. They are to be feared, even by me.

The Igigi watches me carefully from the end of the table, then he starts pacing the room, his eyes scanning my prison for distances and details. The cell is nearly as ancient as I. Artificial light from long tubes affixed to the ceiling grants no warmth to the faded brickwork, in which carvings of unblinking eyes and perpetually poised serpents lurk. The Igigi turns first to the medical equipment, then to the black prism which hosts a single point of menacing red light. The prism is pointed at me, and I feel instinctively that it is yet another eye, watching me.

I study my naked body, which has scarred, but not aged. My skin, once deep bronze, is paler now. I have lost more muscle tone and weight. My forearms are blighted by scars, a story of needles and theft.

They steal my blood.

I taste the bitterness in my soul.

Having completed his study of the room, the Igigi turns his attention to me once more. He looks expectant, as though it were I that had visited him.

His ploy works. Of course it does, how long has it been since I last had a conversation? A year? A decade? My humanity demands some point of connection, even with an Igigi. Even with a man whose soul has been fractured into a thousand shards.

'Who are you?' I venture in English. I do not know what his native tongue is, but English is the language of the Annunaki, and by extension, the Igigi that serve them. The man does not respond.

'Who are you?' I ask again. My voice cracks, it is rusty with disuse.

'Do you not know me?' The Igigi answers with a lyrical fluidity at odds with my voice, and my expectations.

He stares at me with intrusive intensity, and I am reminded of the malevolent prism in my periphery. I study his face, and in doing so, I *see.* I see that he does, truly, expect me to know him. But I do not. I have never seen this face before, and enough divinity remains to me that I can perceive the shape of a man's soul, if not the content. But this man's soul is shattered. Perhaps I knew its shape, once.

'I...' I begin, but falter, not knowing what to say.

Some god I am.

'Me-igrah ramah le-vira amiqtah,' the Igigi prompts in flawless Aramaic. Words that belong to someone I loved. Andrea Bar-Jonah. A man I thought lost, though I never quite abandoned all hope. Could it be him? Parts of my mind have rusted away entirely.

'Andrea?'

'Is that all you have to say?' the man hisses, his voice stripped of all humanity.

Sorrow envelopes me as I move beyond seeing, and I *realise.* Andrea. It is Andrea. I feel the depth of the waters I have shared with this man, no matter how far apart we have drifted. The stories of our lives are irreversibly entangled. We do not share roots of origin, but *essence.* He is part of me, and I am part of him.

I feel every bit of the pain and anguish that my human existence has caused Andrea. I see what Andrea has done, the sacrifices he has made. He has fractured his soul *for me.* He has damned himself, knowingly, willingly. And I am sorry. I had no choice in the matter, but I am sorry nonetheless.

'Andrea, I am so sorry, old friend.' The message carries directly from my soul to my tongue.

'Yes,' a hint of satisfaction breaks Andrea's solemn surface. 'I have come, as you no doubt realise, to get you out.'

'I thought you had become one of them, Andrea. Perhaps you are,' I glance at the eye of the Igigi pinned to his chest. 'Can you get me out? Why would you do this? Hasten your damnation.'

'I am damned in this life too, as *you* taught us, and believe it or not, it was a lesson I absorbed.'

'But what about Symeon?' I ask.

'We can do nothing to change the fact of our damnation,' he spits. '*That* was a lesson I had to learn for myself. So I can, and will get you out. But something like this takes planning, it takes people, and it takes doing the kind of things you never would. That the Ophanim never would. But with an Igigi? With me? Yes, it can be done.'

But at what cost? And what of the cost of my remaining captive? Every path leads to suffering.

'And soon. Which, I appreciate, is a relative term.' And something warm, something *Andrea* is there. For a fleeting moment, the shards of his soul are assembled into something almost whole. And it is beautiful, and tragic.

Andrea turns on his heel, and walks out of the cell. The door slams shut, and I am sucked back into darkness.

CHAPTER TWO

Gethsemane, Jerusalem
Month of Elul, 29 AD

Symeon's mind betrayed his soul. There is no betrayal greater, nor more commonplace.

-BOOK OF YESHUA

Symeon Bar-Jonah grabbed the wineskin from Andrea and drank with relish, testament to his thirst. The light was dying, but the heat remained oppressive and close, and Symeon's sweat-stained shawl clung to his torso. The heat was making Symeon irritable, as he had been so often of late, but he could feel the wine start to take effect, and his mind unclenched, just a little. He leaned back, dropped his arms to the soft grassy ground to support him, and sighed. In but a few weeks the grass would be dry and scratchy, as it had been one year before, during the group's very first meeting in this small, sparse garden at the foot of the Mount of Olives.

It was best to get a little drunk before Yeshua started teaching. Symeon thought back to that meeting, when Yeshua had said as much. At the time, Symeon had been unsure if Yeshua had been joking or not. Yeshua was a master of in-scrutability. It came of being a god, Symeon supposed. Yeshua was a master of just about everything, everything except ka'ab, though whether Yeshua lost on purpose, was truly inept in the art of deceit, or the dice were against him, Symeon could not say.

"It's ka'ab, Symeon," Yeshua had laughed when Symeon pressed him, "it doesn't *mean* anything."

Whether or not Yeshua had been joking about the wine, Netanel had taken Yeshua at his word, and at their second meeting had produced a bulging wineskin from his cloak with a dramatic flourish that had bought cheers from most of the group. Yohanan and Yacob Bar-Zebedee had cheered loudest, and longest. The "Sons of Thunder", so-named for their temperaments, were partial to a drink. They were childhood friends of Yeshua, and he was more forgiving of their frailties and failings, or at least, less likely to notice them. A resentment that Symeon, a latecomer to the group, had tried, unsuccessfully, to banish.

Yeshua had laughed when Yacob and Yohanan had cheered, and when the wineskin had been hesitantly passed to him by Levi, he had drunk deeply.

"Save some for me," Andrea, Symeon's brother by blood, had shouted, only half-joking, as Yeshua proceeded to quaff the entire remaining contents of the skin.

"Oh, ye of little faith."

Yeshua's stern impression of the High-Priest Caiaphas would have been unnerving in its accuracy if Symeon had been unaware of his extraordinary capacity for vocal and facial mimicry.

"Is it not written that a man should not thirst, for the Lord God will provide?" Netanel had chimed in, his own impression capturing something of the High-Priest's manner in its exaggerated pomposity, but falling far short of Yeshua's high standards.

Yeshua had rolled the honey-coloured, rough-cut Kishar Stone across his knuckles, then winked at Andrea and passed him the wineskin, full once more. No-one had been particularly surprised. They'd all seen Yeshua work miracles. Symeon remembered the mischief in Yeshua's eyes just before he had lifted his head to the skies and let out a colossal belch. Everyone had

laughed, Symeon included. Then Yeshua had turned to Taddai
Bar-Yacob with mock-seriousness.

"Perhaps they should call *me* Son of Thunder," he had said.

And timid Taddai had roared with laughter. Netanel,
loathe as he was to let someone get the last word, even a god,
had nudged Taddai then.

"Wait till you hear him fart."

Symeon had laughed so hard with the others that tears
had welled up in his eyes and he had felt as if his chest would
burst.

He had been happier then. What had changed? Nothing,
truly. The changes had taken place outside of this circle, but
nevertheless, *because* of it. Yeshua had encouraged them to relinquish their wealth, and donate it to those most in need. And
so Symeon's wealth now belonged to lepers, men and women
without work, families, or hope. Symeon had been happy to do
so, at the time. Even after Maryam had left, informing Symeon
that she had never intended to marry into poverty, Symeon had
not resented it. *She* had a deficiency of the soul.

It wasn't so much the fact of his losses, as the lack of *recognition* from the group that so rankled. None but Symeon had run
successful businesses and accrued wealth of any significance.
None had lost their wives to ruinous generosity. He should have
been the shining example to the others, the man that Yeshua
pointed to.

*This man, this man gave up everything, his is the selflessness
we aspire to.*

Yeshua had chosen him, as he had chosen the others, it
was true. But only because of Andrea's introduction. Only because of Andrea's persistence, his older brother had served as an
advocate for Symeon's inclusion as a chosen messenger.

*Andrea has always looked out for me, from the earliest age. He
fought Bertel when he set upon me with a stick, even though Bertel
was five years his senior, almost a man grown. He drew Bertel's wrath
and took the beating meant for me. It was I who stole the sweet-bread,
and he took the beating anyway.*

A polite cough interrupted his train of thought.

'Any chance of you passing the wine before the sun sets?' Judah asked.

The wineskin had become tradition, and their meetings were as much merrymaking as they were instruction. Symeon passed the wineskin to Judah.

Amazing. The secrets of the universe are open to us, and Tau'ma has dribbled wine down his front, while Yacob and Yohanan are throwing olives at each other. The chosen few.

Yeshua cleared his throat. 'Shall we begin, before Yacob and Yohanan's olive skirmish escalates to all-out war?'

The younger members of the group chuckled. The Sons of Thunder laughed, settling into still, cross-legged positions to indicate readiness, Yohanan next to Yeshua. The group were sat in a circle, but all attention was directed towards Yeshua. He was on the perimeter with the rest of them, yet also at the very centre. Yeshua could do that. They were hidden, as best anyone could hide in this garden, by waist-high hibiscus. An olive tree, twice the height of a man, stood protectively over Yeshua, it's branches outstretched as though shielding him.

'Who is going to summarise our last meeting for us?' Yeshua's eyes danced around the circle, and settled on Filippos who was sat next to Judah on Symeon's right, directly opposite Yeshua. 'How about... Filippos?'

Something dangerous flashed in the eyes of Symeon, and the merest hint of a scowl appeared on his face. It was always Filippos. Filippos or Judah. Why did Yeshua favour them so? Judah was smart, in a provincial, uneducated, kind of way, but he could not hold a candle to Symeon's intellect. The man spoke no Hebrew and only limited Greek.

How can a man have an understanding of metaphysics without a firm grasp of Greek?

Filippos, on the other hand, spoke excellent Greek, it being his father's native tongue, but he was glib and superficial. A man of semantics, not metaphysics or ontology. A man incapable of questioning the true nature of things.

'I believe,' Filippos began in a mock-formal tone, 'that in the early stages of our previous gathering Yohanan drank far too much, as usual, and after some goading by Yacob, boasted that he could pull a plough better than an ox, and that he would prove this at the next meeting.' He looked around the circle. 'I see neither ox nor plough present, and motion therefore that henceforth the boasts of Yohanan be treated with the contempt they deserve.'

Yohanan laughed. 'Seconded.' His response was laden with exaggerated humility.

Yeshua smiled. This was the structure of their meetings, humour and wine preceded metaphysics. Metaphysics preceded dinner.

'Subsequently, Levi, our illustrious monetary magician,' Filippos continued, enjoying himself, 'promised that he would use his considerable knowledge and skill to help me prove more financially prudent. In this he failed.'

'Not for lack of trying,' Levi protested, palms open in a display of innocence, 'but you have to *have* coin in the first place to be careful with it.'

'Levi's efforts were laudable,' Filippos conceded, 'but as Yeshua once said, "some fell on stony ground."'

Filippos was referencing a phrase Yeshua had used when describing a flaw in his design. It was a moment that would live with Symeon for as long as he walked the earth, for it was the moment that he had learned that his god was imperfect. It seemed obvious now, inevitable and natural, but at the time it had felt like blasphemy, even though the words came from Yeshua's own mouth.

Infrequently, Yeshua had informed them, a spark of the divine would enter and animate a corporeal form inside the womb, give it life, but fail to take root. "Spiritless beings" Yeshua had called those born under such circumstances, without souls. They were primitive creatures, as Symeon understood it, driven only by base instincts and material self-interest, but with human intelligence. Mistakes. Dangerous mistakes.

'I motion, therefore,' Filippos continued, wearing a self-satisfied smirk, 'that one of my good friends lend me the paltry sum of ten denarii as an alternative solution to my financial struggles.'

Symeon laughed with the others, but there was a hint of bitterness. The thirteen of them combined could put up a few denarii at best, having given away most of their wealth to the most desperate and needy in the Lower City. Ten denarii would have been a paltry sum to Symeon once, before he had lost Maryam.

It was the silver that she loved, not me.

'Nobody?' Filippos looked around the circle in mock astonishment. 'You tight-fisted bastards.' He paused, allowing the group to chuckle. 'After these more important matters, Yeshua, having what I consider to be the unfair advantage of divinity, continued his irritating habit of sharing a few minor details about the nature of the world and our souls.'

Pompous ass.

Yeshua chuckled, 'I can go over them again, if you like?'

'No need, no need,' Filippos replied, waving a dismissive hand, 'as unimportant and uninteresting as they were, I happen to have a superb memory. You may not all recall, he told us quite some ago, and he has only mentioned it a few hundred times since, but Yeshua is a god.' Filippos paused. 'Was a god? Is a god?' Helpless, Filippos turned to Yeshua, who merely shrugged, as though the question was unimportant.

'In him burns the One Whole Consciousness. There are others like him, other gods who minister to other worlds, so far away that they cannot be seen in our sky, even on the clearest of nights. As for us mortals, we are granted a small fraction of this same consciousness, a tiny spark of divinity. We call this spark the soul. When we die, if we have not damaged our soul irreparably, we either return to the one whole consciousness, or if the spark remains restless, burn again in a new body, a new incarnation of the soul.'

Filippos sniffed. 'If the life we have lived *has* done major harm, the soul is unable to ever rejoin the One Whole Consciousness without contaminating it. Such souls are...' he looked downward, searching for the right words. '... severed, cast into oblivion. Nothingness. *Damnation.* Yeshua has chosen us to carry his message, down the years and across the Earth, to prevent more souls from being lost. Yeshua, of course, names this responsibility a "burden", I think I speak for the rest of us when I name it "privilege."'

There's some brown on your nose there, Filippos.

'And this, he informed us, was to be the subject of today's discussion. When we leave the comfort of this place, when we travel to the furthest reaches of the planet. What will be our message? What do we tell those who steal, rape, and murder? How are such men taught *kindness*?'

'Right,' said Yeshua casually, 'that pretty much sums it up. Although...' he grinned, the joy in his smile undiminished for the missing tooth, 'I'd have liked a few more words describing my power and glory. "Almighty", "holy", "magnificent," that kind of thing.'

'"Annoying" is the word that springs to mind right now,' Filippos replied, earning smiles.

The group was close-knit, bonded by ties of humour, friendship, laughter and love. At the beginning, Symeon had felt this kinship keenly, but recently he felt apart from it.

'So,' Yeshua addressed the group at large, 'what *is* our message?'

Filippos was itching to answer, Symeon could see, straining against the compulsion to open his mouth once more. To his credit, he did not. Instead, and to Symeon's surprise, it was Levi who spoke. Levi, who was an unerringly practical man, and generally reserved in nature.

'The damage we do to others,' he said cautiously, as though worried about making a mistake, 'is damage we do to ourselves. I think we should *show* them. Show them that we are connected to the One Whole Consciousness, even as we are apart from it. Show them the power of meditation, of self-healing by connecting with the One Whole Consciousness. Show them the joy of kindness. Our message should be one of *example,* the example of a life filled with joy. With the power to perform miracles, if it is still your intention to grant that to us Yeshua, the eyes of the world will be turned to us anyhow. Let us make examples of our lives.'

Yeshua nodded thoughtfully.

'We must explain, too,' Judah added, 'we must explain that too often people's minds fight against the will of their souls, inhibit them from happiness, from mending. Explain how they can overcome the instincts that lead to suffering. Explain how overcoming such instincts is not a form of self-denial, but steps taken on the path to joy.'

'We must drive out darkness with light,' Symeon the Zealot cried out.

The other Symeon. Simple Symeon. Yeshua's bluntest instrument.

'Each of you must deliver the message as best you think,' Yeshua said, 'there is no one correct way. You were chosen for your differences, as much as the kindred kindness within your souls. Judah, I chose you for your ability to reveal the truth of someone's soul, with your patience, and insight. Levi, you I chose for precisely the reasons you outlined, your ability to lead by example. Yohanan... I honestly can't think, now, why I chose you. I probably made a mistake.'

Yeshua grinned. Yohanan pretended that he wasn't listening, but the smallest hint of a smile gave him away.

'Why have you chosen no women for our mission?' Little Yacob asked. 'You've given your reasons for choosing each of us for your ministry, but why no women, if the divine spark burns just as brightly in them?'

Little Yacob had the unfortunate habit of just blurting out whatever question popped in to his head. Symeon just about caught his snort of contempt.

The mysteries of the universe laid bare, and Little Yacob wants to know why there are no women here. Fool.

'Why, are you missing female company?' Yeshua joked.

Little Yacob shook his head vigorously, and Yeshua burst out laughing. This was how Yeshua taught, by encouraging questions. The trick to understanding, true understanding that transcended Filippos' superficial thinking, was asking the right questions. The others might not see it, but how Yeshua judged them, how he ranked them, depended on the questions they asked.

Yacob Bar-Alpheus, known to the group as Little Yacob, though he stood only an inch shorter than Yacob Bar-Zebedee, was one of the youngest in the group, his beard and his mind both fledgling. He was also one of the most naïve.

'Good question,' Yeshua replied

He always says that.

'Why am I here, Yacob?'

'To build a dam to stem the flow of severed souls.' The answer sounded prosaic and profound, even in Yacob's coarse tongue. Symeon suspected that it was a rehearsed response.

Yeshua nodded thoughtfully.

'Yes, too many souls are lost. Each and every lost soul hurts me, fills me with a sorrow and pain you could not even begin to understand. But *which* souls, predominantly, are lost?'

'Souls that rail. The male soul,' Yacob responded with pride.

Well done Yacob, for carrying information in your head for an entire week. Your mental feats astound and amaze.

'You speak truly.'

'Well, you made it obvious.'

Yeshua chuckled. 'Few souls that nurture are lost. The problem is with the soul that rails, and the soul that rails must be the source of the solution. When you head out into the wider world Yacob, what will be *your* message?'

'Do no harm.' The youth's answer was immediate and confident.

A simple answer. A simple boy.

'Indeed. A message from the soul that rails, for the soul that rails. That is why there are no women here. I was also concerned that women, many of them at least, have a certain charm and appeal that... obscures the message.'

'Aye,' Yohanan interrupted, 'if a woman is pretty enough, you often don't hear what they have to say at all.'

'I wonder,' Yeshua replied 'why it is that you remain unmarried?'

Yohanan laughed.

'Yacob,' Yeshua continued, 'there is a reason I took this corporeal form. The message must take precedence.'

'You mean you *chose* the bald-spot, not to mention those eyes, which, by the way, are far too close together?' Netanel asked, with feigned incredulity.

'Well, no,' Yeshua smiled, 'beyond choosing the male form and a sufficiently capacious mind, I left everything else to chance.' He paused, looking serious. 'Though I count myself fortunate to have avoided a nose such as yours Netanel.'

'Aye, hard to avoid a nose like his, it near took my eye out earlier,' quipped Yohanan, who laughed alone at his joke.

'Are souls that rail always found in men, Yeshua?' Tau'ma enquired.

'Not always. As you have learned, my system is imperfect. There are rare mistakes, souls that nurture manifest in male form, and souls that rail manifest in female form.'

Symeon was growing frustrated with discussion of peripheral issues, and so was, atypically, glad when Judah spoke. For all his many faults, Judah could not be accused of a lack of focus.

'Why not carry this message yourself, Yeshua?' asked Judah, stroking his beard thoughtfully. 'The word of a God carries more authority than the word of Judah of Kerioth. There would be no need for soul imprinting, no need for powers.'

Powers and soul imprinting were the reasons they were there. Why question the necessity, when it was what they all yearned for? Symeon was irritated by Yeshua's wide-eyed expression, which seemed to say *particularly good question, Judah.*

'I love being here,' Yeshua answered, 'I have experienced more joy in twenty-nine years as a human being than in the preceding eternity as a god. Truth be told, I had not experienced joy until I became human. It is hard to explain, my brothers, to those who cannot fully comprehend infinity, or immortality, but beauty and joy reside firmly and solely within the realms of the fragile and finite. But as long as I am here, souls cannot return to the One Whole Consciousness. They must, of necessity, return in corporeal form.'

So no soul can be damned, either.

Something seditious stirred deep within Symeon.

'All souls are reincarnated,' Yeshua continued, 'and I am in dereliction of my duty as a god. I cannot remain here, and not suffer from the further sorrow I inflict on settled souls forced to reincarnate. The balance of the world, and the One Whole Consciousness are in jeopardy, should I remain here too long. I must return, and this is why I lay this burden on you.'

'How does soul-imprinting work, exactly?' Levi asked.

At last, information of significance.

Of the whole group, excluding his brother Andrea, Symeon loved Levi best.

Yeshua glanced at Symeon. It was subtle, but Symeon caught it.

'That is something I will be discussing today, but... later,' Yeshua said.

This was unlike Yeshua. Never before had he refused to answer a question there and then. He was unfailingly patient and generous with his knowledge.

He wouldn't hold out on me, *would he?*

Symeon could see that others in the group seemed perplexed. He wanted to put forward the question he was burning to ask, but little Yacob jumped in to the uncomfortable silence with all the grace of a drunk fat man falling into a river.

'When will you leave us, Yeshi?'

Yeshi? You talk to a god, Yacob, you imbecile.

Yeshua's face pouted, his expression that of a child whose favourite toy had been taken away. Sometimes Yeshua could be so infantile.

'Soon. Too soon, I'm loathe to give this up, but we are entering the final stages of preparation for your ministry. Yossef tells me that the Sanhedrin intend to move against me soon, and I intend to let them.'

'Why?' Yohanan shouted, 'why let them?'

'Spectacle,' Yeshua replied calmly, 'an art of great importance, my humanity has taught me. The most important men in the province gathered under one roof, and the opportunity to demonstrate my divinity to each and every one. With their belief, my message will spread further, faster.'

'Careful, Yeshua,' said Judah, 'there will be those who will witness your divinity, and they will fear and resent you for it.'

'I will keep the Kishar Stone with me, my friend. I have nothing to fear. None of us should fear. All of you will have a part to play in the years that follow. But... perhaps not all of you need undergo soul imprinting.'

Aramaic, though ill-suited at times to discussions of higher matters, was a maddeningly subtle language. That a single sentence could have several different meanings, dependant on inflection.

Is he reiterating the choice, or removing it?

The group were silent once more, as they reflected on the path that lay ahead of them. They would be despised, in many quarters. Their message, as simple as it was, threatened to overthrow people of power, people whose positions in life were dependent on the suffering of others. The crickets paid no heed to this period of contemplation, stridulating with the intensity customary to their dusk gatherings.

'Yeshua...' began Yohanan, but Yeshua brought up his hand to silence him.

'I will answer your questions Yohanan, I will. But right now, I think some dinner is in order. Would you and Yacob be kind enough to fetch wood for a fire?'

A bit early for dinner.

'I suppose,' Yohanan grumbled.

'I'll start gutting the fish,' Taddai volunteered eagerly, as though such a job would give him great delight.

'Thank you, Taddai. Symeon, would you walk with me? I need to stretch my legs, and there is something we must discuss.'

Symeon hesitated for just a heartbeat.

'Of... of course.'

CHAPTER THREE

Oxford, England
Month of June, 2024 AD

When the mind reaches maturity, it must be hoped that it is strong enough to support a soul heavy from centuries of suffering. In my experience, it never is.

-BOOK OF YESHUA

'This song, is the absolute bollocks,' Rock pronounced, as the opening drumbeats of New Order's *Blue Monday* reverberated throughout *To Be Square*.

Elliott Ambrose rolled his eyes, an instinctive, almost habitual response to Rock. He needn't look up from the sticky, black and once white chequered floor to ascertain that all his group would be doing likewise. The Andy Warhol inspired garish murals on the walls depicting buxom young women in bold reds, greens and purples, the revolving faux-silver dance floor, *Winds of Change* by Scorpion, both the first and second pitchers of Woo-Woo, Max's Hawaiian shirt, and Rock's own pork pie hat had all been declared "the absolute bollocks."

Elliot couldn't, on this occasion at least, disagree with Rock's assessment. Blue Monday was a song that spoke directly to Elliot's soul, evocative of a sorrow he had no conscious memory of, but nevertheless felt. If ever Elliot were to dance, in public, with witnesses, this would be the time. He didn't though.

'I need a drink. Anyone else want one?'

'*You're* not buying tonight,' Max said, 'I'll grab another pitcher.' Max stood up decisively, a gesture that brooked no arguments.

'Anything but Woo-Woo,' Elliot shouted at his friend, who was starting a polite, skillful slalom through the mass of bodies that obscured Elliot's view of the bar entirely. The acidic, sour remnants of cranberry and vodka pulverised his tongue. It was water that he yearned for, but there was no way he would be allowed anything non-alcoholic without facing a barrage of objections and mockery.

'Time to dance,' Claire said, and stood. She was tall and, with her high heels, stood taller than all of them, save Elliot. She walked off with tipsy feminine grace towards the tight circles of students moving with uncoordinated reckless abandon.

'Yeah, me too,' Rock said excitedly, and trotted off after Claire, a loyal puppy. Rock would never pull Claire, not so long as the acne continued to mark his face, and at twenty-one years of age, it showed no signs of abating. Claire was on the larger side, but her extra weight accentuated her curves, and her soft, symmetrical face, dazzling smile, wit, and confidence meant that she was never short of suitors. Everyone apart from Rock himself knew that his pursuit was futile. But his gentle, confident persistence was to be admired, Elliot supposed.

Many people had questioned why Elliot bothered hanging around with Rock. His cricket teammates couldn't understand it. They all thought Rock a little slow, no match for their sharp wits. Elliot's law class-mates didn't understand it either. The intelligence of University of Oxford law undergraduates at St Peter's College was effortless, and they were scornful of Rock, and his Computer Science degree. Computer Science had lower entry requirements than Law, but Rock had had to study for every waking hour for months to achieve the requisite A level grades for admission.

Even Lucy, Elliot's girlfriend, hadn't understood at first. But Rock was harmless enough that it didn't bother her too much, and after a couple of years of him hanging around, she was now fond of him, Elliot knew, though fonder perhaps in his absence than his presence.

If Elliot was honest with himself, as he was most inclined to be in the midst of the morose, dull, drunkenness he felt at that precise moment, he had questioned it himself too. The heart of the matter was this: Elliot was cool, and Rock was anything but. Elliot's achievements, both academic and sporting, and his social skills had the glamour of effortlessness, while Rock had to grind and toil for everything. Rock came to Oxford with Elliot from Harrow, the public school they had attended together, and Rock had needed Elliot. Elliot had carried Rock socially, but Elliot saw in Rock what others didn't.

If hard work is a talent, Rock might be one of the most talented men alive.

Rock might not have enjoyed the effortless, eloquent intelligence of many of his peers, but he hammered away relentlessly at a problem until he broke through.

Elliot had even tried to persuade Rock to study law with him, when they were both still at Harrow. He knew that Rock would have made an exceptional lawyer. Not, perhaps, the type to schmooze large clients and retire a wealthy man while still shy of fifty. But the type someone would choose if they were smart, and forced to place the balance of their life in someone else's hands. Natural abilities were useful, but diligence and persistence were far better indicators of the likelihood of someone completing a job to a high standard, Elliot had come to realise.

But though no-one but Elliot knew it, Rock would probably end up making more money than those who sneered at him. Elliot was sworn to secrecy on the matter, but he, and he alone, knew that Rock was an extremely gifted computer hacker. Rock called it his "hobby", and never used it to make money. His greatest triumph, Elliot knew, was when he had successfully hacked the Federal Bureau of Investigations website, replacing all the information on the Most Wanted page with a video of 1980s pop star Rick Astley performing *Never Gonna Give You Up*. Though the FBI had removed the video, in the end, they were still none-the-wiser as to who was responsible. One day, though, Elliot would persuade Rock to parlay his skills into well-paying, legitimate, meaningful work. Elliot caught a glimpse of his friend across the dance-floor, his dance moves designed more to amuse Claire than to showcase any coordination and rhythm, which was probably sensible, because he was entirely lacking in both.

Rock was unfailingly generous. This manifested itself materially, which went pretty much unnoticed by the law students who almost invariably came from wealthy backgrounds, or benefited from generous bursaries and scholarships. But more importantly, Rock also expressed a quiet generosity of spirit. Rock allowed others to feel superior to him without resentment, he made those around him feel better, even if it was, sometimes, at his expense.

More than anything, Elliot just liked having Rock around. Not for any particular reason, and even when Rock was being annoying - a common occurrence. This bond, this fraternity, preceded any personality traits or compatibility, it simply was.

When the trumpets heralded the start of Gloria Estefan's *Conga*, Elliot expected Lucy to join the others on the dance floor, but instead, she floated over to the seat Max vacated, her fragile pointed flat shoes seemingly unaffected by the glue of sugary alcohol and filth that covered the floor.

'Hey, you.' She sat flirtatiously, her bare legs swinging over the edge of the chair towards Elliot. With thin, delicate fingers, she swept her fringe from her hazel eyes. Lucy was, and always had been, pixie-like. Petite, and, despite her ferocious legal mind, childish.

'You don't seem like your usual Elliot self.'

Elliot laughed. 'And what's that, my Elliot self?'

'You know, Elliot-like. How you seem to be floating in a happy little bubble, even in Contract seminars with Dr Fuckwit. That *all is well* vibe you give off. What's up? We're supposed to be celebrating your birthday, not mourning your lost youth.'

'I don't know Luce, it just sort of feels like the end of something, you know? Three weeks from now, and we'll be gone. I'll miss this place, everyone. I won't stay in contact with them all, that's just how... life works.'

'Nope, not good enough El.' She put her face to his, and kissed him, her tongue softly parting his lips and finding his.

'Mmmm,' she said as she pulled away, her eyes remaining shut, 'that might be the last time I kiss a twenty-year-old.'

Elliot motioned to his watch. 'Too late for that, it's thirteen minutes past midnight. I was born, as my mother has informed you on no fewer than fifteen thousand occasions, just after midnight.'

Elliot paused, then smiled, as though a delightful and wicked thought had just occurred to him. 'I am officially old enough to apply for my helicopter licence.'

Lucy scowled playfully. She knew Elliot was teasing her about her fear of unchartered flying.

'Do that and I'll break up with you so hard that you'll never love again.'

'Shut up,' said Elliot, and kissed her again.

'Suppose I'll fuck off, shall I?' Max interjected in his best barrister-to-be baritone. How Max had already returned with a full pitcher in such a short time was nothing short of miraculous. Only Claire could rival Max for the ability to navigate a crowded bar and return with alcohol so quickly, and she had the distinct advantage of ample cleavage, a significant portion of which was often on display.

Lucy edged away from Elliot and Max sat down. Rock came slinking back from the dance floor, shoulders slumped in the honesty of defeat.

'Where's Claire?' Lucy asked carefully.

'Dancing with some douchebag,' Rock replied sullenly. No-one pursued the topic.

Uncomfortable with the silence, Elliot poured himself a glass from the pitcher of violently blue cocktail, and took a long sip, carefully limiting the amount of alcohol actually passing his lips. He was feeling really quite ill, he realised. Nauseous. And angry, and scared, and sad. He felt these things, but they weren't quite his, like they belonged to someone else, as if he had just finished watching a film about someone else's life. Nevertheless, he could *feel* them, jealousy in his gut, the taste of spite. And fear, more than anything else. Fear.

What Elliot hadn't told Lucy, perhaps the main reason for his uncharacteristic solemnity, was the decision he had made.

Have I made it? I suppose I have.

His decision didn't fill him with joy. It would, he hoped, bring joy in the end. But for now, he was unable to see beyond the falling dominoes of difficult conversations and feelings of vicarious disappointment for which he would be responsible. Elliot would not be taking up his training contract with *Ott & Dobbs*, one of the most prestigious, and best paying law firms in London. The problem, Elliot came to realise not long after his final exam, was that he had no idea what he actually did want to do with his life. But he knew it wasn't working at *Ott & Dobbs*, and if he started on that path, he might never leave it.

Lucy and Max, visibly disappointed in Elliot's seeming refusal to cheer up, strode off to the dance floor. Elliot knew that this was some kind of protest from Lucy, who often professed the distaste she shared with Elliot for Queen's *Don't Stop Me Now,* which was, unfortunately, gathering pace.

Elliot slumped into his chair. Rock fiddled awkwardly with his phone, clearly uncomfortable at being left alone with Elliot in such an unnaturally dour mood.

Probably playing Sleuth.

A glimpse at the screen confirmed to Elliott that he was right. *Sleuth* was one of the only games Elliot played, but it was highly addictive, and as such, something Elliot, like Rock, only dared play outside of term time. The game was based in the fictional city of Mina, a cartoon metropolis featuring an eccentrically dressed, amoral citizenry and a ludicrously high murder-rate. During the peak of the game's world-wide popularity in the summer of 2023, over 15,000 murders a day were committed. Top hats and canes featured prominently in the wealthier Upper City, while, inexplicably, a large number of murderous clowns were to be found wandering the impoverished Lower City, which Elliot, during his forays into Mina, preferred exploring. Following a murder, the human controlled Sleuths could interview remarkably forthcoming citizens and then (and this was the real skill of the game) track them, unnoticed, hoping to identify inconsistencies in their stories. If an inconsistency and a motive were recorded and verified, *Probable Cause* was awarded, allowing you to break in to the suspect's home where, invariably, the murder weapon could be found.

The great irony of *Sleuth,* Elliot had found, was that high-profile murders were almost never solved, while murdered prostitutes, the homeless, and street orphans were far more likely to receive "justice". Solving the murder of a low-ranking citizen was worth fewer Minara, the currency of Mina, to the sleuth, and so players had a good chance of tracking a suspect without drawing a crowd and alarming the suspect. Solving high profile murders of police, politicians, pop-stars and professional athletes was worth a fortune in Minara, which had such value that it could be exchanged for real-world currencies. But the investigations of high profile murders proved so crowded that large groups of sleuths almost always alerted suspects to their tracking.

'I forgot how much I love that game,' Elliot said wistfully in an attempt to break the awkwardness that persisted, despite Queen's frenetic efforts, 'I should play it again, now exams are over.'

'Yeah man,' Rock said, seizing excitedly on the topic, 'look, this one is an awesome case.'

'Go on...'

'Worth quite a few Minara too, I should reckon, case of a dead homeless guy, at least at first. See this fella right here...'

Rock pointed at the screen, a pixelated cube man boasting a handlebar moustache, flat cap and coral pink cravat stood in line with a paper at *Fagz n' Booz*. This, Elliot knew, must be in the Lower City.

'Well I tracked him, and he did go to chess club in the afternoon, like he said he does every afternoon.'

'Right...' Elliot prompted.

Get to the point, Rock

'But I decided to interview some of the other citizens in the chess club anyway, and it turns out that old flat-cap here joined only two days ago.'

Ha, that is Daniel Theodore Rockett to an absolute tee. No stone unturned.

'Interesting, so what's the motive?' Elliot could see from the flashing *Probable Cause* icon in the bottom left hand corner of the screen that Rock had already determined the motive.

'He's trying to buy the homeless shelter; he wants to build

a casino there. He won't have permission from the city to buy it until there are no homeless people remaining in the shelter. He hasn't just killed one, this is his third, at least! Took me a trip to the planning office and the best part of this afternoon to figure it out.'

'Shit, so he's a serial killer?' Catching a serial killer was worth some serious Minara.

'Yup. Cigarette?'

Elliot didn't smoke very often, only socially. Most often when at night clubs, and particularly when Queen songs were playing.

'Sure.' Elliot stood quickly, then vomited over the floor. Cocktails, bile and half-digested mozzarella sticks hit the floor with force, and spread across the chequered tiles. He straightened himself, and saw one of the bouncers making his way through the crowd towards him. The threat of further vomit burned Elliot's throat. His stomach churned.

'Diborim be-'alma', he cursed. Words he did not recognise in a voice that was barely his.

What the hell was that?

'I need to go home,' Elliot stammered, and Rock took him by the shoulders, and started towards the club's exit.

AΩ

As the vivid images of a dream in which he fled across a desert began to fade, Elliot became aware of aggressive sunshine streaming through the gap in the curtain, applying pressure to his eyelids. Memories of the previous night cycled through his head. The sounds of Queen, Lucy's sulking, vomit hitting the floor.

I made it home, then.

Strange, how the small rented room and the thrown together household of 27 Milton Avenue had become home.

The pillow felt like sun-baked concrete against his fragile head. His jeans chafed against his skin. He was subject to the insistent chirping of birds outside of his window, more unwelcome alarm than peaceful serenade.

'Urghhhhhhhhh,' he groaned.

The Eurasian wren.

How did he know that? Elliot had never taken any interest in ornithology. But this inner voice he did not recognise pressed on, supplying him with information he was sure he had not acquired in his twenty-one years.

Unusual for its polyamorous breeding habits. Generally non-migratory.

Elliot attempted to close his mind. He flipped his pillow and embraced its cold touch.

Misosazai, the Japanese term for wren

Elliot's mind was forced fully open. He *remembered*. The wrens that chirped happily even as he thrust the bokken sword into his gut and sliced that chapter of his soul's journey away. He remembered being Chide Morosuke, four hundred years ago, trained as a youth in the art of Bushido, abandoning his path after his twenty first birthday to fight the battle he had always fought.

It started, of course, with Yossef. And it would always come back to Yossef. More than anyone, more than Chide, more than Kofi, more even than Elliot, he would always be Yossef.

Of course, I could be going mad.

He had been visited by *that* thought every time he came into maturity and recalled who, exactly, he was, and who he had been. It was a thought that availed nothing, changed nothing. If it was madness, it was his madness. Two thousand years of madness weighed heavy on a soul that was too old, too battered. A soul that owed a debt to the entire world.

CHAPTER FOUR

Praetorium of Pontius Pilate, Jerusalem
Month of Nissan, 30 AD

Pilate thought himself a man of great power. But he was a thrall, both to his ego and the machinations of men with lesser titles and greater minds.

-BOOK OF YESHUA

Pontius Pilate was positioned precariously. The prefect of Judea sat at the platform, too close to the edge for his liking. He could not close his giddy mind to the vertical forty-cubit drop to the auditorium floor. He found himself unable to meet the faces staring up from the curved stone benches below him for any length of time. Jewish and Roman alike, the faces lacked the respect and fear they ought to have worn.

Theoretically Pilate could eschew the platform, take any seat he wanted as his own. But he couldn't, not really. Here on the platform he was elevated, with a commanding view of the assembly. The fasces to his left, a statue depicting rods bundled together, and Aquila, the solid gold eagle that saw all, were symbols of his strength, his justice, and his power. Never had it been more important to him that everyone present, everyone in the entire dusty, miserable province it was his misfortune to govern, look up to him, and witness his power.

Pilate was not looking forward to the next case to be

brought before him. It would be theatre, and he did not care for the role that had been scripted for him. It galled him, to act in accordance with the wishes of the Sanhedrin.

He had overplayed his hand, underestimated the strength and resolve of the Jewish faith. On the say so of the Sanhedrin, Jerusalem had rioted in objection to Pilate's attempt to stamp out the absurd and blasphemous practises and rituals of Judaism. The Sanhedrin had known that Rome would frown on instability on the region, would blame the new Prefect. They had created a threat to Pilate's position and standing within the Empire. And so Pilate, unable to crush that threat, was making concessions. This case was one of them. In truth, this was one of the lesser concessions, and Pilate had no interest in the case. But it would prove a visible humiliation, and for that reason, he resented it more than the religious freedoms and political influence he had ceded the Sanhedrin.

Pilate had thought the Sanhedrin manipulators. They had proved to be far, far more dangerous. They were, in fact, *believers*, and insane for it. The Sanhedrin were deluded, drunk on the lies that had fermented in their hearts and minds for centuries.

Monotheism, a ludicrous concept.

The chaos of the world could not be explained by the governance of a single deity. And if there was a sole deity, such a deity was unworthy of worship, or even respect. A despot and narcissist; a divine Tiberius. But Pilate thought such an idea highly unlikely. Judea was a depressing microcosm of the wider world, a tangled web of interests, beliefs, and hatreds. The world only made any kind of sense in the context of divine *conflict*. Now the Sanhedrin felt their delusion to be threatened by a single swindler, one Yeshua of Nazareth. Like all men, rather than accept the truth, they railed against it, fashioned their entire lives into pillars to support the lies they learned from their mothers and fathers.

'Bring in the accused,' Pilate's deep voice boomed across and echoed around the auditorium, drowning the assembly beneath a powerful wave of authority. His was the voice of a military commander, and when he spoke in this echo-chamber, *his* auditorium, it was as if a god made his demands.

The arched doors to the assembly opened. Two legionaries wearing the badge of the bull on their woollen tunics, marking them as members of the Fretensis legion, dragged a beaten, dishevelled figure into the chamber. The soldiers stood erect and resplendent in their gleaming armour. Shining examples of the glory and power of the Empire.

Yeshua was marched past the Roman contingent. Pilate caught the eye of Manius Rufus, and nodded respectfully. The Manius family were powerful players in the slave trade, and Rufus, who had the ear of many senators back in Rome, was a close, and important ally of Pilate's. Next to Rufus was the colourfully dressed and jewellery adorned Falco Flavinnia, who gave Pilate a playful smile. Flavinnia hoped, Pilate knew, to be courted. She, too, had connections in Rome, and it would be a poor decision to shut that particular door. Flavinnia was a widower, and no longer youthful, but she was not without wealth, wit, and a certain mature beauty.

In the very centre of the auditorium, Yeshua of Nazareth was dumped on the floor, a crumpled heap. He rose unsteadily, and glanced nervously at the still and silent figures of the court above and around him.

Pilate was unimpressed. He had been expecting a man like Tavarius, his favoured advisor, a man who had made more of himself. But this man was dressed in rags, he showed no composure, no strength; a wounded sheep in a den of wolves.

Pilate had been hoping for better. He liked swindlers. They took what little they had and made more of it than ordinary men. They manufactured belief, garnered respect and wealth, and commanded servility with nothing more than their imagination and wits. And they were rarely boring. Tavarius of Jericho had been a swindler. Named Eli then, he had travelled Judea, amassing a small fortune selling divine blessings of whatever god or gods gullible local merchants were primed to worship. Eli had been unlucky enough to attempt his ruse on one of Pilate's informants playing the part of a cloth merchant in Hebron.

Pilate saw the first glimpses of Eli's potential shortly before his scheduled trial. Josephus, the captain of his personal guard, reported that the two Fretensis legionaries standing outside of Eli's prison cell, hitherto loyal servants of the Empire, were refusing to remove themselves from the door. Josephus had informed Pilate that the soldiers were willing to die in defence of the man they named "prophet".

"Shall I have them all killed Prefect?" the captain had asked dispassionately in Latin, departing from his usual Greek to show that *he* remained loyal to the Empire, and to Pilate. How very close Pilate had come to saying *yes*. The word had formed in his head, and had he said it aloud, that would have been the end of the matter.

But the word had caught in his throat, and instead Pilate had gone to Eli, irked and intrigued. From inside his cramped, shit-smelling confines, Eli had commanded the two soldiers, *Pilate's* soldiers, to stand aside. Pilate's heckles had been raised, and he had stormed into the cell.

"Do you know who I am?" Pilate had thundered, his voice an expression of the Empire's might.

"Yes, Prefect," Eli had replied, his bent posture obsequious, his face arranged to tell a story of remorse.

Pilate's anger had been punctured.

"I apologise for the scene," Eli had said, "it was not my intention to anger you, or waste your time."

"My time is being wasted now," Pilate had replied, his voice heavy with danger. There had been no questioning inflection in his tone, but Pilate had raised an eyebrow ever so slightly, the merest hint of curiosity and permission to explain.

"It is my sincerest hope that that is not so, Prefect. I required a demonstration. I understand that I have flouted your laws, and in doing so I have done you wrong. Is it not incumbent on a man who has wronged another to make it right?"

Pilate had said nothing.

"I believe, Prefect, that I have no means of righting that wrong, while I remain imprisoned. I needed to show you what I am capable of, what I can do for you." Eli had dipped his head even further to the ground. His posture had bordered on grovelling, and Pilate's anger had remained suppressed, but Eli's words and cadence had been a steady stream of confidence.

"And what is it that you can do, Eli of Jericho?" Pilate had asked, genuinely curious.

"Given my lowly status, any judgement on your governance I could make is unworthy of your consideration. Nevertheless, I feel compelled to say that I have always been mightily impressed by your leadership. It seems to me that you see the ropes, invisible to most, that tether and control people, and are able to manipulate them accordingly. I flatter myself that I have the same qualities, albeit in lesser quantities. It was wrong of me I know, but I borrowed two of your soldiers to show you that I can make them dance. Judea is a large and populous province, Prefect, and there are many ropes. I wanted to show you that I am a lesser puppet master, who could be put to work for your benefit."

Rather than sentencing Eli, or even conducting a trial, Pilate had covertly made the charges, and the money Eli had made, disappear. Eli was granted a new name, employment in the treasury office, and a whipping. Curiosity, more than anything, had been Pilate's motivation for all these decisions.

Tavarius-who-was-Eli became responsible for a new, innovative and highly effective taxation system based on door-to-door collections. Incomes soared across the entire province. Tavarius' brilliance had seen him invited into Pilate's inner circle, and now he stood highest amongst them as his most trusted, and useful, political confidante.

Pilate saw none of Tavarius' potential in this pitiful man beneath him.

'Yeshua of Nazareth,' Pilate began, 'you have been brought here today so that I might pass judgement on crimes of which you have been accused, do you understand this?'

Yeshua nodded, exposing the full extent of the bald spot that dominated his scalp. Evandrus, Pilate's Praetor, had informed him that Yeshua was only thirty years of age, a full decade and a half younger than himself. Yet with the man's sallow skin, skeletal figure, irregular yellow teeth, and distinct lack of vertical bearing, he might have been Pilate's senior. Pilate was greying at the temples, a source of angst, but he remained a robust and, so his concubines told him, attractive man. This Yeshua was neither, and it fuelled Pilate's contempt.

'Are you content for the trial to be conducted in Greek?' Pilate asked, 'Aramaic can be used if you would prefer?'

The man met Pilate's eyes, there was an intensity to his stare that unnerved Pilate a little. For the first time, Pilate saw something that wasn't merely pathetic.

'I have no problem with the trial being conducted in Greek.'

Pilate was impressed. Though Yeshua did retain a flavour of rural Galilean in his accent, his speech was fluent and precise. This was not the broken, second-language Greek of Judean tradesmen.

'You speak Greek well, for a tradesman.'

'Thank you. You speak Greek well, for a Roman.' The man's tone was not mocking, but there was a hint of laughter.

Someone in the ranks of the Sanhedrin sniggered. Pilate swallowed his anger and chuckled. The auditorium chuckled uneasily along with him.

Better they think I have given them permission to chuckle than to have them snigger rebelliously.

Pilate looked over Yeshua to the audience beyond him.

'Who stands to accuse this man of breaking the law of Judea, Province of the Empire?' The words were ritualistic, and Pilate savoured them.

One of the Sanhedrin front-benchers stood. Slowly. At least eighty years in age, the man was stooped and boasted a smoke-grey beard that was impressive in length, but looked thin, and dirty.

'I do,' the old man croaked slowly, 'Boaz Ben-Jada. May it please the Prefect that I have been chosen to represent the Sanhedrin in the charges that I will lay against Yeshua of Nazareth.'

Pilate wondered why the Sanhedrin would choose this man to represent them. Perhaps they thought the court would conflate old age with wisdom. More likely they simply didn't care, knew the outcome guaranteed and were giving this old bastard his moment in the sun.

'And what are these charges, Boaz Ben-Jada?'

'I accuse the man you see before you of breaking the law of Judea on three counts. Firstly, that he claimed to be a king, undermining the rightful authority of the Prefect of Judea, which is to say, yourself'. The old man looked expectantly at Pilate.

Thanks for the clarification, you shrivelled prune.

Pilate nodded. 'Continue.'

'This falls under the charge of fomenting non-aggressive rebellion. Secondly, that he forbade citizens of Judea from paying their taxes, which likewise falls under the charge of fomenting non-aggressive rebellion. Thirdly that he incited the citizenry of Jerusalem to riot, which falls under the charge of fomenting violent rebellion.'

Pilate caught himself from gasping, but it was a close-run thing. The audacity of it. Pilate stared at the faces of the Sanhedrin front-benchers. No smirks were visible, but he could sense them, lurking just beneath the surface.

The bastards, they would pass off their own crimes, knowing I have to play along. There will come a time when they will pay for this insolence.

It was cleverly done. If Yeshua were convicted, and he would be, Pilate could not, at some future date when his power was more secure, hold the Sanhedrin accountable for the Jerusalem riots. It was also an automatic death sentence for Yeshua, there was no discretion in the case of fomenting violent rebellion.

'Praetor,' Pilate boomed, taking temporary solace in the script, 'what are the sentences if guilt is determined for these charges?'

Evandrus, Pilate's praetor, was of an age with Boaz Ben-Jada, but despite his advanced years he held himself straight when he rose on the dais below Pilate. His voice carried clearly throughout the auditorium.

'If found guilty of the charges of fomenting non-aggressive rebellion, the accused will be scourged and imprisoned for a period of time commensurate with the seriousness of the offence at the discretion of the Prefect, or Praetor who serves as his representative.' Evandrus paused, ever the dramatist.

Usually, Pilate enjoyed political theatre, but usually he was the puppet master.

'If found guilty of the charge of fomenting violent rebellion,' Evandrus continued, 'the accused will be sentenced to death, with the method of execution determined by the Prefect, or Praetor who serves as his representative.'

Beneath him, Yeshua squirmed.

Worm.

'Accuser,' Pilate directed his words and steely gaze at Boaz Ben-Jada, 'do you have evidence to bring before us?'

'I do, Prefect,' the old man replied solemnly.

'Yeshua,' said Pilate, turning his attention to the Nazarene, who stood a little straighter now, but still struck a pitiable sight, 'do you have anything to say before the accuser presents his evidence?'

'Two things,' Yeshua said, 'firstly, that Boaz Ben-Jada is an ass, producing nothing but meaningless braying... and foul odours.' Gone, for a moment, was the fear, and the man's eyes suddenly twinkled with youthful rebellion.

Several of the Sanhedrin front-benchers, and many others in the audience turned to Pilate, anticipating a rebuke. This irritated Pilate, and no rebuke was forthcoming. Instead, Pilate smiled, and nodded sagely.

'And the second?'

'That I forsake my right to defend myself from these charges, and instead pass that responsibility to an advocate.'

'And who will this advocate be?'

'Yossef Bar-Elias of Arimathea.'

A tall, young man sat close to the Sanhedrin front-benchers stood up hesitantly, betraying obvious nerves. He was pale for a Judean, his hair light brown. The man's clothes conveyed wealth, his cloak appeared new and was dyed a deep crimson. As he stood, the contempt, but not surprise, of near the entire Sanhedrin was directed towards him, with hissing, muttering, and murderous stares.

'Very well,' Pilate consented, 'Yossef of Arimathea, do you have anything to say before the accuser presents his evidence?'

'I do, Prefect.' The advocate fidgeted, and looked at his feet. This was not a man who was accustomed to public speaking. Nevertheless, when he spoke, he did so with a clarity and eloquence that suggested good breeding and education.

'I would have the assembly and Prefect made aware that the Sanhedrin, for whom Boaz Ben-Jada speaks and of which, until recently, I counted myself a proud member...'

At this, there was much murmuring and tutting from the Sanhedrin. One front-bencher turned around and spat in Yossef's direction, a large glob of thick, tawny phlegm that landed just short of Yossef's sandals.

They spit in my court. One day they will pay for their insolence.

Yossef was clearly perturbed and paused. 'Are... are not acting in the interests of protecting the law of this land. They are not even acting in the interests of protecting the laws of their own faith. May it please the Prefect to know that yesterday Yeshua of Nazareth was tried by a full complement of the Sanhedrin, presided over by High-Priest Caiaphas himself. The charges presented were not those presented to the Prefect here today.'

'This is not unheard of,' Pilate replied, 'nor do I see the relevance of this. The findings of the Sanhedrin hold no weight in my court.'

Pilate said this last part slowly and deliberately, taking

pleasure in the implications. The scowls that appeared on the faces in the ranks of the Sanhedrin pleased him greatly.

Such a shame Caiaphas isn't here.

'What is unheard of, in Jewish law, Prefect, is such a trial being conducted during Passover. It is also unprecedented that Yeshua should be denied representation before the Sanhedrin. My own request to represent him was denied. Further, it is against the principles of Jewish law that the accused was asked an incriminating question. I inform the assembly of these things because...'

'And what incriminating question was he asked, advocate?' Pilate interjected. He had been impressed by Yossef prior to this point, but this admission, surely, was an error. Perhaps Yeshua had been unwise in his choice of advocate, eloquent though he was.

'Yeshua was asked if he was the King of the Jews.'

'He did not deny it,' one of the Sanhedrin shouted from the back.

Pilate paused, then smiled.

'Boaz Ben-Jada did not deny being an ass when so named.'

There was cruel, cackling laughter from the Roman contingent. Pilate basked in the glow of his own wit.

'Are we to conclude that Boaz Ben-Jada believes himself an ass?'

More laughter. Boaz Ben-Jada scowled, the trenches of wrinkles in his forehead deepened. Pilate turned to Yeshua, who was scratching at his bald spot and looking uneasy.

'Are you the King of the Jews, Yeshua of Nazareth?'

Yeshua looked Pilate directly in the eye. 'No.'

Boaz Ben-Jada cleared his throat, an unpleasant mixture

of phlegm and death. 'I have evidence from one who heard him make such a proclamation, Prefect.'

Yeshua looked down, whether at his torn sandals and blood-caked toes, or the pearl-white marble floor, Pilate could not say. He looked up again, his face set with resolve.

'We shall hear it then,' Pilate snapped.

'I call on the witness testimony of one Hananiah,' Boaz said, 'a well-digger who has lived his whole life here in Jerusalem.'

At the back of the hall, a man stood. Studying the man's thin, pointy features, and awkward scurry to the floor, Pilate was reminded of a rat. The well-digger stood in front of Pilate and Evandrus the Praetor, with the Sanhedrin and the rest of the assembly to his back. He edged away from Yeshua, clearly keen to put as much distance between himself and the Nazarene as possible.

'You are Hananiah, the well-digger?' Pilate enquired.

'I am, Prefect.'

'Very well, provide your testimony.'

'Well, it happened like this, Prefect.' The man's Greek was halting, but he made himself understood. 'In the month of Nissan, I was drinking wine, in a tavern down in the Lower City...'

Drinking piss more like, no wine purchased in the Lower City could accurately be called "wine".

'...and Yeshua the Nazarene entered the tavern, surrounded by followers.'

'You knew him, then?' Pilate asked.

'No, Prefect, that was the first time I ever saw him.'

'Continue.'

'He bought drinks for everyone in the tavern, me included. This made him very popular, and after the second round some men began to chant his name. Yesh-ua, Yesh-ua, Yesh-ua.'

The well-digger's feeble chant echoed awkwardly around the chamber.

'This must have gone to his head, because he jumped up on one of the tables, grabbed a sword from one of his followers and said "I am Yeshua Bar-Yossef, King of the Jews. As I have provided for you, so will I provide for all of Israel. But first we must take it back."'

Pilate could see Boaz Ben-Jada smiling.

You think this subtle, old man? Clever? You and your ilk would be crushed on the political battlefields of Rome in your very first skirmish.

Pilate sighed. He didn't mean to, but he did.

'What happened then, well-digger?'

'His followers, and some of the tavern's revellers took up a new chant. "Hail, King of the Jews."' This time he only spoke the words, and did not chant.

'Yeshua led them out into the streets, and, well, you know the riots?'

Pilate scowled.

'It all started with him,' Hananiah explained, 'Roman soldiers, noble peace-keepers,' he glanced nervously at the legionaries astride Yeshua, 'were attacked with stones and sticks, the houses of tax collectors were burned.'

'Did you witness all of this, well-digger?'

'I did, Prefect.'

'You followed Yeshua out into the streets?'

'I did Prefect, but didn't do any rioting.' Hananiah sounded panicked now, and spoke hurriedly, 'I was concerned was all, and I reported what I saw that night to the authorities.'

'Who, in particular, did you report to?'

'I don't remember his name Prefect. He was a Jewish priest.'

Pilate let this unsatisfactory answer hang in the air.

'He had a beard,' the well-digger added pathetically.

Yes, they nearly all have beards.

'Thank you for your testimony, you may be seated.'

The well-digger scurried off, his relief evident.

'Accuser,' Pilate said, turning to Boaz Ben-Jada, 'do you have any evidence to corroborate this man's story?'

'I do, Prefect,' the old man wheezed. He spoke as if straining to prevent the jaws of death from snapping shut about him.

'Let's hear it then. Wine.' He snapped his fingers at a pretty serving girl hovering behind him. Dark, smooth skin, a toga riding high on slender legs, curves to make a sculptor proud. The sleeping arousal within Pilate stirred, he would have this girl later.

'Zafir Bar-Yacob,' Boaz announced.

Wine was brought to Pilate. At the back of the hall, a large dirty brute of a man rose to his feet, but only when a tiny old woman reached up to tap him on the shoulder. The man lumbered down the aisle. Those encroaching on the pathway parted before this mound of muscle, as they had not done for the well-digger.

Pilate sipped at the wine, he was pleased to feel the coolness against his lips. The taste was clear and crisp.

Praise Bacchus, god of wine.

'What is your story, Zafir Bar-Yacob?'

The man said nothing, but looked around him, bewildered. Pilate repeated the question, this time in Aramaic.

'My name is Zaf,' the large man grunted in response.

'Where do you come from, Zaf?'

'Here,' Zaf grunted again.

The man is clearly simple.

Zaf's simplicity did not evoke Pilate's contempt. It was not stupidity that angered Pilate, but rather stupid men who thought themselves clever. Pilate spoke with more gentleness to the man.

'Tell the court your story Zaf.'

'My name is Zaf and I worked as security for a tax-collector named Caius, at his house'. Zaf ploughed through his words with a plodding rhythm. This was clearly a prepared and rehearsed speech. 'I saw the man called Yeshua from Nazareth come to the house with a group of men, and some women. They had weapons and torches. "Do not give your silver to the man who lives here, but give it to me, your rightful king," Yeshua from Nazareth said. Then he took a torch and threw it into the barn, where Caius kept his animals. "Burn this place" he said. Then the group stormed the house. I couldn't stop them. Caius was killed. So was Mistress and... and... Mistress was raped first. When I saw this, I... I fled.'

'Thank you, Zaf.'

The man turned and set off back up the aisle, a large sea-vessel making an ill-advised trip along a narrow river.

Parts of this story at least are true, his mind is insufficiently capacious to remember all of it, were it entirely fictitious.

'Prefect,' Boaz croaked, 'I have one more witness to present.'

'I shall hear him now. Wine.' The room was hot, and the

heat was starting to get to Pilate. Beads of sweat were forming on his forehead, he wiped his brow.

Cool wine, I need cool wine.

'Fabianus Tulius Catullus.'

Pilate was taken aback by the Roman name. This was not expected. A Roman legionary, another wearing the bull of the Fretensis legion, marched the length of the hall. He stood before Pilate, removed his helmet and bowed deeply. His face was handsome, but dark. This man's Roman roots were shallow.

'Prefect, I am Fabianus Tulius Catullus, and I serve the Empire in the Fretensis legion as Princeps Prior,' the soldier said.

'And what is your part in this, Catullus?'

'At your command, Prefect, conveyed to us by Legate Casca, the legion was deployed throughout the city in response to the rioting in the month of Nissan. The century under my command was sent to the Essene Quarter. After reports from two of my men, I visited the residence of one Herius Pullo Caius, a senior tax collector in the region and employer to the man who just provided testimony. The house was burned to a shell, and the naked, mutilated corpses of Caius and his wife were laid out in front of the building, as if on display. I asked local residents for names connected to these crimes, but given Caius' occupation, he was not a popular figure, and names were not forthcoming. However, the following day, two residents, both Essenes, approached me separately and gave the name of Yeshua of Nazareth, a tradesman not long resident in the city.'

Catullus stood to attention, betraying no sign of whether he anticipated further questioning or dismissal. *This* man was not bought, that much was clear. He was, however, being manipulated; the man's obedience and sense of duty being twisted to the nefarious ends of the Sanhedrin.

We train our soldiers to obedience, and out of thinking.

'You did not see Yeshua in the quarter?'

'No, Prefect.'

'Was Yeshua known to you prior to the riots, as an agitator?'

'Not as an agitator Prefect, but his name was known to me, through hearsay only, as a healer of great skill. Men within my own century spread rumours that the man could heal any ailment, and would not charge for his services.'

'Thank you for your testimony, Princeps.'

Catullus bowed deeply once more, turned on his heel, and marched towards the back of the hall. Pilate directed his attention to Yeshua who, perversely, seemed bored with proceedings and was picking at the grime underneath his nails. The advocate looked agitated.

'Accuser, do you have any final comments to make, before the defence presents its case?'

'Yes, Prefect.'

The Princeps had spoken with a soldier's efficiency, and in contrast, Boaz seemed to be speaking even slower than before. Irritability coursed into the extremities of Pontius Pilate, who drummed sweaty fingers into the arm of his chair.

'Evidence has been presented,' Boaz continued, 'to show that Yeshua of Nazareth has broken the law of Judea, and must be punished accordingly. This man...' he said, pointing a finger that wouldn't quite straighten at Yeshua, 'brought Jerusalem to its knees, and we trust that the court will make the correct decision and punish him accordingly.'

The presumption stole Pilate's breath.

I need more wine.

'We will take recess before we hear from the advocate from the defence.'

And what a waste of time that will be. Yeshua was condemned to die before a word was spoken today.

Below, Yeshua stared at the floor, a defeated man.

CHAPTER FIVE

Dordogne Valley, France
Month of June, 2024 AD

*Returning home is a punishment we are forced to choose over
and over. But it is home, nonetheless.*

-BOOK OF YESHUA

He was being followed, he could feel it. Though the memories
belonged to dead men, Elliot knew the path. Leaving the river
behind, he headed into the forest. The verdant canopy offered
relief from the feeling of exposure. He stopped, turned around,
convinced he would see people watching him. Tracking him.
Hunting him.

But there was no-one. He slumped against a red-fruit
bearing tree, then slid his back down the trunk, hitting the
ground a little harder than he intended. His teeth ached from
the juddering impact. The tree was a Cormier, part of him that
wasn't Elliot knew. He took a half-hearted swig from his water
bottle, then closed his eyes.

Thinking of snails, he chuckled. Everything material that
remained of Elliot Ambrose was tightly packed into the ruck-
sack strapped to his back. For the past few days he hadn't taken
it off, except for sleep. What was the point? He'd only have to
put it back on again.

My "es-cargo".

Elliot laughed aloud, convincing himself in the process that no-one was there to listen.

No-one is here to witness. I am my own witness now. Luce would have found it funny though.

Elliot grimaced. He wasn't supposed to think about Lucy.

Don't look back, that way lies only grief.

Grief particular to those few souls forced to walk away, over and over again. Grief he was forced to choose.

Trying not to think of a topic is inevitably counterproductive. Why is that?

He would have to ask Yeshua. His list of grievances and gripes with Yeshua had grown long in the course of their enduring separation. Elliot didn't know whether he would embrace or slap the man when he finally got the chance. *If* he finally got the chance.

I will embrace him, despite the mistake he made. He chose me, and I chose him. Choose *him, over and over.*

His mother had forgotten to pick him up from cricket practice once. Elliot had been no older than nine or ten. He still remembered the long walk back home, the cricket bag pressed heavy on his aching back, rehearsing the recriminations he would deliver to his neglectful mother. But none had been voiced when he walked through the door. His mother had apologised, genuinely and profusely, and his anger had melted away. He had enjoyed extra time on the PlayStation that night, cutting down vast swathes of zombies with an arsenal of pistols, sub-machine guns, and, he shuddered now at the thought, machetes.

His senses adrift in the soothing gentle breeze, fonder memories of his mother visited him. Her hunching forward, perched on the edge of the sofa, her glasses tied to her head with string, typing with only two fingers on the ancient laptop she refused to replace. His father catching Elliot's eye from across the room and smirking, Elliot trying not to laugh aloud at the description his father had given, more than once, out of his mother's earshot.

Like a monkey trying to work the controls of a helicopter.

He smiled, thinking of his mother's skilled, rhythmic chopping of peppers while listening to Abba at a volume barely detectable to human ears. The volume kept low, Elliot knew, for the unfounded fear of disturbing either Elliot, who would have been in his room with headphones on, or his father who, Elliot suspected, was slightly deaf.

Elliot hugged his knees and thought of his father. Edward Ambrose was a man who lost his explosive temper at TV adverts, failures by the England cricket team, and bad parking. But he showed more patience with those he loved, those in his inner circle, than anyone Elliot had ever met. Perhaps of anyone the sum of his incarnations had met either, save Yeshua.

But then, Elliot thought, each of his incarnations had thought someone they loved incomparable. For Miguel, the boy he had been last, no person could be as loving, gentle and giving as his Abuela. She had proved it, hadn't she? Dying to protect him, refusing to give him up even faced with AR-15s, and then later, machetes.

Not that it had mattered. Dario had found him in the end. It's only possible to hole up in Iztapalapa for so long before someone sniffs you out or sells you out. "You're never far from a rat in this city," Pablo had told him. It had been Pablo who had sold Miguel out. Not that Elliot blamed him, though Miguel certainly had. Pablo had had his little sister to think about.

Faced with AR-15s, Miguel had been bold, defiant. Faced with the machetes, Miguel had broken. He would have given anything, betrayed anyone. Luckily, he had had nothing to give but his life.

Miguel had been fifteen years old when the machete severed his soul from his body. It was only the second incarnation where he had failed to reach maturity. With his grandmother dead, who would have had mourned when his scattered body parts were discovered, half buried in trash? Pablo? Perhaps.

Despite its brutality and premature end, Elliot was glad for the life of Miguel.

"Take care of yourself, Miguel. Be happy. Be strong," his Abuela had said, when he went into hiding. Then she had kissed him on the forehead. A rare parting in love in the ancient journey that his soul had taken. The words had steeled him in the days to come, right up until the first glimpse of his reflection in the machete held to his face.

"Do whatever the fuck you want, then, Elliot," had been Lucy's final words to him, after he told her he was breaking up with her and moving, to "find himself."

"Your mother doesn't deserve this, Elliot." His father's final words to him. New lyrics to the heart-wrenching poem he carried with him, centuries in writing.

AΩ

Elliot awoke suddenly. Diagonal shards of pale light had broken through the canopy, and the heat had intensified. His shirt was soaked in sweat, and was sticking to his body.

Behind him, he could hear rustling. He jerked himself up in panic, turned, and peered through the trees. He saw nothing, but remained on high alert. He reached, instinctively, for his pocket, to check the time. Only then did he remember that he had discarded his phone, had thrown it overboard on the ferry. It had been a liability, a connection to a life that he could no longer have, a connection that could only endanger those he had loved. *Still* loved.

The afternoon was hot, and uncomfortable. His shirt was sticking to his skin, and something sharp in his pack was digging into his back. With a groan more suited to his soul's age than his body's, he hoisted himself up.

Elliot walked back the way he came. He told himself that he wanted one last look at the vista behind before becoming fully burdened by the weight of memories tracing back to Yossef, but in truth, he was checking to see if he was being followed.

Not that I could do much if I were, and besides, why would anyone follow me?

The Annunaki would have all the motivation in the world to hunt him, and there was no group more capable, or dangerous. But nothing and no-one could tie Yossef to Elliot, only the thoughts in his head. That would change, of course, it always did. But for now, he was safe. Still, he continued to head back.

Emerging from the trees, the valley cut a swathe of beauty beneath his feet. His self-pity, his fears, were stilled by something greater. The river moved languidly, shimmering with the gold of the proud, dying sun. The promised glory of the sun's rebirth was reflected in the waters. It was a view he had seen and felt countless times. It had awed Zheng, Femi, and Qara most of all. Those incarnations whose journey to this valley had been longest and hardest.

Miguel would have loved this view.

There had been so little beauty in his short, brutal life.

Elliot started to hit his stride in the forest. The fresh smell of pine was invigorating. He was becoming, as Lucy would say, more Elliot-y. The walking anchored his thoughts, and his true purpose returned to him. The small town of Domme was only a few miles away.

The feeling that he was being followed persisted, no longer at the front of his mind, but lodged in the back, like knowledge not currently needed, but ready to be called upon. He dribbled a pine cone between larger stones, a school boy dreaming of footballing glory. He laughed at a squirrel hastily carrying off an acorn, as though certain of Elliot's intention to take it from him, and he removed his trainers and socks and walked barefoot. He felt a pine needle stab sharp life into his weary, soft sole. He felt connected, once again, with the healing energies of the Earth. Walking barefoot always helped him feel revitalised, and connected. It was something Yeshua had recommended, all those years ago.

For the first time since his soul-memories had returned, he felt present, truly alive. His pack felt less of a burden, more a connection to a life that had been *good*. The uncomplicated life of Elliot Ambrose had been a privilege, distinguished, more than anything, by love.

He could feel *gratitude*. Gratitude for the feeling of purpose. The first time his memories had come back to him, the memories of Yossef only, he had not known what to do, where to go. He had waited, confused, angry, and scared. Judah had found him. Now, he travelled to his brothers, knowing he would be welcomed, and loved.

He thought he heard a stick snapping behind him, but he deflected the anxiety easily, a poorly aimed blow from a feeble foe. He turned around, though not in expectation or fear, but out of habit. He saw nothing, and continued his journey.

On leaving the forest, Elliot was unsettled to see how much the little town had changed. Domme had been a refuge for two centuries, the outer shell of Yamaloka, the place that Yossef called home. And Domme had always *felt* like a refuge. Charming, but dull. Quiet, still. Not dead, but in a deep, peaceful sleep. Imprecise architecture and heavily weathered sandstone had always given the town a chimeric quality, as though it hid inside the pages of a fairy tale. But he could not sense that quality now.

The town glowed and buzzed in the afternoon sun. It was busy, almost frantic. The entire town, which had grown substantially over the last thirty-eight years, resonated with the ominous, mechanical thrum of industry and transportation. He felt a threat from the town that was almost palpable, a bitter, smoky taste in the air.

Perhaps I felt it from afar. Perhaps that's why I felt watched.

He skirted around the edge of the town, buying a cheese and ham sandwich and an orange juice from a petrol garage on the outskirts that he had remembered as a library. CCTV cameras were trained on him. Unblinking red eyes that watched with timeless patience.

They can watch, but they cannot see ancient thoughts.

'Merci beaucoup,' Elliot said, pocketing his change.

The vendor said nothing in return, but watched him exit the soulless shop with careful disdain. Unlike most of his languages, Elliot's French was pretty up to date. It was a language most in Yamaloka knew, and it was used often, though it had been 300 years since it had last been his mother tongue. Elliot attributed the vendor's disdain to contempt for tourists, for though he spoke the language, his oversized backpack and English accent must have marked him as an outsider.

Odd, that contempt. Tourists buy petrol. And cheese and ham sandwiches.

He ate as he walked. The heat was draining from the day, and wearing only a t-shirt and cargo-pants, Elliot was starting to feel cold, a cold he could feel it in the small of his back. Colour began to drain from the world, adding to the sense of threat that was starting, once again, to overwhelm him.

The bread was dry, the cheese tasteless, but he forced

himself to finish half. The other half he passed to a homeless woman, who sat upright on a frayed mat wedged between two faux-marble pillars that separated a bank from a clothes shop. She gave no word of thanks, but Elliot saw the gratitude in her jaundiced eyes. He had never seen a homeless person in Domme before.

The sight of the homeless woman made him feel that the balance of the world was truly tipping out of control, that the great social injustices should reach a place as isolated and idyllic as Domme. The balance of the world *was* in threat, it was why he made this journey, over and over again.

He left the town behind him, and felt relief. Where the road would take him on to the next town, he turned to the cobbled pathway that lead down to the system of ancient caverns for which Domme was famed. Halfway down, as the path veered down to the right, Elliot hopped over the handrail, and tip-toed down a rocky embankment. At the bottom, he passed through a dense thicket of trees and bushes, snagging his cargo-pants on a particularly grabby root, and found himself on a path less well trodden.

Elliot was weary now, his eyelids felt heavy, his breathing forced. The path carried him downward still, away from both the current civilisation of Domme, and the historic civilisation of the Domme caves. Eventually, he came to the edge of a sheer cliff. He walked sideways, guided by memory, until he reached an opening, barely large enough to admit him, even on his hands and knees.

I've never been this tall before.

Yossef was considered a tall man in his time, but he would only have come up to Elliot's shoulders.

Elliot squeezed through the opening, and only just avoided banging his head as he stood, catching the rocks that jutted out from the side with his hand. He remained stooped, to prevent his head from hitting the ceiling. It was dark.

Of course it's dark, you idiot.

Pulling off his pack, he fumbled around in the front pocket for the torch he kept there. When he switched the light on, the cavern was not illuminated. Rather, a white circle of light shone on the blankness of the wall of rock opposite. Slowly, he guided the circle across the wall, until a wooden door was revealed, no more than five-foot-high, set into the wall.

Yamaloka. Home.

For three hundred years, this compound had been home. To his shame, Elliot could no longer remember who had started calling the place Yamaloka.

Probably Tau'ma

Tau'ma had been both Vihaan and Sameera, and it was his kind of joke. An old joke, no longer funny. *Yamaloka*, the Hindu abode in which souls were punished prior to reincarnation. But Elliot's soul was not punished for his own sin, but that of Yeshua. Yeshua's choice.

Would that I had endured a day's torture and then death. I would have been spared millennial suffering. You chose wrong, Yeshi.

But despite it all, Yamaloka was home, and he would see his brothers. Smiling, he walked over. He pounded long-dead oak with the rusty iron knocker, and waited.

From behind him, there was a muffled thud, then a sharp howl of pain.

'Fucking hell,' someone shouted, in obvious pain and distress. It was an English voice. A high pitched voice. A familiar voice. He spun the torch around and trained it on the commotion.

'Fucking hell,' Elliot replied, in disbelief. He was staring at *Rock*, who was clutching the side of his head. The white torchlight made him look deathly pale. The blood trickling down his ear was thick and black, like tar.

What have you done?

Behind Elliot, the ancient door creaked open.

CHAPTER SIX

Praetorium of Pontius Pilate, Jerusalem
Month of Nissan, 30 AD

We who love Yeshua, do not love him for his divinity. I under-
stand those who fear his divinity. I confess, I have feared his
divinity myself.

-BOOK OF YESHUA

Tavarius might have been thought a presumptuous upstart by
his peers, but the man always knew where he stood in relation
to Pilate. It was one of the many things Pilate liked about him.
He came when he was summoned, offered advice when he was
asked, and kept his distance and made himself useful otherwise.
Given this, Pilate was shocked when Tavarius burst through the
door of his tablinum without so much as knocking, an insult
both to him, and Cardea, goddess of the hinge.

He didn't feel the anger that should have exploded in him
though. As a man of great power, most days unfolded according to his expectations and wants. Today was not one of those
days, however, and he felt weary. Besides, knowing Tavarius,
and seeing his flushed face and sweaty brow, Pilate could only
assume that he had significant cause for this disturbing lack of
decorum.

Pilate withdrew an impatient hand from the slave-girl's
hiked toga. It had only been an appetiser anyway. He dismissed

the girl with a slap on the thigh. She looked at him, doe-eyed, a little hurt.

'Later,' Pontius growled. A mixture of promise and demand. The girl smiled, and pranced barefoot towards the open door, a satisfyingly delicate pitter-patter across the mosaic floor. She swept past Tavarius, who paid her no heed. Pilate drained the rest of his wine, and dropped the bowl to the granite table in front of him with a clatter.

Sensing permission, Tavarius slipped gracefully into the centre of the tablinum, stopping when he stood between Pilate's table and the sun-bathed archway to the courtyard beyond. Tavarius' thin, angular face and narrow eyes, spoke, as they always did, of intense intelligence. Somehow, Tavarius' positioning brought the stinging sweet scent of honeysuckle from the blush-red courtyard to the forefront of his nostrils, and his mind. Pilate breathed deep.

'What is the meaning of this, Tavarius?' Pilate tried for angry, but failed, and the result was merely surly.

'I apologise Prefect,' Tavarius replied, bowing deeply, 'it was urgent that I catch you before the trial resumes.'

Pilate was reminded of Eli, the criminal Tavarius had been, before Pilate had raised him high.

'What is it Tavarius? My patience is sorely tested today.'

'And will be further, I fear. One of my sources came to me, about the trial.'

Ah, of course, one of Tavarius' sources.

Pilate's other officials and advisers did not keep low company; thought it beneath them. But Tavarius had his ear to the ground, and so was first to hear the stampede of the herd. Tavarius' friends in low places had provided valuable information to Pilate, particularly in the matter of the riots. It was just a shame that most of it couldn't be put to good use. Yet.

'And?'

'And he informed me that the defence in this trial is going to go in an entirely unexpected direction today. I have investigated his claims, and they do warrant consideration.'

'Tavarius, we both know how this trial is going to play out.'

'I... wouldn't be so sure Prefect. My source, he knows Yossef. And Yossef, he claims, knows that...'

'Yossef?' Pilate enquired irritably; his head heavy with wine despite forenoon not having yet elapsed.

Every other man in the city is named Yossef.

'The advocate, Prefect. He knows that Yeshua is condemned. He knows the, ah, impertinent demands of the Sanhedrin, and he knows that any conventional defence is doomed.'

'So?'

'But the man... and I get the impression, Prefect, that the advocate is exceedingly cunning... isn't prepared to quit on the Nazarene. In fact, my source informs me that Yeshua and Yossef actually *desired* a trial, courted it. They baited the Sanhedrin, and now they bait us.'

'But why?' Pilate asked, nonplussed. 'He will surely die, what will that avail him, in any scheme?'

'Rather than focusing on disputing the evidence the Sanhedrin has presented, which you already know is fabricated, Yossef will attempt to show that you have something to lose by condemning Yeshua to die.'

'What, Tavarius? Besides a little face, which I have already lost, what do I have to lose?'

'Your soul, Prefect. Yossef and Yeshua will attempt to *prove* Yeshua's divinity, and in doing so show that you have more to lose by killing Yeshua than by antagonising the Sanhedrin. They wish to make your courtroom the stage for their greatest deception. They wish to turn even *you* into a believer.'

I just want this farce of a trial to be over.

'And how, Tavarius, will he *prove* his divinity to me?'

Tavarius smirked, then shrugged. 'Illusions, clever rhetoric. Telling you the things he believes you secretly wish to hear.'

'The same tricks that you once employed.'

Tavarius frowned. 'Not on you, Prefect. I was not so foolish as that.'

'No, I suppose not. So tell me, advisor, how do I show that he isn't divine?'

'By having him killed.'

ΑΩ

Pilate's head was spinning. The auditorium floor, far beneath him, was as a choppy sea. The faces in the audience swayed. He sat, and felt physical relief wash over him.

'We shall resume,' Evandrus announced in a voice that pounded at Pilate's fragile head, 'with the defence.'

Yossef of Arimathea stood. Even at distance, and through the vinous fog, Pilate could sense the man's fear.

This really matters to the man. Why?

'Prefect, Boaz Ben-Jada has painted a picture for you of a violent agitator. I do not intend to waste your time counteracting the ridiculous claims put forward. I have too much respect for your intellect to consider such an approach necessary. The Sanhedrin are as transparent as they are false.'

There was a collective animal reaction from the Sanhedrin, hissing, snarling and muttering. Pilate did not bother to steel himself against the flattery. He enjoyed flattery, perhaps even encouraged it from time to time, but he was practised in ensuring that it would not avail petitioners too much.

'Instead I hope to show you the type of *man* Yeshua is.'

Did Tavarius speaking truly? Does the advocate mean to prove that a god stands before me, awaiting my judgement? Well, good luck, advocate.

Pilate looked at Yeshua, whose hands worried over each other, while his eyes darted about the auditorium. Nothing could seem less powerful, less divine. And then, the man was *transformed.* His posture became straight, his body and face steel. It was a look Pilate associated with his strongest military commanders. Men who would not bend, and would die before they broke, men who would use their very corpses as obstacles to Rome's many enemies. Yeshua stared directly at Pilate then, and the Prefect of Judea wilted beneath the man's gaze.

Fire. This man is fire, and he has come to burn me.

'To do this,' the advocate continued, affecting legal normality, 'Yeshua requires a...demonstration. This demonstration requires someone impartial. In the first instance, we would ask yourself, Prefect, as the ultimate figurehead of impartiality in this courtroom.'

Pilate laughed. It was slightly manic, and no-one, not even his lackeys in the Roman contingent, joined in.

Absurd.

Pilate looked at Yeshua, who was daring Pilate with his eyes, though whether to accept, or refuse, he could not say. Pilate looked, then, to the Roman contingent, where he knew Tavarius sat, he caught the man's eye, and saw Tavarius shake his head, barely perceptibly.

He presumes too much.

'Very well.'

Yeshua stepped forward. He stared directly at Pilate, with an intensity that the Prefect of Judea simply could not match.

'Prefect, I knew you, intimately, for the first fifteen years of your life.'

Despite the intense heat of the afternoon, Pilate felt the chill of exposure.

'Better than any man or woman has known you. Better, certainly, than you have known yourself, for as a man of power, the lies you tell yourself are not contradicted by the world. No-one dares tell you a truth that does not serve your self-image.'

Pilate was roused to anger. He gripped the sides of his chair tightly and scowled.

Anger is good, I can work with anger.

'You are a fool, tradesman. Do you forget that I hold the power of life and death over you?'

This is a public trial, be the statesman.

'See. Truth drives you to anger. It is an unwelcome guest in the soul of Pontius Pilate.'

'And what, tradesman,' Pilate replied with forced calm, 'would you know of the soul of Pontius Pilate?'

'Do you recall, Prefect, *Livia*?'

Pilate froze.

No.

'I would be surprised if you did not. After all, you would wake with her name on your lips in the dead of night. You would save her from drowning, in those dreams, as you had not in life.'

No. No. No. That chapter is done.

'It makes sense,' Yeshua said, nodding, 'after all, you reached out to her. Told her how you felt, and she did not feel the same. "Scrawny", she said. "Provincial". "Runt." Attacks on you. No wonder you attacked her.'

'I DID NOT!' Pilate shrieked, standing.

Be the statesman. Tavarius was right.

'She drowned. You pushed her into the river and you did not pull her out. But you were thirteen Prefect. You did not do so much damage to your soul that you made damnation inevitable.'

'Who are *you* to speak of damnation, tradesman?'

'A God. I tell you this not because of any need for worship or sacrifice or adoration. I am not Jupiter. I tell you this only because it is *your* soul, not my life, that hangs in the balance.'

Where was the wounded sheep? This man cowed Pilate, the most powerful man in the province, in his own courtroom. Pilate could hear the susurrus of whispered suspicions from the audience.

I should have the man gagged and flogged. But it would lend credence to his words, too many people have witnessed this.

Absurdly, Pilate turned to Josephus, captain of his guard, who stood behind him on the platform. For a fleeting moment he was concerned that Josephus would apprehend him. But this was nonsense. Pilate took heart in the man's erect stature, unmoving jaw and calm, chipped blue eyes.

'You are a madman,' Pilate said with forced nonchalance, turning back to Yeshua.

'She was reborn, you know,' Yeshua said with a kindliness that was every bit as natural and believable as Pilate's nonchalance had been unconvincing and contrived.

There was a pause. Pilate said nothing.

'She lives in far-off Aksum. Or at least she did. I hope she still does. Her family loved her. She was full of joy, when I still knew her, as a little child. Much happier than she ever was as Livia. Her soul is settling.

Livia. Strange how the name alone can torment me as much as the girl herself had.

As Yeshua spoke, he rolled a rough, tamarisk coloured stone between thin, deft fingers.

What is that? Why was it not confiscated?

'Remember Tacitus, Prefect.' Yeshua's voice was powerful now, a match for his own, which had been honed to booming perfection by a thousand tedious military exercises.

'Remember the boy beneath your station who shared in your games, the boy you loved, the boy you laughed with, at your father's pomposity. Remember the horse that would snort with indignation, just like your father, when Tacitus tickled him in the right place.'

Pilate smiled, then caught himself.

'You can be that boy again, Prefect. The boy who loved Tacitus. It is not too late to save your soul.'

'Enough!' Pilate bellowed. 'Wine!'

'Allow me,' Yeshua said, and then *winked*.

Pilate glanced at his bowl. Where it had been empty, now it was filled, a deep burgundy with a heady scent that promised. He sipped at it suspiciously. It was exquisite, full-bodied with the distinctive oaky flavour he associated with wealth. As though the man *knew* the perfect vintage for him.

When Pilate lifted his head, he witnessed a swirling vortex of dust, dust brought into his courtroom on the sandals of those who gaped at the whirlwind with the incredulous open mouths of dying fish. Then, with no warning, the dust arranged itself into the likeness of a willowy, beautiful young woman with high cheekbones and stern eyes.

Livia. This is no illusion. My soul hangs in the balance.

Yossef stood, with trepidation. If he feigned nervousness at interrupting a god's games, it was a consummate performance from a skilled mummer, worthy of Suadela, the goddess of Persuasion herself. And suddenly, the dust fell to the floor, and nothing of the shadow of the girl Pilate had loved, and who had rejected him, remained.

Yossef coughed, nervously. 'If it please the Prefect, we have character witnesses. May I present them.'

The man speaks as though he did not just witness a display of divine power.

Pilate glared at the advocate. The promise of retribution burned bright within. Anger he could not direct at Yeshua, for fear, burned brightly. He would punish the lanky streak of shit orchestrating this.

You will pay for what you've wrought here today, Yossef of Arimathea.

'You may,' Pilate replied through gritted teeth.

Yossef left his place, giving the Sanhedrin a wide berth. He skirted to the back of the hall, where two Fretensis legionaries blocked his path. The soldiers, Pilate was reassured to see, gave no sign that they had just witnessed something miraculous. Something... habit perhaps, kept them loyal, preserved the façade of normality. At a nod from Pilate, the legionaries removed themselves, and Yossef pulled the large oak doors open. Outside, an unruly score of commoners shuffled anxiously. They followed Yossef inside the auditorium. Yossef returned to his place, while the commoners formed a line.

'Will you hear them Prefect?' Yossef asked.

If I must.

'If I must.'

Where is my filter? This insanity has stripped me of my wits.

An old woman at the head of the line moved to the front of the audience chamber, and stood below Pilate. Though bent with age, comprised of curves where straight lines should be, she held herself with a certain poise and dignity. Her clothing was made from fraying undyed wool, but the overall effect was cared for, almost well put together. Her hair was entirely grey, but remained thick and, unusually for a woman of her lowly station, clean. There was a total lack of fear when she met Pilate's eyes. Pilate's gaze had reduced seasoned soldiers, veterans of numerous campaigns, to nervous wrecks. But this woman, of a station so far below Pilate that she ought to pass entirely beneath his notice, was staring at him as if he were an unruly grandchild she wished to scold.

She would be a good wife for Evandrus.

It was an absurd thought. Though Evandrus had been a widower these past few years, he was a Roman of high standing and noble blood. Nevertheless, he couldn't help but picture his Praetor embracing this old woman.

The day has broken my mind.

'Prefect,' the old woman began in Aramaic, 'I am called Bina, a widower of ten years, and a resident in the Lower City. I come before you today to speak of Yeshua's divinity, which I have witnessed, and felt. In the winter, in the month of Kislev, I came down with a fever. I could not move, I could not eat, and I could not drink. My sons, good boys, summoned a healer, Tuviya. The healer informed us that nothing could be done. The fever had hit hard and fast, and I was not likely to survive the night, and certain to die within the week. I could not speak with my sons, from weakness. But I prayed, and I prepared to welcome death.'

'My sons, though, were not as willing to welcome death in to our home as I. My youngest, Yossef...'

Another bloody Yossef.

'...Had heard tell of a healer who could work miracles, and would not charge for his services. My sons went out, and found that man that evening. That man was Yeshua the Nazarene, the carpenter who stands accused here today. Yeshua came to my bed side. Placed his hands on my head. And the fever lifted.'

The woman's voice was full of wonder.

'I was a dead woman, and this man gave me life back. Who else could have done what he did, but a god?'

'A better healer,' some wit in the Sanhedrin back benches shouted. But the laughter was sparse, and did not catch around the auditorium.

Did they not witness his power? Did they not see that he can command even dust?

'Fraud!' another shouted. A few others took up the cry. 'Fraud! Fraud!'

Pilate clapped his hands together once, and silence washed over the hall.

I am Prefect still. I am the authority here.

'Thank you for your testimony, I would hear the next witness.'

Bina gave a small perfunctory bow, that fell only a little short of disrespect, and moved to the back of the auditorium. The man that took her place had her look, and indeed, turned out to be her youngest son, Yossef. He, too, spoke only Aramaic.

'I am Yossef, son of Bina, who just spoke.'

The man was shaking, and sweating. Terror, Pilate suspected, rather than the heat, which, though intense, was no more ferocious than usual for this time of year. Yossef son of Bina was as fearful as his mother had been fearless, but he asserted the truth of everything Bina had just asserted.

As the line of commoners thinned, Pilate's heart thickened with fear. There were too many stories, too well corroborated. The Livia made of dust, and the wine that just *appeared*, were not singular instances of divine power that might, conceivably, be dismissed as tricks. There was Baruch, the builder, whose leg was crushed, and then healed by Yeshua. His fellow builders, the brothers Osip and Orli provided corroboration. There was the mother, Mana, whose girl was cured of the bloody flux through a simple touch of Yeshua's hand. The girl's uncles witnessed, and proclaimed Yeshua a god before the court. Last came the household of Pau, who had been a leper, and after a touch from Yeshua, was a leper no longer. Pau's wife and mother-in-law wept as they told the court how they had banished Pau from their home, as a leper, and rejoiced when he had returned to them clean, thanking Yeshua of Nazareth.

'I have heard all that I need to hear from the defence today,' Pilate announced wearily, after the parade of commoners ceased.

The man conjured wine from thin air. Who could do that if not a god?

CHAPTER SEVEN

*To be born without a soul seems a great plight, to one who
has a soul. To one without a soul, the lack means nothing. At
times, I have wondered if being without a soul wouldn't be
liberating. In defence of such thoughts, I can only say that my
soul is particularly heavy.*

-BOOK OF YESHUA

Urday squeezed the trigger with careful thoughtlessness, put-
ting instinct and training in control.

Got the fucker.

The sulphurous stench of the gun's explosion mingled
pleasingly with the smell of dying grass. The M16 was a part
of him. He used the assault rifle as effortlessly and skilfully as
James Rodriguez used his left foot. Urday idolised James Rodriguez, perhaps the greatest Columbian ever to play the beautiful game, and had recently dispensed with a small portion of
his considerable wealth to purchase the boots that Rodriguez
had worn when he had scored *that* goal in the 2014 world cup.
Urday's mental picture of the goal was clear and sharp. The
cushioned header from Cuadrado, the chest control from Rodriguez, the instinctive, balletic swivel, and the strike, as gentle as
a lover's caress and as deadly and accurate as the bullet from a
Dragunov sniper rifle. He pictured the way the ball cannoned off

the underside of the crossbar and into the net, heard the Colombian roar, sensed the Uruguayan dejection.

The face of the person he had known best, by contrast, was blurred. Before he killed his mother, he had always turned from the stern looks, the visage of worry and disappointment, the hectoring, scolding, nagging voice. Now only a vague impression of the woman remained.

'I will pray for you, hijo.' How'd that work out for you, bitch? She always wanted me to be someone else, but I am Urday.

Urday had always been glad of that. Movement, a flash of white in the flaxen grass of the plain.

400 metres.

Urday liked to be tested. The hare leapt. Urday had the hares specially bought in. They came from stock originally bred for coursing, but these hares were trained in fleeing humans. They made for the best hunting, Urday found, even though they did not come cheap. Urday raised the M16 and pulled the hare into the line of his gun sight. He squeezed the trigger, and there was rapid burst fire, followed by blood, stillness and calm.

This was his meditation. He had told Ksawery, the one they all called "Polack", about his meditation once.

"What the fuck," Polack had replied in the deep, guttural masculine voice that Urday so envied, "does a man without a soul want to meditate for?"

Urday hoped he would be given the chance to kill Polack one day, but it didn't seem likely. They were, after all, both Igigi. Both on the same team. You didn't kick Colombians while Uruguayans remained on the pitch.

Still, Polack's words had lodged themselves into Urday's brain. Why *did* he meditate? The answer had come to him, fittingly, while he was meditating.

I reflect, he had realised, *because the* mind *reflects, and the mind is greater than the soul. The soul is an anchor, a weight that drags the mind down, hinders it.*

Urday had known enough minds, both soulless and soul-burdened, to know that the soulless were greater. He was soulless. So was Polack, as it happened, but they were a rare breed. Most minds, it had been learned over the course of nearly two millennia of Initiations, bore souls.

Urday crouched in stillness, scanning the grassy expanse for pestilential movement. He narrowed his eyes against the afternoon sun, which seemed Colombian, rather than English, in its intensity. The sulphurous, grassy smell that persisted reminded him of the arid field behind his parent's house in Agua de Dios. That field had burned during one particularly hot summer, destroying his parents' home.

The whole world seems ready to burn.

Most of his fellow Igigi would not talk, or think about their Initiation. For them, Urday had learned, it was something painful that they had to do; the price of admission to a better world. But for Urday, there had been no cost. The little boy's crying, and later screaming. The terror, blood, piss, and shit. The sickly sweet smell, like overdone pork, of the small, broken body as it burned. None of it had meant anything to Urday.

Urday felt instinctively what Tavarius had taught all the Igigi Initiates. That the cost *was* illusory. That little boy, all the children that were butchered, would benefit from what was done to them. They would be reborn. They would live forever. Experience everything. By serving the Annunaki, Urday and his fellow Igigi gave those children the ultimate gift, everlasting life.

It was, in Urday's case, a particularly generous gift. Urday himself would not benefit from it. Tavarius had taken him aside after the Initiation, and told him that he was special. To do what he had done, without anger, hatred or revulsion, and to feel nothing, meant that he was soulless. He would not be reborn. His oblivion, his *damnation*, was predetermined, and assured.

Still this is the only life that matters. Here. Now.

Urday had never been able to envisage life in another body, another time. The possibility of his damnation, as frequently raised by his mother, had never bothered him before the Initiation; the fact of oblivion didn't bother him after either.

The only thing that had really bothered Urday was the short span of a human life, another problem solved by serving the Igigi. By reaching the rank of Ugula, as he done, he was gifted extended life by the Annunaki. As a man taking Kansarrum, he could be expected to live for up to two hundred years. He had never been explicitly told the source of Kansarrum, but he had his suspicions. The Annunaki paid extremely well, but no amount of money could ever replace the gift of extended life, and his loyalty was assured, and absolute.

His senses alerted, he pivoted, and shot a hare at 200 metres. All three bullets tore through its fragile body. He laughed.

Urday felt a buzz in his trouser pockets, he was being paged. It was a message from Tavarius.

Assemble at Ekugnuna HQ, ten minutes.

AΩ

Urday was the last to arrive at Ekugnuna, the large underground bunker underneath the living quarters in their compound on the plains. He had no recollection of why it was called Ekugnuna. Something to do with ancient history, no doubt. One of Tavarius' many obsessions, beyond and beneath Urday's comprehension.

Ekugnuna was impregnable, unless you had a large army at your disposal. It was undetectable by air, and contained enough provisions to support a small civilisation for many years. It was used as a base for high-level operations. Urday felt excitement course through him.

Something big must be going down, if Tavarius has come here in person.

He took his seat at one end of the conference table, opposite to where he knew Tavarius would sit. That was his right, as the highest ranking Igigi present. As an Ugula, a commander, he outranked everyone save the Annunaki themselves, and reported directly to Tavarius. It was never explicitly stated, but was nevertheless well known by his fellow Igigi that Tavarius was the Annunaki's de facto leader.

Urday scanned the room, to see who else had been called in. Polack leaned against the dirty-white brick wall near the door, with his buzz-cut and harder-than-you scowl. He wore black leathers, the Inu on his lapel, the ruby eye that marked him as an Igigi, his only concession to colour.

Mack sat in one of the chairs, minimalist in design and the comfort they offered, with a straight posture and handlebar moustache, he had more of a look of a gentle grandfather than trained killer. Mack was far away in thought, his eyes directed at the symbol of the Annunaki that adorned the heavy steel door, a myrtle-green serpent swallowing its own tail. Mack was older than the rest of them, forty at least. His Initiation had taken place ten years prior to Urday's own.

He's all right, is Mack. Good at what he does, keeps his head of out of his ass, mostly.

Sonny was there too, his frame towering over the table on which he leaned. Yellow eyes, yellower teeth, and skin blacker than the puny soul he carried around with him. Tavarius confessed to Urday once that he had wondered, briefly, if Sonny, too, was soulless. It was there, Tavarius had assured Urday, a withered, small thing with mere embers of the divine. Sonny was smiling, which was not unusual. Very little failed to amuse him. Even nothingness, it would seem.

Dominique was slumped in her chair, as though bored. Urday scowled. He had no reason to hate her, but for the fact that she wouldn't fuck him. She wasn't pretty, not exactly. More handsome. But her features were symmetrical, she had that feline French accent, and a lean, hard body with just enough feminine promise. He felt his cock twitch. He wanted her now, to bend her over the table, pull down her fatigues and thrust himself inside her. But she was a good soldier, and a dangerous adversary. Another thing he would probably never have. Urday gritted his teeth.

The group kept their silence, tense and expectant, right until the moment Tavarius entered the room. He was followed by Symeon and Pilate.

The entire Annunaki. This must be some serious shit.

The triumvirate were followed into the room by the two bodyguards that Tavarius was never without. Urday thought of them as Tavarius' shadow, split by twin light sources. They were white, skin-heads, and possibly mutes, for Urday had never heard them issue any kind of noise from their mouths. The bodyguards melted into the background, against the wall. Tavarius pushed himself into the foreground, standing at the head of the table, opposite Urday. Tavarius was a small, frail looking Chinese man in his late sixties. But he was a man of immense *power*, the sort that Urday respected, and craved. Possibly, Tavarius possessed a greater power than any man living, certainly more enduring, and so his weak body and soft voice didn't matter. Tavarius commanded Urday's respect, something not freely given.

As always, Tavarius wore a chain, tucked into his shirt. He would stroke whatever hung from the bottom of that chain through his shirt whenever he was agitated. Urday suspected that it was some kind of totem. Such was the man's power that the behaviour, rather than seeming the irrationality that it was, gave him a kind of mystique, a connection to a world outside of Urday's understanding, and interest.

Tavarius leaned on the table, flanked by Symeon and Pilate. Symeon was a bland, bespectacled, chubby man of middling height and middle age. He looked decidedly non-threatening, nice even.

Urday didn't bother to hide the contempt he felt for Symeon, only Tavarius' opinion mattered.

Pilate, in contrast to Symeon and Tavarius, *did* look threatening. He was Caucasian, like Symeon, but that was their only similarity. Pilate was heavy, but not obscenely so, his body more like that of a niche sportsman who welcomed the extra weight. A sumo-wrestler, perhaps, or an offensive lineman. His thinning hair was slicked back into a pony tail. He was tall, and wore a practised scowl that contrasted with Symeon's benign smile.

Still, there was a weakness in Pilate. Urday could sense it. Maybe even smell it.

Great as they are, these are soul-burdened men.

'Oh good,' Tavarius said amiably in an English accent that wasn't native, but was nonetheless flawless, 'we're all here.'

Tavarius sat. Symeon and Pilate followed suit.

Tavarius beamed at them all.

Some kind of good news, it would seem.

Tavarius nodded to the bodyguard on the left, who peeled away from the wall to place a laptop on the table. Polack moved away from the wall too, walked behind Urday, who resisted the urge to flinch as Polack moved into his blind spot, around the table, and sat opposite Mack and Dominique.

Tavarius fiddled with the laptop, then turned it to face the group. There was a grainy colour photo of an elderly olive-skinned man with a moustache walking along a stony path. The man looked a little like Mack, but older.

'As you have probably guessed, this is a matter of the greatest importance. We have flown here directly from Kur.'

Kur was the headquarters of the Annunaki, hidden from the world in the Zagros mountains. Urday had been there only once, for his Initiation. It was a matter of considerable pride, only those Igigi who showed exceptional potential were Initiated at Kur. For his fellow Igigi, Kur was a place of dread. But not for him.

'We have located it, my friends. *Araboth.*' He spoke the word with the zeal of a man who saw an ancient goal realised at last. 'Our intelligence analysts have found the place we call Araboth, the headquarters of the Ophanim. Those servants of darkness who would subject us all to the tyranny of damnation.

Araboth is in the Dordogne valley, our surveillance has verified this information beyond any shadow of doubt. We know where they are, and who is there. This is our best chance to take the one we need alive in *five hundred* years.'

The Ophanim. The enemy.

Dominique smiled and bit her bottom lip as though aroused.

She's never aroused though, frigid bitch.

Sonny's eyes widened. Mack didn't react at all.

'Fuck,' Polack growled appreciatively, 'how did we find them?'

Tavarius beamed, his expression one of corrupted rapture.

My face probably looked like that when I killed for the first time. That teenager who was waving a gun around like he had the first idea of how to use it. Well, I showed him how to use it, though it was a short-lived lesson.

Urday smiled at the memory.

Tavarius was answering Polack's question. 'The Ophanim made a mistake. Five months ago they put too much money into a Swiss bank account they didn't know was compromised. We've followed that money around the world, and watched it all trickle back. We've followed the rivers, and now we know where they originate. They're in France, in the Dordogne valley. We've had them under surveillance. And *Filippos is there.*'

Why Filippos?

It was always Filippos that Tavarius wanted, but he would never say why.

'But how can we know which one is Filippos?' Sonny asked, somewhat unexpectedly. He was a man of few words, and little curiosity.

Tavarius studied Sonny, as if deciding whether or not the big man deserved an answer. Evidently, Tavarius did not find him wanting.

'We have,' he explained, 'Soul Trackers working for us. Some of the foremost minds in the fields of mathematics and statistics that this world has to offer. They plot all of the known facts of the Ophanims' journeys through their lives. Over time, certain... patterns have started to emerge. Combining the soul-trackers work with that of our agents in Interpol, feeding us information about young men who go missing shortly after their twenty-first birthdays, and our recent surveillance, I can tell you with certainty which one Filippos is. And he is in the Dordogne Valley. And you, my friends, are going to bring him to me.'

'Urday will lead, Polack, you're his second. There's a helicopter waiting outside. There's a doctor, in case Filippos swallows his L-pill and requires medical attention. There are also... other assets. Urday, I'm trusting you to get this done. If Filippos dies you may have set us back another five hundred years.'

Urday nodded. He wouldn't fuck this up.

Tavarius pointed to the picture of the man on the laptop. 'This, is Filippos' he said, 'let him slip through our fingers, and my rage will know no limits.'

Dominique laughed. A *French* laugh, arrogant, as though she, and she alone, could perceive the absurdity of things. 'Is he Greek?' she asked.

'Italian,' Tavarius answered flatly, 'it doesn't matter, just bring him in.'

'What about the others' Polack asked.

'I don't really give a shit. Kill them. Kill them all if you can, but bring Filippos in, he's the priority, the only thing that matters.'

'No unnecessary cruelty,' Symeon added softly.

Polack scoffed.

Tavarius stood, indicating an end to the briefing.

'Eat, drink, piss, and shit if you have to,' Urday told his team, 'then meet me in the armoury.'

CHAPTER EIGHT

Dordogne Valley, France
Month of June, 2024 AD

Yamaloka, we came to call it. An old joke, for old souls. It is our refuge and punishment still. We should have picked somewhere warmer for the winter months, but, at the time of writing at least, it remains safe.

-BOOK OF YESHUA

The fingers around his throat tightened, his windpipe would be crushed in mere moments. Such pain.

'Mapiqta... Mapiqta. It's... me... Yossef,' Elliot managed to gasp. The grip around his throat loosened, and the password saved him from the fate of Rock, who lay a whimpering mess on the floor.

'Sit,' the man growled.

Elliot did as he was told, perching on an old stool he remembered well. The inadequate electric light, once a marvel to him, was now a century old, and barely illuminated the antechamber to Yamaloka. Behind him, he knew, stood a south-east Asian man, Chinese at a guess, and in his mid-forties. He guarded the small oak door through which Elliot and Rock had been dragged.

Directly in front of Elliot, Rock was pulled roughly to his feet by the man whose hands had been wrapped around Elliot's neck moments ago. He was burly, also in his forties. Slavic looking, with hairy arms and a broad chest. The man twisted Rock's arm behind his back, poised to break it. This seemed unnecessary to Elliot, given that Rock was clearly broken in spirit, and likely in body.

'What the fuck were you thinking Yossef?'

Yohanan, then, or Yacob.

Such wrath surely belonged to one of the Sons of Thunder.

Elliot detected a flavour of Russian to the man's accent. All business was conducted in English, and had been for a couple of centuries. Most casual conversations too, unless the group was brushing up on a particular language, or speaking Japanese to wind up Levi, a perennial Japanophile and the only one of their number not to have been Japanese.

'What the fuck, were you thinking?' the man repeated, perhaps confusing Elliot's slow thoughts for a refusal to answer. 'You gave the password. This one,' he used his free arm to jab at Rock in the small of his back, eliciting a yelp of pain, 'did not. Who is he, why is he here?'

Elliot did not respond. He had no response to give. He was yet to wrap his head around what Rock had done, what it would mean. Rock's persistent sleuthing had triumphed over centuries of caution and evasion.

From behind Elliot, a soothing voice replied for him.

'Take it easy, brother.'

Yohanan's grip on Rock loosened, but the taut anger in his face remained.

Judah.

Only Judah could prove such a calming influence on the wrath of a Son of Thunder. Judah placed a hand on Elliot's shoulder. A skeletal white hand. Thin, and bony, with long, pale fingers. When Elliot had known him last, he had been a stocky Russian, squat, and strong.

The most notorious villain in all of human history, and my friend.

It seemed wrong that Judah's hand should be so thin, now. But Elliot placed his hand on Judah's.

'Judah, it is good to see you.'

'And you.'

Judah walked over to the man who held Rock. Judah was tall now. Very tall, and slender, with thinning blond hair, despite being, Elliot guessed, in his late twenties. Elliot also suspected that he was Scandinavian, or perhaps Dutch.

'I will handle this, Yohanan.'

Yohanan mumbled something, released Rock by shoving him forward, and stormed off to the unburnished steel door, behind which lay Yamaloka's living quarters. The door slammed shut with such force that Elliot was momentarily worried about the cavern collapsing in on itself.

Judah raised his eyebrows and shook his head at Elliot, a parent exasperated and amused by a toddler's choleric tantrum. Despite the circumstances, Elliot laughed. Judah's soul had always had that gift. He was like Yeshua in that.

'Yossef, brother, who is this boy, why is here?'

'We still use the old names then?'

I am not ready to address what Rock has done, what I have allowed to happen.

'Certainly. Much has changed while you were gone, but not that. Yossef, we must know who the boy is.'

'He is a man, Judah. He has reached maturity. His name is Daniel, and he is a trusted friend.'

Not once in their friendship had Elliot called Rock "Daniel." But in this place, "Rock" or "Dan" hardly seemed appropriate.

'He followed me here. How, and why, I am not sure. I discovered this only moments before Yohanan found us. At the door. But I can vouch for him.'

'Not good enough, old friend. I do not mistrust your word, or your judgement. But this is against our creed. I will not suffer any blood but ours on our hands again.'

'I could leave,' Rock interjected, in a terrified, high-pitched squeak.

Judah shook his head.

'I wouldn't tell anybody a thing, not that there's much to tell, I really have no idea what's going on.'

Judah continued shaking his head solemnly. 'They might track you down.'

Rock was burning to ask who "they" were, Elliot knew. He had never known anyone for impertinent curiosity like Rock, and he had known more men and women than any soul, save his brothers who inhabited this compound, and, of course, the Annunaki, their ancient stalkers.

'We must discuss what to do with the rest of our brothers,' Judah said to no-one in particular. 'Taddai, will you keep a watch over... Daniel?' This was directed at the Chinese looking man who had been guarding the door, who nodded.

It never ceases to be strange, seeing familiar souls in unfamiliar bodies.

'Welcome back, brother,' Taddai said to Elliot in a clipped New York accent that surprised him.

Judah addressed Rock directly. 'You must remain in this room. For how long, I do not know. You will be watched at all times. You will not be harmed. You have my word on that. If you doubt the value of my word, ask Yossef.'

'Elliot,' Elliot mumbled 'He knows me as Elliot.'

'Ask Elliot then.'

'You can trust him, Rock.' Elliot tried to reassure his friend with a smile, but the resultant grimace did nothing to penetrate the bubble of fear that surrounded his oldest new friend.

'Yossef, we must visit Tau'ma.'

'Yes, of course, but...' Elliot turned to Rock.

'Rock, why? Why did you follow me?' Elliot shook his head, tears welling in the corner of his eyes.

He has no idea what he has done.

'I...' Rock answered, in a wheezing voice, 'I needed to know what was really happening. I knew that everything you said, going off to find yourself, leaving Lucy, I knew it was all bullshit. I was worried, that was all.'

'How?' was all Elliot could say.

'I hacked your phone and set it up so that I could track you. It wasn't that hard. I could have hacked it remotely, but, Jesus El, you made your pin-code 1-2-3-4.'

'Yeah, but, I threw my phone overboard on the ferry, it's somewhere at the bottom of the Channel now.'

'True,' Rock said, 'and since then I've used the old fashioned technique of watching you, and walking in the same direction you do.' Rock gave a weak smile that Elliot was unable to reciprocate.

'Do you still have your phone, Daniel?' Judah asked.

'Umm, yeah?' Rock said.

'I need it. Now.'

Reluctantly, Rock passed Judah his phone.

'No phones here. It's one of our rules,' Judah said, walking off hurriedly, heading through the doors that lead to the living quarters.

'What's he going to do with it?' Rock asked Elliot.

He's going to burn it in the fire pit, I should think.

'I wouldn't bank on getting it back, Rock.'

'Ah. Right.'

ΑΩ

Tau'ma was in the library. Not for nothing was he known to the brothers as "Librarian". He sat at his desk, books and scrolls boxing him in. Unlike the others, Tau'ma was the same man Elliot remembered. It calmed him, this familiar face. He was older, much older, certainly. Tau'ma had been in his late fifties when Yossef had known him last. Now he was an old man. His skin sagged, only a few tufts of hair above each large ear remained to him. But the eyes still twinkled, and his warm smile was unmistakable.

'Yossef, it 'as been too long.' Tau'ma's voice had thickened, and was now a Gallic purr so deep that Elliot was reminded of a lion.

'Sixteen years too long.'

'Quite. What 'appened?'

'I died before I reached maturity.'

'I am sorry to 'ear that. But... it was for the best, per'aps.'

'Why, what happened?'

Stress twitched through Tau'ma's face, then he swatted the air dismissively with a thin, wrinkled hand.

'We must update the records.'

Tau'ma stood and turned to the safe embedded in the wall behind him, and turned the dial with a dexterity that belied his years, entering the combination that only he and Judah knew. He pulled out a new-looking leather bound book, no larger than the copy of James Joyce's Ulysses that had sat untouched on Elliot's bed-side table for the past couple of years. It always seemed too small, the *Book of Yeshua*. It was, perhaps, the most remarkable book in existence, a record of the lives of those who had imprinted their souls, determined to exercise the ministry of Yeshua. The book was also a record of the life of Yeshua himself, or at least the part they knew about.

An incomplete book.

The lives of Miguel and Elliot were missing. Most of Yeshua's life was missing. Perhaps others were missing too. The book had obviously been replaced recently. Every half century or so, Tau'ma copied out everything from the book into a new tome.

Tau'ma opened the book, then turned the pages carefully until he came to the back of the section titled "Yossef of Arimathea."

'You left us as Qara. Who have you been? Who have you returned to us as?'

Judah pulled up a chair, and sat near Elliot. 'You don't mind?'

And so Elliot told Judah and Tau'ma the missing stories of Yossef of Arimathea. He spoke of Miguel, his short life, and messy death. He told them about Elliot, his joys, privileges and capabilities. In the telling he relived his childhood in Surrey, his education at Harrow, his friends, his family, his loves, and his study of law at Oxford. And Lucy, though it mattered little to Judah or Tau'ma on a practical level. Elliot spoke of Lucy's fear of goldfish, her love of Scandinavian crime novels, and the way her nose would wrinkle at even the slightest hint of any less-than-pleasant odour. All the small things that made Lucy... *Lucy.*

He relived the sorrow, pain and grief of departure when he spoke of his soul's reawakening. The telling felt good even as it hurt, like the physical pain of exercise. Sharing something of his soul's burden with his brothers lightened the load, just a little.

'As Elliot, I am blessed with a sharp mind,' he finished.

Tau'ma nodded, but did not lift his eyes from the paper on which he continued to scrawl in his cramped, neat handwriting which seemed to have remained *his* throughout every incarnation of Tau'ma.

'That is good,' Judah said, beside him, 'we have need of every advantage at the moment. We are diminished.'

'Diminished? Why, how many others are here?'

'There are six of us,' Judah said with uncharacteristic solemnity.

'That... you're joking, right?'

'Would that I were. Yohanan, Taddai, Tau'ma, Filippos, and Judah of Kerioth reside here, and now Yossef of Arimathea is returned to us.

'What happened Judah?'

They had been eleven. Most were the chosen, Judah of Kerioth, made infamous through the Great Lie as Judas Iscariot. Tau'ma, another with a reputation sullied by the Great Lie. Yohanan and Yacob Boanerges, the "Sons of Thunder." Levi and Yacob Bar-Alpheus, the tax collector and his brother. Netanel Bar-Talemei, Symeon the zealot, Taddai, and Filippos. Immortal names, to match immortal souls. The apostles, as fraudulent history knew them, all but the traitors: Andrea, whose soul had not been imprinted, and Symeon, one of the Annunaki.

Then there was Yossef. Chosen by circumstances, not by Yeshua, initially at least. But no less committed, or welcomed, to the brotherhood.

Eleven they had been, though it was rare that all of them were together at any one time, for when one of them died, they did not return for the time it took to reach maturity, and their soul-memories to return to them. But for only six of them to be gathered, something must have gone wrong. Very wrong.

'Islamabad. Islamabad happened. A false trail planted by the Annunaki. We thought Yeshua was there, we had good reason, good intelligence Yossef, we had to go.'

'*Was* he there?'

'No. We were outsmarted.'

Again.

'Who was killed?'

'Only Yohanan and I escaped. Yacob gave his life so that I might get away. I must remember to thank him. Everyone else was shot or took their L pill. Both Yacobs, Levi and Netanel. Taddai had stayed with Filippos and Tau'ma.'

'Shit.'

But not as bad as it could have been, at least they weren't captured.

'Who manages our money while Levi is gone?'

'I do, and Filippos helps out'.

'What of the Zealot?'

'Little Symeon died shortly before Islamabad. An old man. He is not due back to us for nineteen years.'

Six of us, as diminished as we have been in a thousand years.

Inexplicably, Judah smiled.

'What?'

You have been away from us too long. Tonight at least, you must be a brother only, not an asset, or co-conspirator. Eat, drink, talk. We missed you, Yossef.'

'But Judah...'

'*Tomorrow*, old friend.'

'I will not eat or drink a thing until Daniel is treated as one of us.'

'He endangers us, Yossef.'

'He endangers us more as a prisoner. Yeshua didn't choose me any less than he chose...Daniel. Circumstances lead us both here. He *is* here, and we have no other choice.'

'Is this Yossef who speaks, or Elliot Ambrose?'

'Does it matter Judah? What else would you do, keep him captive indefinitely? Kill him?'

'I suppose not. Jesus fucking Christ, Yossef.'

AΩ

Elliot took a long drag on the Shisha pipe, as Rock emerged from his meditation. Elliot could see that Rock had experienced the transcendent, and truly tapped into the One Whole Consciousness. The meditation techniques Yeshua had taught them had not yet lost their power.

'Fucking. Wow,' Rock said, a grin plastered all over his face.

As Elliot, he had tried Shisha once before, while at Oxford. It hadn't done much for him then, but *this*, this was the good stuff. Mint filled his mouth, stinging his lips, sweet on his tongue, soothing in his lungs. Relaxation swamped his mind, body and soul.

'How was it?' Judah asked.

'It was... all the joy of existence, with... with every trace of suffering removed. It was as you said it would be, I *became* this collective consciousness you described. It was... awesome.'

Elliot turned to Rock, who sat, now, as part of their circle. Judah, Tau'ma, Filippos, Taddai, Yohanan and the two of them. Elliot's mind travelled to a time in Milton Avenue, his rented accommodation in Oxford, when the household had sat in a similar circle, passing around a couple of joints, listening to Dead Prez on an HP laptop with tinny speakers. Rock had been there, as he was here now, surrounded by individuals with different skin colours, different accents, glued together by circumstance.

But where in the front room of their rented house in Milton Avenue there had been Clockwork Orange posters and artwork depicting 1930s New York construction workers lunching high above Rockefeller Plaza, the grey rock of Yamaloka, jagged and uneven, allowed for no such adornments. And while Rock and Daisy had argued over the relative artistic merits of *The Simpsons* and *South Park,* they now discussed factions that governed the course of human history, and a god who had walked the Earth, now lost.

'Did you feel the infinite?' Tau'ma asked Rock, as Elliot passed his friend the shisha pipe.

'I think so,' Rock said, still smiling. 'I was here, and yet I was... everywhere. I could sense... love. In a pure, abstract form. As a pure power, uncomplicated and... universal.'

'This. *This*, is the absolute bollocks,' Elliot said quietly through a mouth thick with smoke, and passed the hose to Rock. He was full, stuffed with Taddai's portable gas stove cooked wontons, the veined blue cheese with fresh, crusty bread that Judah had served subsequently, and the forgotten pleasure of true, unending kinship. He would meditate himself later. It had been far too long.

Rock managed a weak smile, then took a drag before coughing and spluttering. Yohanan slapped Rock on the back with a fist the size of a small dinner plate, nearly knocking him into the hookah.

'Easy kid,' Yohanan said with affection.

Yohanan's friendship came as swiftly and powerfully as his rage, though while the latter was temporary, the former was permanent. In two thousand years, only the traitors, Andrea and Symeon, had had the friendship of Yohanan revoked.

'I'm fine,' Rock said, tears in his eyes, 'I'm fine. Before meditation, you were speaking of the Annunaki, and their goals.

But... aren't they kind of right? I mean, isn't it better that we are reborn, over and over again?'

'You must trust me Daniel, when I tell you, that after living many lives, a soul becomes so burdened that it desires nothing more than to be reunited with the One Whole Consciousness. And there is this to consider: the Annunaki cannot prevent damnation forever. Even if they last till the very end of humanity, at some point humanity *itself* will die out. Then damnation will come, and for souls that reincarnate over and over, it makes damnation a likely proposition.'

Rock stroked his chin pensively, then seemed to accept the point, nodding to himself.

'What is more,' Yohanan added, 'the Annunaki have created great imbalance. With souls unable to settle, the One Whole Consciousness feels it, more and more souls split off from the whole, and none are able to re-join. At some point, some point soon perhaps, this planet will be overrun by souls, and the One Whole Consciousness itself fatally destabilised. If Yeshua cannot resume godhead, all consciousness, life itself might implode, and cease to be.'

'And the Annunaki do not see this?' Rock asked.

'They see no further than their fear of damnation,' Judah answered, 'perhaps they do see it, but if so, they simply do not care. They would postpone their own damnation, even at the cost of an entire world of souls.'

'So, why don't they simply kill Yeshua?' Rock asked with characteristic bluntness.

'He cannot be killed,' Judah said. 'I have watched the man be dismembered, and survive. He wanted the human experience, for the most part, but he did make himself immortal, he wanted to leave on his own terms. Don't forget, Daniel, that Yeshua is a god. But he cannot release himself from this world, as he intended to do two millennia ago, not so long as he is held by the Annunaki.'

'But who, exactly, are the "Annunaki"?'

'Three men... and an empire. Two you know, or at least,

you know their names. Pontius Pilate, and Simon Peter. The third you do not, but he is called Tavarius. The most dangerous of the three. They are responsible for the capture and imprisonment of the man known as Jesus of Nazareth. Like us, they have imprinted their souls so that they reincarnate with the memories of their previous lives intact. They have endured and grown in power throughout the ages. When Yeshua was captured, they had a significant head start on us, and their ruthlessness and lack of worry about what harm they do has allowed them to build an empire far greater than ours. They have extraordinary wealth, legions of followers, some knowing, most unknowing. Some drawn to their cause, but most to their wealth. The Roman Catholic church is of their design. They laid the foundations of lies on which the church is founded, authored the Great Lie.'

'The New Testament?' Rock guessed.

'Exactly. Did you ever ponder, Daniel, the sheer absurdity of the story told there? That humanity's redemption lay in the execution of god's only son?'

'I never gave the story much credence,' Rock admitted.

'Would that more people had seen through the lie perpetuated by the Annunaki and those that serve them,' Judah said, 'they are devoted to their cause: continuous, unending reincarnation. But they do not hunt us simply to frustrate us in our search for Yeshua. There is something else that they want.'

'What?'

Rock's curiosity always trumped his scepticism. It was the reason Rock had watched old episodes of *Great Haunts* when they had been at Oxford together, a show in which a camp, charismatic TV psychic and an easily frightened middle aged woman would enter castles, old hotels or pubs, spend the night in darkness, terrified by contrived, mundane bangs and creaks, and exchange stories of great tragedies alleged to have occurred at these locations.

That feels like a life-time ago, but it was only last week.

'What do men of power always want?' Judah replied,

'more power. Before he was captured, it was Yeshua's intention to grant us, well most of us here at least, the ability to... perform miracles, for want of a better phrase. To channel the very spirit of this planet and mould our immediate environment according to our will. Yeshua told Filippos how we might do this. And because of Andrea and Symeon, the traitors, the Annunaki know that Filippos is the key. They hunt us, certainly, but more than anything, they hunt Filippos.'

'You can perform miracles?' Rock asked Filippos, his tone now sceptical.

'No. The ability to perform miracles requires something that we do not possess. We call it the Kishar Stone.'

'What is it?'

Filippos did not answer, but Judah did. It was, Elliot knew, a display of commitment and trust. More for Elliot's benefit than Rock's.

'A stone, zircon I have come to believe, though I may be wrong. Nothing extraordinary to look at. Yeshua did not want to live his childhood being able to perform miracles, or being aware of his divinity. He pre-ordained this realisation to occur on maturity, at twenty-one. At that age, he travelled to Egypt, where Yeshua had had it buried while he was in godhead still, and unearthed it.'

'So long as Yeshua held the Kishar Stone, he could channel extraordinary powers, perform what you might call "miracles". His plan, before returning to godhead, was to break the Kishar Stone into twelve pieces to give to his chosen messengers, the men history knows as "the apostles". However, simply holding a piece of the Kishar Stone is not enough, it requires... activation. The secret of which, only Filippos knows.'

'The Annunaki have it,' Elliot explained to his friend, 'but they have yet to figure out the secret of activation. Hopefully, that shall remain the case until Yeshua is freed.'

'But if they do,' Rock said, 'they will possess divine powers?'

'They would be able to channel the planet's own power,

Earth's own divinity. To what extent, I am not sure. But I do know that everyone is significantly better off so long as the Stone remains deactivated.'

'And will it?' Rock asked.

'Twice the Annunaki have captured Filippos,' Judah said, 'twice they have subjected him to the worst imaginable tortures. But he has never broken.' There was immense pride in Judah's voice.

'What kind of torture?'

Elliot winced at the insensitivity of Rock's unapologetic question, not for the first time in their friendship.

'He will not speak of it,' Judah said brusquely.

'No, Judah,' Filippos interjected in his heavy Italian accent, 'on this occasion, I will. This young man, wants, and perhaps needs to know of our enemy. I can think of no better way of explaining the Annunaki.'

The group fell into reverent silence. Taddai, who had the shisha pipe, placed it carefully on the ground in front of him. Elliot was reminded of the speech given at the Oxford Union by Eman Divjak, a survivor of the massacre of Bosniaks at Srebrenica. The scale of some suffering and tragedy, Elliot reflected, conferred a perverse holiness onto events.

'The first time the Annunaki captured me,' Filippos began, 'they tortured my body, consistently, for many years until my death. I thought, afterwards, that no suffering could be greater. But the Annunaki... Tavarius... showed me how wrong I was.'

CHAPTER NINE

Dordogne Valley, France
Month of June, 2024 AD

The lieutenants of the Annunaki they call the Igigi. No loyalty could be more assured than that of damned men tasked with preventing posthumous judgement.

-BOOK OF YESHUA

The Puma attack helicopter landed in darkness, in a field a mile away from where Araboth was marked on the map.

'Stay here,' Urday told the pilot through the comms device in his helmet, controlled through the touch screen interface on his digital wrist coach, 'I'll be in radio contact when I want extraction.'

Urday switched the comms device to Channel 2. 'Ok, we're on.'

He hopped out on to the grass. The slowing rotor blades sent energy and noise into the otherwise still and quiet night. Polack, Dominique, Mack, and Sonny all followed. Like Urday, they sported M16 rifles, while rappels and other climbing equipment were strapped to their backs. They wore Glock 17 handguns on their waists, a belt equipped with flash bangs, and around their foreheads they had Yukon Advanced Optics with night vision capability. Sonny also had a small blond-haired girl, about two years old, harnessed to his chest. She was crying, a sharp wail, almost a screech that pierced the chuff of the rotor blades. It was a noise that grated, and made Urday's fingers twitch. He wanted to snap the girl's neck, one quick, satisfying crack that would end the noise, but she was an asset.

Sonny was unhappy with this arrangement, and had complained bitterly about it during the flight. But, as Urday had pointed out with uncharacteristic patience, Sonny was the biggest and strongest of their group, and would be least hampered by the girl.

Sonny had relented, eventually, on condition that the girl was sedated. Which wasn't, Urday reflected, a bad idea anyway. It was just irksome that it wasn't *his* idea.

The doctor hopped down. He too was equipped with Yukon Advanced Optics, and he had a backpack in which he carried his medical equipment.

'Doctor,' Urday said, 'sedate the girl.'

The man nodded, and then put his backpack on the ground. He opened it, and pulled out a syringe with, Urday was pleased to note, dexterity and urgency. That boded well, the speed of this man's work may well prove crucial to the mission. The doctor put the syringe to the girl's neck.

'Careful,' Urday warned, 'if the girl dies, you die.'

But not until I have Filippos.

To Urday's surprise, and the man's credit, the doctor wasn't unduly cowed.

'It's ketamine, in the appropriate dosage. It will knock her out for a couple of hours.'

Urday turned to his team, who were awaiting his command. 'Squad, on me. Optics activated. We move on the sharp.'

On alert, and in silence. That's how I like this lot best.

Urday took the lead across the field, following the map on his digital wrist coach. He stayed low, and moved quickly. Intelligence hadn't observed any security on the approach, but that didn't mean there wasn't any. At the end of the field was a cliff face, a sheer 250 metre drop into the glistening darkness of the river Domme, quietly making its way through the valley. Urday moved towards a row of trees, fifteen metres from the cliff edge, he raised his left fist, indicating to the others that they should stop. He waggled the index and middle fingers of his left hand alternately, and taking the lead, Urday took the rappelling equipment out of his bag, and secured the clutch to the two anchors, tying the rope tail to his corbelette in a secure knot, before looping the ropes around the sturdiest looking tree.

The rest of the team busied themselves with their own rappelling equipment, while Urday tightened the loop around his waist. He walked to the very edge of the deadly drop. The night was still. Secure both in his knot and his abilities, he turned his back to death, and edged out over the precipice.

With each jump away from the wall, Urday felt *alive.* His stomach dropped quicker than the rest of him, and for a split second, he was held hostage by hope, the hope that his knot would hold, prevent the death his body felt was inevitable. With every stop, every survival, he would savour the adrenaline flooding his system, it was hard to stop himself from laughing, so powerful was the experience; something that approximated joy.

This is as close to "God" as I can comprehend. Faith. One needs no soul to appreciate these things when descending a cliff face and defying death. `

The doctor had assured Urday that he was a competent rappeller. Nonetheless, he was slower than the rest of the group on the descent. His push offs and drops were neither as far reaching, or as confident, as his team. Even Sonny, who wasn't a natural, and had the girl strapped to his chest.

They moved down the cliff, the only sounds the excited whizz of the ropes sliding through the carabiners, the grunts of the doctor, and the ominous churn of the river below. Urday reached the bottom first, and was quickly joined by Dominique, Polack and Mack. They crouched on a large rock by the edge of the river. Waiting in stillness and silence.

Lucky the river runs low. Out of summer, this route would be inaccessible.

Sonny dropped to the floor and unhooked his corbelette two minutes later. The doctor was another three minutes. He thudded to the floor with a grunt, panting and gasping for air.

'Shhhh,' Urday hissed.

He gave the signal to continue, a forward motion with his left arm. As point, it was on Urday to find passage over the boulders and rocks. The green of his optics gave the night an artificial feel and showed him the clearest path.

The doctor was able to keep up, as Urday moved slowly. It would be easy enough to turn an ankle in better conditions than this. So he moved like the river, cautiously and circuitously.

Urday checked his watch, they were near the entrance to the cavern compound. All they needed to do was scale the 120 metres of rock-face above them. Urday pulled out his climbing spikes, and his team did likewise. He pulled himself up the cliff face, snarling, filled with anticipation.

This is it Urday.

With each movement, Urday felt his excitement rise, the anticipation of combat, the feeling of *mission*. This was what he lived for, what gave his life meaning. It was the thing that he was best at, the thing that separated him from other men.

His right index finger slipped, for just a moment, and a shadow of death rushed up from the ground, where it had lurked during the climb. He caught himself, felt the rush of adrenaline and *life* surge through his body.

Circumstances had been unkind to him, Urday reflected. He should have been born in some historic age, where warriors were heroes, celebrated. Became rulers, even demi-gods. He would, he had no doubt, have been a great conqueror, a man whose name would live through the ages, a man whose violent passage through life became first history, then legend. But Urday's fate was to skulk in the shadows, his greatness dimmed, largely unappreciated. Still, that was his lot. Better a warrior now, than something weak, something that can be dominated. And though his name might not live on, what he did, was truly great. He gave the world eternal life.

Gasping, Urday pulled himself over the precipice, and felt his body relax.

Christ, I could do with a fucking cigarette.

Once the doctor had joined them on the precipice, Urday gave the signal to edge around the sheer wall of rock. He was searching for an entrance, and 50 metres in from the river, he found it. It was a small opening at the base. Just large enough to crawl through, though it would be a very tight squeeze for Sonny, with the girl strapped to his chest.

The opening gave Urday pause. It was a bottle neck. And if *he* were planning the defence of this compound, he would have had an unpleasant surprise waiting for any unwelcome guests. But time was of the essence here, if they wanted to bring Filippos in alive. And besides, the Ophanim were known to be non-violent. Their answer was always to flee, rather than fight.

Still, everyone is non-violent, until they're not.

People were like dogs; one day, one might turn and bite you. Unless you stayed vigilant, you just wouldn't see it coming.

Urday lowered himself to the ground and crawled through, expecting explosion, pain or death with every tiny movement. And then, he was through.

Nothing.

Urday smiled. It was a missed opportunity for the Ophanim. A perfect murder hole, unmanned.

This is why we win. This is why it's better to be soulless.

CHAPTER TEN

Dordogne Valley, France
Month of June, 2024 AD

We buried their broken bodies, those friends and brothers who had joined our cause. We all wondered if we had put them on the path to damnation. After, we swore that it would not happen again.

-BOOK OF YESHUA

All, including Elliot, sat as though hearing Filippos' tale for the first time.

'The second time the Annunaki captured me,' Filippos continued in a voice that was slow, deliberate, and curiously flat, 'was late in the thirteenth century. We were based in Toledo, in Spain. The very heartlands of the enemy. I was born an Englishman, but my skin was dark enough, and my Spanish good enough that I passed as a local without problem. At the time we were recruiting followers, men to fight our battle alongside us. If you are any kind of student of history, Daniel, you will know these men as the Knights Templar. Legend tells us that these men sought the Ark of the Covenant. Or the Holy Grail. And so even the Annunaki believed, for a time. But the truth is that they gave up their families, their lives, to the search for Yeshua. We were cautious with our trust, operating with cells, each of which reported to one leader, an intermediary who acted as the conduit for all communications between us and the knights who fought our battles.'

'But, as was inevitable, I suppose, the Annunaki learned of the Templar's true purpose. The leader of one unit, the accursed Bernard de St Amand, had been bought with promises of gold and immortality. With his help, the Annunaki learned the identity of the Templar's true leader, Arnaud de Orleans. Not as history would have you believe, Renaud de Vichiers, who served only as titular leader and little more than a decoy. Arnaud was captured, subjected to the flaying knives of the Annunaki's most deranged Igigi servants, and gave up names and locations. False names, true locations.'

'Those who had taken up our cause, out of love, were tortured and slaughtered. Many were... sodomised before the relief of death. We vowed, after that, never to let others fight in our name, to take up our cause. Their blood was on our hands, and we have never been able to wash it off.'

A memory, hazy for distance, visited Elliot. Judah, then a small north African man, weeping, shaking. Telling Yossef what had transpired in painful, breathless sentences. Elliot had seen Judah, stoic, solid Judah, broken that day.

'I was taken in the dead of night,' Filippos continued, in a voice so quiet that it commanded absolute silence, 'the knights who stood guard while I slept were slaughtered, a bag was placed over my head, and I was taken to a location that I would later learn was Igelisa de Santo Tome. For three days and three nights, I festered in the bowels of the place, kept in darkness, given only horse piss to drink.'

'If you have never drunk horse piss, I do not advise it. Most all of it is vomited back up, it burns your throat and causes you to contemplate the extraordinary capacity this world offers for suffering and misery. I was a hunchback then, and greatly feared for the new tortures they would be able to inflict on a part of my body that already caused me to suffer daily.'

'Then *they* came. Tavarius, himself crippled with a twisted leg, lead a procession of torch bearing Igigi. As the torches filled the dungeon, the true scale and horror of that place was revealed to me, and the darkness I had despised was suddenly all that I yearned for. The dungeon was as large as the church above, at least, perhaps larger. There was certainly more in the dungeon that was hidden to me than was visible. Nevertheless, what I saw was enough to make me piss myself with fear. Closest to me was an iron chair, barbed with spikes. Next to it was a rack, designed to tear limbs from the body. Beyond that I could see a small brazen bull, large enough only to accommodate a child, designed to burn alive whoever may be put into it. In the flickering light I could see racks with knives, pliers and branding irons. It was an artist's impression of hell made real.'

'Following the torches and the Igigi, women and children were herded into the room, twenty or so. Wives and children of the poor, Tavarius explained to me. Those who would be missed and mourned, but not avenged. From inside his cloak, Tavarius produced a sand glass, turned it over, and placed it on the floor in front of me. Whether by luck or judgement, though I have always suspected it to be the latter, he had placed it only just beyond the full extension of my manacled leg. I had until the sand ran out to tell him... what he needed to know. If I did not, one of the women or children in the room would be given to his Igigi for "creative execution". At the time, I did not know how long the sand in the glass would take to run out, though I would come to learn that it was approximately six hours, or ninety recitations of Blow, Northern Wind.'

'I could not tell Tavarius what he wanted to know, for it would have given him the divine powers of the Earth, by allowing him to activate the Kishar Stone. More than the lives of the poor souls in that dungeon depended on it, and so I closed my eyes. One might expect the time to have flown, but it did not. It dragged, as no period of time had ever dragged before. Were I to have guessed the amount of time it took for the sand to run out, I might have guessed at days. Women sobbed, or screamed. Children whimpered or hid. Tavarius and his hooded Igigi were completely silent.'

'When the sand ran out, the horror and dread had built in me, so that I thought my heart would burst with the pain.'

'"Asi es," Tavarius had said then, "*So it is.*" One of the hooded Igigi, I would never learn their names, chose a woman first. Mother to two boys in the room. Two of the Igigi strapped the woman to the rack, while two others held the children, but left their mouths unimpeded so I might hear their screams. The woman's left arm came off first. The gruesome squelching sound and the scream I still hear, the sound echoes round my head, even now. Her right arm followed moments later. She had bled to death by the time her legs were pulled away, despite the cauterisation of her wounds. But they finished the job anyway.'

'Throughout all of this, Tavarius had said nothing. When it was over, he walked up to the sand glass, and casually flipped it over. Over the course of that first day, or perhaps it was night, I had no way of knowing, I watched a woman have the skin peeled from her body so that she did not so much die as disintegrate. I watched a boy no older than seven or eight bleed to death on the spiked chair. I smelled an infant being burned to death in that brazen bull. I never heard the cries of the infant, for the screams of the mother were too loud. Screams that reached into my very heart, and threatened to rip it out. Would that they had.'

'But the first day, if that's what it was, was not the worst. No, that came when the final woman died, boiled in a large pot as if she were nothing more than a potato. As the crimson sludge from that pot was poured away into some gutter, another two score of women and children came whimpering into the dungeon at sword point. It was then, that I realised, it would never stop.'

'I was fed, and watered. At times, the animal within me betrayed my soul, and I ate willingly. Mostly, though, I had to be force fed, thin, scalding soups funnelled down my throat. Sometimes, the most delicious meals would be prepared for me, exotic fruits and spiced meats. Those I never touched. No-one, save Tavarius, would talk to me, unless you counted the begging of relatives of those who died in front of me.'

'"Tell me," Tavarius would say, "and you will not live just as a king till the end of your days, but as a god till the end of time."'

'As I endured, more and more evil was brought into that dungeon. Crates of scorpions that could paralyse victims without deadening the capacity for pain. Bags of starving rats, and buckets that could be strapped to the waist, or head. The women and children would come from further afield. Sometimes men would be killed. Tavarius would visit every couple of days, and he would always ask the same question. Then, "Tell me, and you will not live just as a king till the end of your days, but as a god until the end of time."'

'For what I believed to be about one year, I endured this. My body would simply not do what I beseeched it to do with every fibre of my being, and die. And then Tavarius changed his tactics. One mother at a time, with one child, would be sent into my dungeon, and then left. A pair of Igigi would stand outside the door to the dungeon, but would otherwise pay me no attention. The mother and child would be left for an indeterminate amount of time. Sometimes a day or two, sometimes a month. But they would always die. In agony. With Tavarius watching, and me helpless, and broken.'

'For the most part, I would try never to interact with those left with me, for it would increase the grief I felt when they were slaughtered, and threaten my resolve, when I was forced to tell myself that the suffering in that dungeon would be nothing compared to the suffering that would result from my telling Tavarius what he wanted to know.'

'But then came Esme,' Filippos' voice softened, 'Esme was beautiful. She possessed such beauty as should have seemed obscene in a place as foul as that dungeon, but it did not, for her beauty shone, and everything else was dimmed.'

'I realise, looking back, that Esme had been chosen deliberately. Her beauty was incomparable, and her soul was so gentle, how could anybody *not* have fallen in love with her. She had no child with her, and she was left for a long time, longer than any other poor soul thrown into that dungeon, save myself.'

'Tavarius hoped that I would fall in love with her, and do anything to protect her, to preserve her life.' For the first time since had he started talking, a smile flickered across Filippos' face.

'And he was probably right, but he underestimated *her*. Esme was beautiful and pure, but she was also resourceful, clever, and brave. She seduced one of the Igigi guards, convinced him to kill the other. Took his weapon from him, killed him, and before making her escape, killed me. Being stabbed through the heart with that dagger was the sweetest feeling in my many lives. As I slumped against the wall to which I was still manacled, surrounded by my own shit and blood, I gave thanks to Esme, the beautiful soul who saved me from years of further torment, and the lives of countless future victims.'

A long period of reflective silence followed Filippos' tale, for even though all but Rock had heard it before, the subject was still too large and powerful to be confronted directly.

'Filippos lives the first twenty-one years of each life in blissful ignorance,' Yohanan said, after a while, 'and the rest of his life in Yamaloka. We all suffer, but none more than Filippos. He does not tell us the secret of miracles, so as to protect us.'

'What...what happened to the Knights Templar?' Rock asked, uncharacteristically embarrassed to address the hell that Filippos had endured.

'They were hunted down and slaughtered,' Judah replied, though the question had been directed at Filippos.

'And... what of Esme, what happened to her? After she escaped.'

Filippos went to answer, but Elliot interrupted. His brother had relived enough pain for one day.

'You can ask more questions tomorrow, Rock.' The flow of questions would be ceaseless, Elliot knew.

'I have a question for you, Daniel,' Yohanan said, 'do you believe us?'

Rock paused and looked thoughtful, his face screwed up

in concentration.

'I believe,' he said finally, 'that *you* believe all this. And some, much of it, must be based in truth. No mind could conceive of such relentless coherent insanity.'

Yohanan laughed with thunder and slapped Rock on the back once more. Elliot smiled.

What a strange and wonderful man Rock is. I have known men to accept insane lies before. Never have I seen someone so open to insane truths.

And Elliot knew that he could trust in Rock's diligent research, in his unrelenting pursuit of truth. That Rock would become a true brother was not something Elliot doubted, and it made some part of his heart glad, but the greater part was filled with sorrow, for what Rock would have to give up.

Besides, he is not soul-imprinted, this is... temporary.

'Come,' Judah said, more to Rock than Elliot, 'I will show you to your rooms.'

They followed Judah through the living quarters, down to where they would sleep. Rock leaned in to Elliot's shoulder.

'Why doesn't Filippos simply kill himself, every time he reaches maturity?' he whispered.

Elliot was glad that Rock had had the tact to wait until now to ask, and to ask him.

'There may come a time when we need the information he guards,' Elliot said, 'and besides, it could fracture his soul, committing such violence against the self over and over again, without need. He would do it though, even at the cost of his soul, but Judah has forbidden him.'

'Oh, right,' said Rock, looking thoughtful.

They were walking into the sleeping quarters when Elliot heard the first explosion.

CHAPTER ELEVEN

Dordogne Valley, France
Month of June, 2024 AD

I have been asphyxiated, drowned, stabbed, poisoned and
burned. I have endured terrible illness, and extreme violence.
I do not embrace death. I still cower and whimper when faced
with it. But I can, at least, accept it.

-BOOK OF YESHUA

His team followed Urday through the small opening. Sonny un-
strapped the girl from his chest and pushed her through with
callous carelessness, as if she were a sack of potatoes he wasn't
particularly bothered about.

On the inside of the cavern opening, a small oak door
stood at the back. Sonny pulled the girl up towards him, and
reattached her to his chest harness. Urday motioned Mack towards the door, and grabbed a flash bang from his belt. Mack
pulled the C4 from his belt, then turned his head to Urday,
awaiting his command. Dominique, Mack, Polack and Sonny all
imitated Urday in drawing their rifles from their backs, disengaging the safeties with the satisfying clicking noise that Urday
savoured. Urday made a fist, followed by extending all his fingers, and Mack slammed the C4 against the hinge of the door, activated it on his digital wrist coach, then spun and crouched so
that he wouldn't be in the blast range.

Urday winced at the sound of the muted explosion The door burst inward, flying off its hinges through the now exposed ante-chamber. Mack tossed in a flash bang, waited for the blast of blinding white light, before rushing through. Urday followed, breathing in deep the smell of burning plastic, and destruction.

No targets. Is the intelligence wrong? Is Araboth deserted? Is this even Araboth?

From this point, they were moving blind, they had no idea of the layout of the compound. Pollack, Dominique, Sonny, and the Doctor stood in the room, all awaiting instructions.

Urday wanted to move quickly. If he could trust the intelligence given to him, they had come through the only way in and out of Araboth, but Urday couldn't be sure that the Ophanim didn't have some other way out, and they were almost certainly now alerted to the presence of intruders. There were two doors in the ante-chamber. One on the far left of the wall they faced, the other more central.

The left door will take us closer to the river.

There simply wasn't enough space to travel too far in that direction, the majority of the compound would surely be found to the right.

Urday motioned for Dominique to stay and watch the door on the left. She scowled, but fixed her gaze, and rifle, to the door. The rest, he motioned over to the other door. Mack took another pack of C4 from his belt. The team lined up against the wall. This was a heavy steel door, and the explosion was only strong enough to cause the door to pop open reluctantly. Mack nudged the door open the rest of the way with the barrel of his M16, and moved smoothly into the room. Urday followed.

There was a burst of gun fire from Mack's rifle. Urday surveyed the scene in a split second. Three hostiles, no weaponry. One body, that of a middle-aged Chinaman, his face half-blown away, little more than a crimson smear.

There *he* was. An elderly man with a drooping moustache. As still as the corpse of the Chinaman. Sat, while everything around him was panic. Saliva foamed from his mouth. He was smiling, intermittently, through obvious pain.

Shit, he's already taken the L Pill.

A large Slavic man charged at Mack. He roared as he did. Pure rage. He stepped on a plate, cracking it, and sending bits of food across the room. Urday and Mack both fired on him. Six bullets ripped through his body. Blood sprayed behind him, and Urday was reminded of a jet ski. The man continued to stumble forward, falling at Mack's feet. Mack casually put a round of burst fire through his head, which at close range, exploded like melon. Red splashed Mack's trousers.

Stupid man. What did he hope to accomplish? Besides, I was closer than Mack. Souls stop men from thinking.

Urday was pleased to see that Pollack and Sonny had had the same idea with regards to the last remaining mobile hostile. Wait to see which door he was heading for. He was an elderly man. Older than Filippos, and even with urgency, he moved slowly. He had now reached the door at the back of this room, which Urday judged to be some kind of living quarters, based on the furniture and remnants of dinner scattered across the floor.

Sonny and Polack both took aim as the old man touched the door handle, but Polack beat Sonny to it, and it was his bullets that tore through the old man's chest and throat, and the wooden door behind him.

Souls, even puny little one like Sonny's, cause men to hesitate.

Froth was now covering Filippos' chin. He looked absurd, like a man in a bubble bath pretending to be Santa Claus.

'Filippos,' Urday said, hating his thin, reedy voice. It was no fair representation of the strength of his mind, 'just so you know, if you die, the little girl dies too. And her death will not be clean.'

Not that he can do much about it now. Still...

Fear flashed, dispelling the calm that had been in his eyes.

'Doctor, get to work,' Urday commanded.

The doctor worked quickly, placing his pack on the ground, and taking a syringe from the front pocket. He sank the syringe into Filippos' neck, and he immediately slumped, but the doctor was ready to catch him. Then he pulled out a gas canister attached to a mask. He placed the mask around Filippos' head, then opened the vent. Gas hissed. The doctor took out another syringe, and inserted it into the other side of his neck.

The doctor pulled open Filippos' eyelids, and shone a penlight into both pupils. He then opened the man's mouth and peered inside. Evidently, he was satisfied with what he saw. He turned and nodded to Urday, who realised that he had been holding his breath. Not a sensation he could honestly say he was familiar with outside of climbing. He exhaled relief.

'Stable, but at risk of a heart attack. I want him on that helicopter as quickly as possible,' said the Doctor.

'Ok. Polack, Mack, Sonny go with the doctor outside. Polack, you take point. Sonny, you carry Filippos. Sonny...?'

But Sonny was not there. He must have gone through one of the doors, perhaps his attention caught by some threat.

Urday switched his comms device to Channel 1, using the wrist coach.

'Uttu do you copy?'

'Yes, awaiting instructions.' The reply came immediately, with crystal clarity.

'Extraction from designated location 1A.'

The Puma would land, Urday knew, just outside the entrance to the cavern system. There was limited room, but Urday knew Alexander, the pilot, to be extremely skilled, and it was a calm night. Turning his head back to his wrist coach, Urday switched back to Channel 2.

'Sonny, do you copy?'

Something is wrong.

Polack set off, back towards the entrance, Mack and the doctor in his wake, holding the unconscious Filippos between them, draped across their shoulders.

'Dominique,' Urday said, 'we're going to sweep this building. The main objective has been accomplished, but I want to take everything this place has to give. Start with that door you've been staring at.'

Dominique gave a seditious pause.

'Understood,' she growled eventually.

I could probably go over to her and have her, right now. There's no-one to stop me. No-one except Dominque. Besides, I have a job to do.

Urday walked over to the door that the old man had made for. He stepped over his corpse, pulled the handle, and nudged the door open with his left hand. Leading with his M16, he walked through. There were sofas, armchairs and wooden stools. There was a chessboard, with a game half finished. There were cabinets housing books and board games, and there were eleven doors cut into the uneven stone wall, such as it was.

Shit.

These must have been the sleeping quarters. If there was an escape route, it could have been built into any single one.

Or perhaps all of them. That's what I would have done, if I was designing the place.

Urday decided to act on his instincts. If there were eleven escape routes, they would all likely end up at the same place. Intelligence would have picked up at least one or two of the different exit points if there were eleven of them.

He walked into the first dormitory. A bed and nothing else. Urday dragged the bed across the floor, grunting with the exertion as he did, exposing a trap door, dusty and ancient. He pulled it open with the large brass circular pull, and pointed his M16 into darkness. When he flicked down his optics, the world below revealed itself in murky green.

Nothing but floor.

He dropped down, no more than a two-metre fall, and found himself in a tunnel. A tunnel that lead upwards, in only one direction.

There was crackling. Dominique was saying something over the comms device. Something about a safe and a book, but the signal was faint, and Urday ignored her. Instead, he sprinted, flying through the tunnels. He was quicker than any quarry, he knew. There were some backpacks on the floor, he ignored them, and ran right past. There were rocks, right in his path, some as high as his shin. He hurdled them with speed and ease. The roof was sloping downward, while the floor continued up. He was stooping as he ran to avoid banging his head on the ceiling.

He could see an opening up ahead. Where daylight would have been, had there been any. Instead, it was represented by a lighter shade of night vision green. And just in front of it, a group was moving. A skinny teenager, two tall men, and a large black man with a colossal frame and a child strapped to his chest.

Sonny was leading them out. Protecting them, the enemy. *Betrayal.*

They were near the opening. Urday raised his rifle and fired. The high pitched screaming told him that that his burst fire had secured a hit on the teenager, but not a major organ, probably a leg shot. His wounded prey pulled itself through the opening. Urday ran, but he was still 200 metres away.

Still, they won't get far.

Then the opening started to disappear. A large boulder was being rolled across the gap, and the gap was no more. Urday bellowed, and ran. He reached the boulder, and threw his weight at it, but it would not budge. The boulder was heavy, and it was sitting in a dip. Rage consumed Urday, he aimed back down the tunnel, and sent a hail of burst fire bullets into nothingness.

'SHIT!' he screamed. 'Shit. Shit. Shit.'

CHAPTER TWELVE

Praetorium of Pontius Pilate, Jerusalem
Month of Nissan, 30 AD

*That minds can be directed against the souls to which they are
yoked is something Yeshua never truly understood. No man
was more skilled at directing another's mind against his own
soul than Tavarius.*

-BOOK OF YESHUA

'I'm going to release him, Tavarius. By Clementia, goddess of
clemency, I'm going to release him,' Pilate informed his advisor,
sipping wine, studying Tavarius closely for his reaction.

*And why should I care for the man's reaction? Why does his
estimation matter to me so?*

'Then your career is done,' Tavarius said bluntly.

Pilate gave Tavarius his most threatening stare. They sat
either side of the granite table that stood at the centre of his
tablinum.

He has grown too blunt, he forgets himself.

It became clear to Pilate that his advisor was not going to
amend his statement.

'More than my political career is at stake here, Tavarius. I
will not kill a god. You saw what he did, that was no trick, no illusion, only a god could do what he did.'

'I share your misgivings, Prefect,' Tavarius said, leaning
back in his chair.

Pilate sipped his wine, inhaling the distinctive citrus notes, and contemplated Tavarius' response for a moment.

'*Do* you, Tavarius?'

If he thought for even a moment that Yeshua was a god, he would not still argue for his execution. And yet, he was there, he saw.

'I do, Prefect. I argue not for his actual execution.'

It's as if the man can read minds.

'The man's life, or death, means nothing to me. To *us*. What matters is that we give the Sanhedrin no cause to incite riot, and incite riot they will, unless we do as they wish.'

Pilate scoffed at this.

'The Sanhedrin want Yeshua *dead*, Tavarius, as well you know. They want me to kill a god. What fate awaits a man who kills a god? Can he even be killed?'

This gave Tavarius pause. Then he smiled, as though a thought had just come to him. Pilate doubted this, however. Tavarius hatched all his schemes in the quiet, solitary darkness of his soul, not in the course of conversation.

'Prefect, what if there was a way that we could give the Sanhedrin what they want, and avoid deicide?'

'Well obviously, Tavarius, I would be open to that,' Pilate said testily, 'tell me of your plan.'

'Sentence Yeshua to death. The Sanhedrin will be appeased and will have no cause to blame us for what happens afterwards.'

'When *what* happens afterwards?'

'Have you heard, Prefect, of *Chen*?'

Pilate shook his head reluctantly. He recognised the word as Hebrew, but had no recollection of its meaning.

I know too little of the Jewish faith. Do I underestimate it still?

'It is an ancient custom in Jewish law, limited to the time of Passover. It is many years since it was last used, since Sanhedrin brought prosecutions are now forbidden during the Passover. Nevertheless, it still stands. If just one of the Sanhedrin makes the request, you would be legally and honour bound to allow them to choose one Jewish prisoner convicted during the

Passover for release.'

Pilate sighed, and kneaded his forehead with his knuckles, disappointed.

'Fool,' he spat, 'they would not choose Yeshua for release.'

'I believe they would, Prefect. I have conferred with Evandrus, only one other Jewish prisoner has been convicted during the Passover. A prosecution brought not by the Sanhedrin, but by Linus.'

Linus. As a Judean legate posted in Jerusalem, whose jurisdiction covered the Lower City, Linus brought the majority of prosecutions to the Praetorium. Most were handled by Evandrus as Praetor in Pilate's absence. Pilate trusted Linus, and thought highly of his skills, and had never been given cause to doubt his loyalty to Pilate and the Empire both.

'Who is the prisoner?'

'Another Yeshua, Yeshua Bar-Abba.'

The name was familiar to Pilate, from one of Evandrus' reports that had landed with him only the day before.

'The one who...?'

'Raped children, yes,' Tavarius replied matter-of-factly.

Pilate gave this some thought.

Surely Tavarius is right. The Sanhedrin would not free a child-rapist whose crimes are well known. Their own followers would turn against them if they did. But, can I sign the death warrant of a god?

'Even if you speak truly, Tavarius, I am sentencing a god to death. Whether or not he will actually die, I will be guilty of that crime in his eyes.'

'Not if he knows what you have done. When a man tells his father-in-law that he would never beat his wife, but then proceeds to do so, is he judged by his words or his actions?'

'His actions,' Pilate conceded.

'Words give lie to the truth of a man's soul, Prefect. And your soul will be innocent, even if your words are not.'

This unsettled Pilate, but he could find no fault with the logic.

'But they will not evoke this Chen, surely.'

'It takes only one to evoke it, Prefect,' Tavarius smiled, 'and it just so happens that one of their number is mine.'

This was news to Pilate, though he knew Tavarius had many agents. 'Really? Who?'

'I think it's best if I do not say for now.'

'I... do not understand this, Tavarius. Why do the Sanhedrin continue to push for his execution? They witnessed his divinity as well as you and I.'

'Yeshua made the leaders of the Jewish faith his enemies, by preaching about their hypocrisy, their perversions, their vanities. But many *have* walked away of late, witness the young man who stands as advocate for Yeshua. What remains are the hardened core of the Sanhedrin, those who would kill a god, and the truth with it, in order to preserve their lies, and their standing.'

'And you would have me do the *same thing*, preserve my standing, at the risk of my soul. I will not wager my soul Tavarius. Do you swear to me that your man will do as you say? Do you swear it on... your life?'

I can think of nothing else that is precious enough to him to make any such vow worthwhile.

'I swear to you on my life Prefect. And think on this: taking this path might make Yeshua a friend, or at least an ally. He will be indebted to you when he learns the truth of what you have done. And I will ensure that he learns the truth. If Yeshua is all that he appears to be, his allegiance may be more important, and beneficial, than that of Tiberius himself.'

'See it done, then.'

ΑΩ

The audience chamber awaited Yeshua's sentencing with baited breath.

Little do they know of what is to come.

The thought brought a smile to Pilate, who moved quickly to suppress it and arrange his face into a picture of solemn authority.

'Prefect,' Evandrus began. He was the only other man in the chamber standing.

How reassuring Evandrus' voice is to me. It never cracks or wavers. He would use the same tone in some meaningless, inconsequential trial as he does for a man who performed miracles in front of a packed assembly.

'Have you considered all the evidence presented to you, both for and against the accused?'

Pilate looked at the floor. 'I have.'

'And have you reached a verdict as to the guilt or innocence relating to all the charges brought against the accused?'

'I have.' Pilate heard his voice waver, and hated it.

This plan will work.

'And what are the verdicts?'

Pilate sought Yeshua's eyes, and found them. He couldn't discern what he found there, but he trusted that the man, a god, might read his intentions through his face.

Please, see that I do not truly condemn you.

Something flickered in Yeshua's face. Something that might even have been acknowledgement.

'On the two counts of fomenting non-aggressive rebellion,' Pilate boomed, 'I find Yeshua of Nazareth to be guilty. On the count of fomenting aggressive rebellion, I find Yeshua of Nazareth to be guilty.'

An explosion of noise followed. The Sanhedrin thundered their applause. The witnesses who had attested to Yeshua's divinity *howled* their disapproval. Boaz Ben-Jada thumped the air with a vigour Pilate would not have thought possible from the old man. He left his seat and tottered over to a group of soldiers in the hall, and shook their hands.

Two Fretensis legionaries grabbed Yeshua, who turned to Pilate with hurt and disappointment written across his face.

Pilate felt his heart drop.

Perhaps... perhaps he plays the mummer too. Or perhaps he's only a man after all.

The sentencing was not yet complete, and so Pilate raised his arm, and silence fell across the hall.

I am Prefect still.

'There is no discretion concerning the charge of fomenting aggressive rebellion. The sentence is death,' Evandrus informed the hall.

The legionaries started to march Yeshua towards the back of the audience chamber.

'Wait,' a feeble voice croaked.

Everyone was looking around for the source of this impertinence.

Surely not.

'Wait,' Boaz Ben-Jada repeated.

Boaz is Tavarius' man? What game is he playing?

'It is the Passover. I wish to evoke Chen.'

This time, the howling came from the Sanhedrin. There was a collective bemusement in the Roman contingent, who were evidently unfamiliar with this obscure concept. Boaz cowered behind the two legionaries, who braced themselves.

Pilate raised his hand for silence once more, then sought Yeshua's eyes with his own.

Please, see what I am doing. This is the only way.

This time, Yeshua shook his head sadly.

I... I don't understand.

'You have that right,' Evandrus informed the court, lacking his usual certainty.

Pilate did his level best to appear confused and frustrated. It was not a hard act. 'What is this meaning of this Praetor?' Pilate boomed.

'By law, Prefect, when Chen is evoked, we must release one Jewish prisoner convicted during the Passover.'

'I see,' Pilate said, affecting to sound perturbed, 'and... who chooses which prisoner?'

'The Sanhedrin, Prefect.'

'And I am bound by this?'

'Yes, Prefect.'

Pilate paused, as though contemplating what other options might be open to him, before scowling as though he had concluded that he had been successfully trapped.

A consummate performance.

'I see. Evandrus, what other Jewish prisoners meet these criteria.'

'There is only one, Prefect. Yeshua Bar-Abba.'

Phlegmy disgust rose in the throats of those in the chamber. It seemed that the man's crimes were well known.

That is good.

'Very well, if the court is bound, either Yeshua of Nazareth or Yeshua Bar-Abba will be released. I would advise that the Sanhedrin take recess and come to a decision.'

'There will be no need,' a voice replied from the front of the Sanhedrin benches. A powerful voice.

Caiaphas.

The man was smirking.

This is not good.

'As High-Priest, I speak with the authority of the entire Sanhedrin. Give us Bar-Abba. Yeshua of Nazareth dies.'

Pilate felt bile rise in the back of his throat. He looked at Yeshua, who stared back, with a blank expression. Pilate searched the hall desperately with his eyes. Tavarius was nowhere to be seen.

'So. Be. It,' Yeshua said over the furore, and the power of his voice commanded silence.

'So be it,' he said again, 'you have made your choices. And you *will* reap what you sow.'

What have I done?

Pilate bowed his head, and wept, silently, not caring for the shame of such a womanly act.

What have I done?

CHAPTER THIRTEEN

Dordogne Valley, France
Month of June, 2024 AD

*Two millennia of searching, all the while being hunted, and
I am tired. Being tired, unfortunately, is no excuse, when the
world suffers more with our every failure.*

-BOOK OF YESHUA

Rock had never been heavy, but draped between Elliot and the
man who called himself "Sonny", he certainly felt burdensome,
even though Judah and Sonny had carried Rock for the bulk of
the past couple of hours.

Elliot, who was struggling now, marvelled at the strength
and resilience of this Sonny, who not only held Rock across one
of his shoulders, but a small, unconscious blonde girl strapped
to his chest, and an assault rifle to his back. Rock was barely
more conscious than the girl. His eyes were wide with the horror and threat of death when opened, but shut more often than
not.

*Who is this man who wears the red eye of the Igigi? A man
damned, and yet one who knows us, and saved us, gave us the head
start we needed to get out.*

But asking the question was pointless. They needed him,
else Sarlat, and safety, would be beyond their reach.

Keep going, I must keep going.

Judah could see that Elliot was struggling. 'We must stop.'

'We can't, not yet,' Sonny said in his booming voice. 'You know they'll still be looking for us. The further we are from Araboth, the better.'

'Araboth?' Elliot asked.

'Your compound.'

'Urghhhhhh,' Rock moaned weakly.

'If we don't hurry,' Elliot groaned, 'he's going to bleed out.'

Rock's bandaged left leg was soaked, ominously, in burgundy. The bandages that had allowed Judah to save Rock's life, using the skills of a physician acquired over many years, had come from the escape packs that Judah had stowed in each tunnel.

But it would have all been for nothing, were it not for the large, black-painted aluminium foil sheets that Sonny had had stashed in his pack. Elliot wasn't sure if he could actually hear the helicopter, a Puma attack helicopter Sonny had informed then, or not. There had definitely been two genuine occasions when the thrum of the Puma had filled the air, vibrations Elliot could feel, while blinking lights beamed through the frustratingly cloudless night sky, seeking them. They had crouched, still, breathing heavily, under the foil that allowed them to avoid infra-red detection.

The sound of the Puma had taken root in Elliot's head, a constant pulsing threat.

When Elliot nearly collapsed, Judah took Rock from him once more. The small, hunted party trudged on through the fields, a hundred meters or so in from the road, walking parallel to it. Or so Elliot trusted, for Judah knew this route better than he. Sarlat-le-Caneda wasn't the closest town, which was why Judah insisted that they make for it. Besides, Judah knew a doctor there with an emergency set-up, who could help Rock, and provide a safe-house. They couldn't walk in to a hospital, all the local hospitals would be monitored, Sonny had told them.

Elliot was hungry now, they had mint cakes in their packs, but he was too hungry to eat. Judah had insisted that Rock eat, once Rock had finished his vomiting. He had tried to force Elliot to eat too, but in the end, had settled for Elliot taking a few sips of water from an aluminium bottle.

Discomfort and hope kept grief and horror at bay. Elliot wore only a t-shirt, and the cold of the night pressed hard against Elliot's bare face and the small of his back. Sickly hunger gnawed at his stomach, and his shoulder ached and throbbed. He didn't complain though, he knew Judah had shouldered more of the burden. And Sonny, whoever he was, made no complaints, and betrayed no weakness. Judah carried Rock's pack, as well as his own. Sonny seemed to barely notice Rock's weight against his frame, nor the girl strapped to his chest, looking fragile, even peaceful. The few times Elliot had looked directly at Sonny, the man had looked agitated, as though he would like to move quicker, but was being held back by the others' feebleness.

Hope drove Elliot on. They had not seen the Puma that hunted them for quite some time, and Judah insisted he had not heard it either.

'The Puma would not have lingered too long,' Sonny said, into the silence. 'You... we... are not their priority, capturing Filippos was.'

'But,' Judah said, sounding panicked, 'they can't know which...'

'The elderly Mediterranean man, with the moustache. They know.'

'But... how?'

'Surveillance, financial forensics, Interpol, and mathematicians plotting your lives like pins on a map. Tavarius' resources are limitless, and his cunning boundless.'

'Shit,' said Judah, who looked as though he was going to weep. 'Yossef, we can't let them take him again.'

'He is already taken,' Sonny said firmly.

AΩ

The merest hint of grey light was starting to seep into the dark world. Enough to feed their hope, but not enough to expose them; so long as they kept up their pace, they would make it to Sarlat before the dawn.

Elliot could see that Judah was now struggling badly, and despite his pain, took on Rock's weight once more, Rock's limp arm, though thin, was like granite, crushing his muscles. They were stumbling along the edge of a copse when Elliot turned his ankle on a stone, smooth and slippery with early morning fog. He fell, and lost his grip on Rock, who fell clumsily in to Judah, without so much as a grunt.

The ankle hurt, but it wasn't broken, or sprained. Elliot had broken and sprained enough ankles in his lifetimes to know.

'When did he lose consciousness?' Elliot asked.

'Not sure, a while back, I think. Sarlat isn't far.' But Judah sounded worried.

'Will he live?' Elliot finally dared to ask.

Neither Judah nor Sonny replied. Sonny pulled Rock up as though he were a log, and braced him horizontally across his back. They walked on, down a track of dried mud, the imprint of tractor tyres preserved by the drought. Their backs were turned to the threat of sun, the barest sliver of which was peeking nervously above the horizon.

At the bottom of the dried mud track, they started up a steep hill. Every step was effort.

One more step. And another, just one more.

At the top of the hill, Sarlat twinkled into view through the gloom and mists.

Beautiful.

It was peaceful still, very little noise. Grief hit Elliot then. Certain forms of grief at least. Elliot was an expert in grief. Grief was to Elliot as snow was to an Inuit.

This grief was sharp, pricking at him, with no room for sedentary melancholy. It was comprised of smaller griefs. Grief for the suffering of his brothers. Death hurt, he knew, and the boys they had been before maturity were gone.

Beneath this he could sense grief for the unknown. Elliot had not known *this* Taddai, *this* Yohanan. And now he never would.

The deepest layer of grief was for the known. True mourning. Tau'ma and Filippos. Dead, hopefully, though Sonny was certain that Filippos had been taken alive. Men who had made him laugh, made him feel alive. Men who had loved him.

But this composite grief was tempered. He mourned the departure of the visage, not the essence. Perversely, for they had caused this suffering, Elliot felt fleeting kinship with the Annunaki. There was comfort, and safety, in the guarantee of reincarnation. The animal that gnawed at his innards would not destroy him because of what he knew about the reincarnation of the souls.

But life *was* suffering in the end. The more lives he had lived, the more Elliot felt the truth of this. Yeshua had taught him this, as Yossef, and though he had accepted it, he had not understood it, not truly. Life, even now, was not without joy. But becoming one with divinity was an end to suffering. A different kind of consciousness awaited, one hard to conceive, but one experienced, fleetingly. Through his meditations, Elliot had some idea of what reunification with the One Whole Consciousness meant. He had felt the joy of existence beyond and outside identity. After far too many lives, trapped with a single point of consciousness, he craved reunion with the divinity. Not just for himself, but for all settled souls.

Elliot slumped to the ground, heedless of Judah's exhortations to continue. He wept. There was no shame, not in front of Judah, and at this moment, he did not know who Sonny was, and he did not care. Centuries of grief welled within him, and needed at outlet. He had seen all his brothers weep like this.

All except Rock, he is a brother now. But for how long?

Elliot stood. The sooner they got Rock into proper medical care, the better his chances of survival. They started down the hill, towards the nearest sprawling tentacle of the stirring monster that was Sarlat-la-Caneda.

CHAPTER FOURTEEN

Praetorium of Pontius Pilate, Jerusalem
Month of Nissan, 30 AD

The distinction between salvation and damnation is subtle.
Symeon, fool that he is, mistook subtlety for irrelevance. The
whole world suffers for one man's misunderstanding.

-BOOK OF YESHUA

'You are bound by your authority, Prefect,' Evandrus informed him, 'there is no precedent for overturning a Prefect's determination of guilt, even by the self-same Prefect. I am sorry.'

There was never any curiosity voiced by Evandrus. When alone with Pilate, he would always speak Latin, the language of procedure. He did not ask why Pilate wanted to overturn his decision. He was good at what he did, and he could be a flexible thinker when it was asked of him. But you always had to ask, with Evandrus.

'If I were adamant, Praetor, I could simply set a new precedent, could I not? By Justitia, I will not let Yeshua of Nazareth die, *if* he can die. I do not intend to find out.'

Evandrus watched Pilate for a moment from across the stone table, as though unsure of Pilate's sincerity.

'I see, Prefect,' he said eventually, 'will you give me some time to think of the best path to take? Ultimately, you are the authority, and your will shall be done.'

'Think quickly then Evandrus, Yeshua is being taken to

Golgotha as we speak.'

There was an insistent knock on the door to Pilate's tablinum that fell just short of pounding.

What? What now?

'Go Evandrus, think on it, I will call on you for your solution shortly. Enter,' Pilate said more loudly, for the ears of the supplicant without.

It wasn't one supplicant, however. It was two. One man, Pilate didn't know. He was Jewish, dressed poorly, brown skinned, low-born. The other was Tavarius. The man his personal guard had been out hunting all day without success had come to him willingly, and seemingly unarmed.

Never a good idea to trust to appearances with Tavarius of Jericho.

Pilate felt a chill then, that wasn't down entirely to the setting of the sun and the warmth draining from the stones that had, not long ago, cooked his feet through his sandals.

'Guards!' Pilate bellowed.

The two remaining guards he had kept at the Praetorium, Cornelius and Felix, had been posted outside in the courtyard. At Pilate's command, they came clanking through the archway, preceded by their long shadows.

'Seize this man,' Pilate said, pointing an accusatory finger at Tavarius. The guards moved over and grasped Tavarius by the arms. Tavarius seemed unperturbed.

'We've been here before, it seems,' Tavarius said calmly.

'I have no time for your games Tavarius. You either betrayed me, or failed me. I would have chosen my soul over my career, and your slippery tongue took that choice away from me. I should have it cut out.'

'Are we Cherusci barbarians now, meting out cruel and undeserved punishments? I came here to help, Prefect. As I have always done. Why else would I be here?'

'Which was it, Tavarius? Did you betray me, or fail me? Did you know Caiaphas would ask for the release of Bar-Abba, or with all your sources and intellect, did you fail to anticipate it?'

'I knew that Caiaphas wanted him dead, Prefect. But I did not betray you, truly. Take my head if you must, but hear me first, I implore you.'

Yes, I will take his head. Though it is poor compensation for my soul.

'You swore on your life, Tavarius. Your life is mine. I would pray, if I were you, to Laverna, goddess of thieves and charlatans. Speak, if you must, then I *will* take your head.'

'It will not only be I that speaks Prefect, I have brought with me one Symeon Bar-Jonah. The man was a disciple to Yeshua. Studied with him, travelled with him, and Yeshua confided in him.'

'*You* speak, then, Symeon Bar-Jonah,' Pilate leered at the caste-menial, 'perhaps I shall take your head too.'

'Prefect,' Symeon Bar-Jonah said nervously, 'I have known Yeshua of Nazareth, these past five years.'

The man spoke Greek every bit as fluently as Yeshua, with less provincial stink to his accent. Though poor, dressed barely better than a beggar, this was a man of learning.

'Tavarius has assured me,' Symeon continued, 'that you will at least entertain the possibility that Yeshua is a god.'

Pilate said nothing, but inclined his head ever so slightly.

Who else but a god could know what he knew, do what he did?

'I can tell you, with absolute certainty, that he is. I have seen him do things that only a god could do. I have heard him explain the workings of our world with the clarity and understanding that could only belong to one who is its architect. And though I am part of his inner circle no longer, he has shared secrets with me, about the world, about me, about souls, that you may find... interesting.'

'Indulge my curiosity for a time, then.'

'When a man dies, Yeshua taught us, one of three fates await that soul. Some souls are reabsorbed into the divine from which they came, some are reborn, and live a mortal life once again. And some souls, those who have been truly wicked, are cast off into oblivion. Damnation.'

Livia was reborn, Yeshua said.

'But salvation and damnation are impossible, so long as Yeshua remains out of godhead. You *are* damned, Prefect. Yeshua told Caiaphas and Boaz Ben-Jada as much. And their crimes are lesser than yours.'

'Watch your tongue, I have committed no crimes Jew.'

'How could you, when you are the law? I speak not of crimes but of *sin*. The damage the soul can do to itself. But even were you not damned, would becoming one with divinity be much better? You would still lose your essence. Better, surely, to be reborn?'

Yes.

Death had always terrified Pilate. Rebirth, though not a Roman notion, was an appealing antidote. Pilate had no desire to ever pass through the gates of Dis.

'If Yeshua is killed, Prefect, he cannot return to his full divinity. We know that he needs to go to a certain location to re-assume his godhead. If that can be prevented, every soul will be reborn. What a gift, for humanity. Release the shackles of your own damnation. You have it in your power to stop Yeshua's death, but why would you? You do not benefit, no-one benefits.'

Pilate gave no response; he was lost in thought.

Is it the man, or his arguments that are persuasive? Does he obscure truth, or reveal it?

'Prefect', Tavarius said, clearly sensing an opportunity, 'if Symeon speaks truly, it would be better if Yeshua died. We would be liberators, like Sisyphus.'

Sisyphus, the mortal who overcame a god, and was loved for it. A story, but...

'If Symeon speaks falsely,' Tavarius continued, 'and Yeshua is no god, then it would still be better if Yeshua died, the Sanhedrin are appeased, and you keep your career.'

'But the crime of deicide...'

'Is no crime if there is no god to declare it so. Besides, Symeon hasn't told it all yet.'

Pilate said nothing.

Silence can be interpreted as ignorance or wisdom. That is the best I can do at the moment. I have been ignorant ever since Yeshua of Nazareth was dragged in to my Praetorium.

'I was one of Yeshua's chosen, Prefect,' Symeon said, 'we who were chosen were promised a different type of rebirth. We need not face each life with ignorance of those that came before. *Soul-imprinting* Yeshua names it. Allowing the soul to remember itself.'

'In less than one life time, think of how much power you have accumulated, Prefect,' Tavarius said, with a simpering obsequiousness that made Pilate feel nostalgic, 'imagine what a soul such as yours could accomplish across hundreds of lifetimes, thousands. A number beyond counting. We... you could become as a god.'

'How is it, Symeon, that you were one of Yeshua's chosen, and yet you sit here, ready to condemn him?' Pilate asked.

'I made the decision to forsake my teacher before this moment, Prefect. When I first approached Caiaphas.'

'Caiaphas!?' Pilate spluttered, turning to Tavarius, 'you schemed with *Caiaphas?*'

'I... did. Prefect.'

'You scheme with my enemy. Why should I permit you to live?'

'Because,' Tavarius replied firmly, 'it is in your interest to do so. Do not pretend that you have not known how much I do beneath the murky depths of the Judean political swamp. If I do not tell you everything, it is to *protect* you if my schemes go awry. But when have I ever not acted in your best interests? I left you out of this scheme until I could no longer avoid doing so, because it insulated you from reprisals, should things go wrong.'

Pilate ignored his advisor, for the moment. He turned instead to Symeon.

'The scheming of Tavarius is second nature to him, the man is a serpent. But you... I do not understand, explain to me why you have done what you have.'

'My responsibility to every soul in this world outweighs

my responsibility to Yeshua, a man I still love, in many ways. I see damnation and salvation both as burdens no soul should have to bare.'

'I see,' Pilate said, though he did not, not truly.

Is this a game, in which I am once again being played?

'How does it work, this *soul-imprinting*?'

'It's fairly simple, Prefect. One must drink some of Yeshua's blood. If this is done, upon reaching maturity, twenty-one years of age, Andrea tells me...'

'Andrea?' Pilate asked irritably.

'My brother by blood, Prefect. Another of Yeshua's chosen. Though loyal to Yeshua, he loves me still. Yeshua did not teach me the secrets of soul-imprinting. But he did teach my brother, and Andrea keeps no secrets from me. There is a phrase one must state, shortly after supping on Yeshua's blood, else the soul-imprinting will not work. But if all is done right, upon reaching maturity the soul will remember its past lives. Until Yeshua, in godhead, declares otherwise. If we prevent him from returning to godhead by killing him...'

'But *how*? How can we kill a god?'

'Yeshua wanted to live, truly, as a human being. All divine capabilities, including healing, can be attributed to the Kishar Stone that he carries on his person. If that is taken from him, I believe that he can be killed.'

Pilate pondered this.

'If Symeon is wrong about Yeshua's divinity,' Tavarius piped up, 'we lose nothing by drinking Yeshua's blood. If he is right, we have *everything* to gain. Including the Kishar Stone, the power of a *god*.'

There was a hunger to Tavarius. Pilate didn't trust the man any more, if he ever had, but he trusted his greed. Trusted to the greed in all men, and Tavarius' greed was palpable, something Pilate could almost taste in the air.

The prize of immortality.

Pilate noticed, then, that Tavarius was no longer in the grasp of his guards, though Pilate had not given such an order.

What kind of power is it that this man possesses? What kind of power will he yield if gifted an immortal mind?

CHAPTER FIFTEEN

Dordogne Valley, France
Month of June, 2024 AD

*Wounds heal, unless you pick at them. I have known wounds
that itch and itch so that I felt as if I had no choice but to pick
at them. This was a lie I told myself, but still, I pick at wounds.
Symeon's betrayal is such a wound.*

-BOOK OF YESHUA

The house seemed like every other in Sarlat, a restored building,
thin and tall. Ancient in memories, but rebuilt several times
and new in stone. It was, Elliot thought, stoic.

The doctor, who boasted a neat, greying beard, was
handsome in an unassuming, middle-aged way. He spoke only
French, and seemed to know and like Judah well, his smile upon
seeing him overwriting immediately and completely the an-
noyance at an early morning disturbance.

'It has been many months since you called here, Willem.
Your rare social visits are never this early.' The doctor's eyes
flicked to the unconscious bodies supported by Sonny, the girl
strapped to his chest and Rock, who looked but a boy, slung over
the man's broad shoulders. Elliot was glad that Sonny had had
the foresight to hide his rifle in a skip in Sarlat's outskirts.

'So this must be something professional, no?' he said with
unapologetic French lyrical rapidity.

This was a man, Elliot realised, conditioned to perpetual

busyness.

'Nazaire, we must come in quickly, I'm afraid.'

Elliot noticed that Judah's French was impeccable, and up to date, though the man had not been French in almost a millennium. There was, almost certainly, no greater linguist in the world than Judah of Kerioth.

'Our friend has been shot, can you help him?'

'I will do what I can, come in, come in,' the doctor said.

Elliot was reassured by the man's bearing and visage. Despite being in pyjamas, and slippers, he did not look crumpled or sleepy. He gave off an air of confidence and competence. They were bustled through the hallway, into the front room.

'The girl?' Nazaire asked.

'Sedated,' Sonny replied, 'she will wake soon, but... she must stay here, for a time at least.'

Nazaire scowled at this, but said nothing. In the living room, the doctor walked towards an old wooden door, out of keeping with the clean, white, modern decor of the living space. Nazaire opened it, and ushered them down narrow stairs, so narrow that Sonny was forced to turn sideways, in order to protect Rock's head from bouncing against the wall.

The basement, which clearly served as a medical room, was spacious, well lit, well-equipped and scrupulously clean. Sonny laid Rock with care on the operating table at the far end of the basement. Rock's left trouser leg had already been cut away, and Nazaire began to do likewise with the improvised bandaging.

Judah, Sonny, and Elliot were banished from the basement while Nazaire worked.

'Your presence here does no-one any good. Go, make coffee, sit on the balcony, get some sleep, whatever. There is food in the fridge. But leave us.'

Reluctantly, Judah and Elliot stumbled up the stairs. Exhaustion weighed heavy on Elliot now, as if his head was made from a much denser material than the rest of his body. He collapsed on the nearest sofa in the living room. Judah joined him. Sonny perched nervously on an armchair, as far away from Judah and Elliot as possible. He began to unstrap the girl from his chest, then laid her next to him. His size made the armchair seem absurdly small.

'Nazaire is a good doctor, Yossef,' Judah glanced at Sonny, who seemed oblivious, 'if Daniel can be saved, Nazaire will do it.'

The words delivered no comfort to Elliot. He needed distraction.

'The doctor, Nazaire, he called you "Willem."'

'A name I use. Not my given name.'

'So, what is your given name?'

Inexplicably, Judah laughed then. An uncharacteristically bitter, almost scornful laugh.

'Thijmen.'

Elliot laughed.

A Dutch iteration of the traitor's name. Symeon Bar-Jonah, like some creature, lurking beneath the surface of the world, with slimy tentacles that reach across space and time, breaking the surface every so often. Sometimes harmlessly, as with Judah's given name, sometimes devastatingly.

In the corner, Sonny cleared his throat. 'You know,' he said softly in a voice that still, somehow, boomed across the room, 'who I am.'

It was not a question. Elliot glanced at Judah, who blinked slowly, and sighed deeply.

'You know,' he said, this time in Aramaic, 'who I am.'

Andrea. Of course Elliot had known.

'I...we...yes,' Judah said, at last, 'but, how can it be? You were not with us when we were imprinted.'

A wall of silence halved the room.

'You will need some time, I understand this,' Sonny said, 'we will get some sleep, then we will have a conversation as old friends. Saving your lives is worth that much at least.'

As though permission, or instruction, was all he needed, Elliot closed his eyes, and darkness took him.

ΑΩ

Elliot awoke from a deep, and mercifully dreamless sleep. He stretched, feeling aches all over his body. Some of it, like the cramping in his leg was almost bittersweet, while the throbbing in his shoulder was a pain that made him grit his teeth. He was sweating, and so kicked off a throw that hadn't been there when he had fallen asleep.

Judah was awake. He looked awful, very pale. He was crouched on the floor, near a transparent and empty coffee table, feeding slices of banana to the little blonde girl, who was hunched like a monkey and eating furtively. There was no sign of Sonny... Andrea.

'Shhhh, you are safe now,' Judah was saying to the little girl, his French pitched to be soothing.

The girl did not respond. The trauma of events was too close, and even Judah's usually calming presence was failing.

'Any word on Rock?' Elliot asked.

Judah was startled, and evidently, had not noticed Elliot waking, or stretching.

'He's stable,' Judah said, 'one of the bullets has been removed. The other was too close to an artery. He's had a blood transfusion.'

'Whose blood?' Elliot asked, knowing the answer.

It should have been my blood.

'Mine. I'm O-positive. Nazaire needed it done quickly, and he's used my blood before.'

Judah knows my soul so well.

The banana finished, the girl crawled behind the arm of the black leather sofa, and cowered there like a beaten dog.

Judah sighed, then motioned to Elliot to retract his legs. Elliot did so, and Judah sat beside him.

'Have you spoken with *him?*' Elliot asked.

The traitor's brother. A traitor himself.

'No.'

'Where is he?'

'Out.'

'Is it definitely him?' Elliot asked, knowing the answer in his soul.

'I believe it is. Yeshua talked with Andrea, alone, before we fled in our different ways. Andrea to Symeon, us into the desert. It is possible that Andrea was imprinted then. Who else could know... what he knows?'

'The Annunaki.'

'Then why help us?'

Elliot was stumped. 'What does he want, then?'

'We must find out, Yossef. He wants to meet... at Place de la Liberté. Come with me, see what he has to say. What do we have to lose? Let us forget what we feel and *think*. He did save our lives, he's right when he says that we owe him that much. And besides, if he truly is Andrea, and served as an Igigi, deplorable as that is, *think* of what he must know, how he can help us.'

'"What do we have to lose?" Judah! It could be a trap. Perhaps he isn't Andrea. And *even if he is*, there is no soul in this world less trustworthy, save perhaps his accursed brother.'

'It's just us now, old friend. Let us find out what he knows. We have nothing else to do but run and hide and wait years for our brothers to return.'

'And what of Filippos?'

'At present, we do not even know where he is. Andrea might be our best chance of finding Filippos too.'

Elliot had no response to this, so instead, he changed course.

'Why does he want to meet out in public? Are we not safer here?'

Judah shrugged. 'If the Annunaki know we are in Sarlat, we are done. If they do not... well, we cannot stay here forever.'

'What about Daniel, and the girl?'

'They will stay with Nazaire, for a period of convalescence. And the further away we are from this house, the safer all of them will be.'

'And the Doctor, he's happy with such an arrangement?'

Why am I being argumentative? Judah is not to blame for this.

'He is... resigned to it. I can be quite persuasive, you know.'

Despite himself, Elliot smiled. 'I will meet with him, for your sake. But I cannot forgive him.'

'I don't ask it of you.'

ΑΩ

The sense of doom that coursed through Elliot was compounded by stepping out of the house and into night. There was always something unsettling about waking to night, something that tightened his stomach. The last time had been half a year's previous, on New Year's Eve, back at his parents house in Cornwall. He had drank until the dawn, and awakened in darkness. The memory of the hangover felt real, as though it had travelled across time and space and now manifested itself in the headache and sickness he felt. Since departing Yamaloka the previous night he had had only a banana, at Judah's insistence. He would have to get something to eat at Place de la Liberté.

They walked the narrow cobbled streets of Sarlat in silence, as the town around them bustled with nocturnal nonchalant merriment. Elliot had showered before leaving, and Nazaire had provided them with a fresh set of clothing. A group of young women, tottering in high heels and talking at alcohol inspired volume watched Elliot pass with frank admiration, presumably at his height and facial symmetry.

It felt good, for a second, to be desired. And then he felt guilt.

Yet again I betray Lucy. She deserved so much better from me.

Place de la Liberté glittered and reverberated with the relentless bass emanating from one of the bars. Despite hundreds of people milling around, Sonny...Andrea was hard to miss. The man was perched on a small plastic chair like a circus elephant on a stool at an otherwise empty table outside *La Ruche*. *La Ruche* was one of the quieter bars in the square, both in volume and density of revellers. Andrea was sipping slowly at a bottle of lager and picking at the label, bored and agitated.

Elliot and Judah walked over and joined Andrea. Before anything could be said, an over eager waiter swooped in, clearly relieved at having something to do. They ordered some fries and bottles of lager.

'Thank you', Judah started in quiet Aramaic 'for saving our lives.'

Elliot grunted in reluctant agreement.

'It was always my plan,' Andrea replied also in Aramaic, 'I understand that you may not trust me, at the moment, history speaks against me, I...

'You betrayed us,' Elliot hissed in English, 'you condemned Yeshua, us, the entire fucking world.'

'Yes,' said Andrea, without remorse, 'and no. Do not confuse the incidental for the essential. I was saving my brother's soul. All I did, I did for love of my little brother, fool that he was...is. Yeshua saw only love in me, and that is why he imprinted my soul. Yeshua is... was... at least, somewhat naïve. He could not foresee how love can lead people astray. Symeon is as dear to me as any of you *still*, despite what he did... what he does.'

'So we were all, collateral damage, is that it?' Elliot spat back.

'Yes. When I realised what Symeon had done, I knew then that his soul was damned if Yeshua were to ever return to godhead. I loved Yeshua, but not as much as I loved Symeon. I did not choose my treachery. I did not choose my path.'

'That is always the lie men tell themselves,.' Elliot said.

'And you?' 'How many lives have you lived? Have you never walked away from those who needed you, loved you, and told yourself that you *had no choice*?'

'I... that's different.'

'How?'

'How? I did not make choices *for me*. I chose what was *right* over what I wanted.'

'As I did not,' Andrea admitted, 'I cannot change the past, but I can change the future. I am... exceptionally placed to do this.'

'And how is that?' Elliot asked, 'how is it that you wear the red eye of the Igigi?' We know, Andrea, what a man must do to join their order. What *evil* a man must willingly embrace.'

Elliot was talking more loudly than he had intended. He was practically shouting.

'Shhhh, brother, calm down.' Judah said.

All eyes on the table across from them were trained on Elliot, who realised he was half standing, his palms pressed flat on the flimsy plastic table.

The waiter brought over the fries, Elliot began to pick at them slowly. It was hard eating them, but it felt good, warmth seemed to spread through his body.

'You wear the red eye of the Igigi, Andrea,' Judah said with pointed calm, 'do you deny that you are one of them, Andrea? Do you deny that you are damned?'

'I do not,' Andrea said solemnly, 'and you do not know the half of it. Not only am I damned, my soul is more fractured than any man living, save Tavarius perhaps. Over the past few centuries I have joined, and rejoined the Igigi, undergoing *Initiation* over and over again.'

The horrifying implication of this knocked all the anger from Elliot. They had learned of the Initiations, the unspeakable acts those undertaking it were required to perform. To do so repeatedly... who knew what such exposure to evil could do to a soul? Perhaps only the man who sat across from him.

'But... why?' Judah asked, looking every bit as horrified as Elliot felt.

'For *this*' Andrea replied, with anger, 'for this moment. To make sure that when the Annunaki found you, I would be there, so that *I* could find you.'

'Why?' Judah asked.

'To undo what I have done. To return Yeshua to godhead. I know where he is. I know where the Kishar Stone is. With your help, we can set him free and return him to godhead. And I need your help. I need men I trust absolutely. I could attempt it myself, or with the help of mercenaries, but if it goes wrong, they will encase Yeshua in stone and drop him in the bottom of the ocean rather than risk future attempts at liberation.'

'And why haven't they done that?' Elliot asked, 'that was always our greatest fear. We would almost certainly never find Yeshua, so why haven't they done that?'

'They have found that his blood contains certain properties that grant health and long life. Something they take for themselves, and bestow on their most loyal servants, though of course the secrets of soul-imprinting they guard jealously.'

'And you can take us to Yeshua? And would do, so we might liberate him?' Judah asked.

'I have told you this. Yes.'

'But you are damned!' Elliot exclaimed, 'why would you want this?'

'Because I *suffer.* Oblivion is preferable to what I endure. And I desire the same for my brother. He would not admit as much, I think, though it is two millennia since we last spoke.'

'You have not spoken with your brother? He does not know you were soul-imprinted?' Judah asked, sounding surprised.

'He knows. Though Pilate and Tavarius do not. He made me a promise that he would not tell. Think what you will of my brother, but never has he broken his word to me. Never. But we have not spoken. At first I stayed away, tried to live life... lives outside of the Annunaki's sphere of influence. Until that sphere grew too great, encircled most of the world. And after that... when I decided that I must undo what I have done... I could not have him know of my intentions, for I could never lie to him. Not being able to talk to my brother, reveal myself, when we have been so close together for many lives, is a source of great frustration to me. At least, it was. I am, now, largely deadened to feeling. Shattering your soul over and over does that. I am driven, now, by the memories of feelings.'

'But my brother *must* now feel as I once felt,' Andrea added forcefully, 'purposeless, endless reincarnation. Surely he, too, would embrace his damnation.'

There was a pause, while Judah and Elliot contemplated this. Elliot sipped at his beer, it tasted cheap, and bitter.

'Where is he, then?' Judah asked finally, as though he did not expect an answer, or at least, an honest one, 'where is Yeshua?'

The question we have asked for two thousand years.

'Vatican City,' Andrea answered, not missing a beat, 'under a level of protection, it would require an army to penetrate. You ask yourselves why I need you, if I am being truthful about my intentions. Because, old friends, I have tried to liberate Yeshua myself, before. At the beginning of the fourth century I, and some recruits, men I paid good gold to, stormed the underground prison in Constantinople in which Yeshua had been held. One of the men, curse him, had informed Tavarius of our plan. He did not meet us at the arranged safe house on the day of the assault. That should have caused me to postpone, or even abandon the plan. But I did not. Instead, we proceeded, only to encounter a century of Roman soldiers. They cut us to pieces, and I feared that they would not allow any such opportunity again. But I was lucky. They never assumed I might be responsible, for my brother remained true to his word. They blamed you. I was also lucky that they continued to need, or at least want, Yeshua's blood. Tavarius is a greedy man, loathe to forsake an asset. He is, at heart, a gambler. And Vatican City, the great fortress that started as a basilica, and became the seat of the most terrible empire the world has ever known, was his throw of the die. They believe it impregnable.'

'But believe me, my brothers, if we come close, and fail, Yeshua will be lost to us for an eternity.'

Elliot and Judah exchanged knowing looks. They had always suspected that Vatican City held answers for them. Perhaps even Yeshua himself. But the bowels and hierarchy of that place were always beyond them. One could not climb as high, or delve as deep as one needed to access the secrets of the Vatican without wearing the eye of the Igigi. And now, if Andrea spoke truth, they finally had their in.

'A fortress,' Judah said slowly, 'requires an army to overcome it.'

'An army, or inside men, and it is this that I offer you. Me, and my colleague. You must meet with him, Judah. This man is one entrusted by the Annunaki, as I am. An Initiate... an Igigi. But not your enemy. You must meet with him, and speak with him, as I have. You will see the truth of him, when you meet him.'

'We can't,' Elliot said to Judah.

'You must,' Andrea said, with a passion in his voice that did not reach his eyes, 'this opportunity might be unique. I do not know for a certainty that they will not figure out the motivations behind my betrayal, perhaps even learn the truth of me. My brother, if questioned sharply enough, might crack. And time is of the essence. You know as well as I how close we stand to the abyss. The balance of the world is in threat. How many souls are trapped here now? Eight billion? Though I lack the capacity to experience the One Whole Consciousness these days, the memory of my meditations are enough. The world and the One Whole Consciousness both stand on the brink of terminal imbalance. How much longer can this go on for? A century or two? Mere decades?

'We know this,' Elliot said dismissively.

'Then you must also appreciate the importance of acting *now*. Take this chance, we may not have another. Come with me to Rome.'

'But...' Elliot said, shaking his head.

'But what? We *must*,' Judah said firmly, 'if there is even the slightest chance that Andrea speaks any truth here, we must try. If you will not, I still will. Will you come with me?'

Elliot sighed. 'Do you even have to ask that?'
Judah turned to Andrea.
'You will take us to Rome, then.'

CHAPTER SIXTEEN

Gate of the Column, Jerusalem
Month of Nissan, 30 AD

If any man could appreciate that remembered lives stack atop
each other until they crush the soul beneath them, they would
surely flee from soul-imprinting. Even if they were damned.

-BOOK OF YESHUA

With Josephus, captain of his personal guard, and Cornelius his
chosen second, Pilate rode out of the city, through the towering Gate of the Column. The gate was wide enough to admit
the entire mounted party. Only Symeon was uncomfortable on
a horse. He had, apparently, ridden a mule only once or twice.
Pilate smirked at the sight of the man, balanced precariously,
without any sense of the fact that he sat atop a living creature.

By Neptunus, god of horses, he looks a fool.

The execution party could be seen in the distance headed
towards Golgotha, walking into the rising sun, against which Pilate now shielded his eyes. Pilate, himself a skilled horseman,
took his Arabian to a trot, then a canter, enjoying the thud of
hoof on dry turf and the way his long crimson cloak whipped up
behind him. It made him look regal, perhaps even divine.

'Hail,' he cried in Latin to the six Fretensis legionaries who escorted Yeshua on his death walk, bearing his own
method of torture and execution across his back and shoulders.
'Hail.'

The shining, clanking, execution party stopped near a thicket, the rest of the land around them as barren as the sandy half-road they travelled.

More a beaten sand-track than a road. Rome is like a different world, in a different time. These people, my people, are savages, truly.

One legionary walked over to Pilate, and removed his pristine, polished galea.

'Prefect,' he said, his tone and his bow both low and reverent, 'I serve as Princeps Posterior here.'

'Princeps, my advisers and I need a word with the prisoner.'

The Princeps hesitated, this was, after all, against protocol. However, Pilate was Prefect, *the* authority. 'Yes, Prefect.'

'And we require... some privacy.'

'Yes, Prefect.' The Princeps bowed again, then turned and nodded towards Josephus, a display of respect. Josephus had served in the Fretensis legion before he had joined Pilate's personal guard. Pilate never had the impression that Josephus had been well liked, but his skills had certainly been respected, and Josephus had climbed the ranks to the position of Pilus Prior.

The Princeps and his contingent retreated some thirty cubits from the side of the road, such as it was.

Pilate approached Yeshua, who stood, looking perplexed, the stake to which he would be nailed across his shoulders. 'You may put that down, for a moment.'

'Oh, thank you,' Yeshua said, his voice dripping in sarcasm, 'you are too kind.'

Pilate ignored the quip, and Yeshua did indeed drop the stake from his shoulders, and the ropes from around his arms to the floor.

'Why are you here, Pilate?' Yeshua asked, his voice weary.

Pilate said nothing.

Why am *I here?*

Tavarius answered for him. 'There is something we need.' He walked over to the thicket, and snapped off a large thorn, large enough that it required two hands to do so.

Yeshua's face betrayed miserable understanding.

'You condemn yourselves. To suffering, and ultimately damnation.'

'No,' from inside his tunic, Tavarius produced a small bowl. He walked over to Yeshua raising the thorn high.

'*No*,' Yeshua said, with divine force in his voice, 'I cannot allow this.'

And a wall of *fire* appeared before him, twice the size of a man. The fire forced Tavarius back, stumbling and coughing. Pilate's skin prickled with the intense heat, and he shielded his face against the unnatural blaze.

Josephus pulled free his sword, as though he intended to attack the fire. Cornelius, Josephus' second, made no such movement, Pilate noted.

We are over-matched.

'Tavarius...' Pilate began.

'Yeshua!' Tavarius bellowed, the sound carrying over the roar of the unnatural fire, 'listen to me. Whatever you are, man or God, you cannot escape the law of *consequence*. There will be consequences for your actions here today. Best discover what they are, and make a reasoned decision.'

Something, perhaps the force, the *certainty* in Tavarius' voice, gave Yeshua pause, and the wall of fire dropped to shin height, though licks of flame lashed out menacingly.

'Whatever game it is you play, Eli, I will take no part in it. Return to the city, and I will spare you my wrath.'

'Oh, you *will* spare me,' Tavarius said calmly, 'unless you would be responsible for the torture and execution of every single man and woman who testified on your behalf. I have had them all rounded up, and my men, vicious men, *damned* men, have been ordered to kill them all, in a manner of their choosing. Osip, Orli, Bina, *all of them*. Funnily enough, fire is one of the methods I suggested. Unless, of course, I return to negate the orders. Unless I return in a *good mood*.'

Yeshua studied Tavarius then, as though the man were a puzzle. Clearly, he divined truth in the man, for he did not contest Tavarius' words.

'Their pain, their blood, they will weigh on your soul, not on mine.'

Tavarius turned to Pilate. 'See, Gods do lie, just like men.'

Then Tavarius turned to face Yeshua once more. 'But even if that *were* true, would you take the gamble, Yeshua, that they will not carry the violence I will mark them with into the next life? That I am incapable of branding a *soul* with the ferocity of my violence. Do you know, with absolute certainty that their suffering will not put them on a path to eventual damnation?'

Yeshua said nothing.

'The price,' Tavarius continued, 'for an alternative fate for those who stood up for you in Pilate's court, and named you a God, is the Kishar Stone. I will have it Yeshua, or tonight the gutters of the Lower City will run red.'

Yeshua hesitated, then spat his disgust at Tavarius' sandals.

'So be it. But know, Tavarius, that it will not work for you.' Yeshua reached inside his tunic, pulled out an unremarkable looking stone, and tossed it on the floor.

Tavarius put down the bowl he held, picked up the Kishar Stone, and examined it. He walked over to Symeon, and held it up to his face.

'Is this is, is this the Kishar Stone?' Tavarius asked.

Symeon studied it, then nodded.

'It... I think so... yes.'

Tavarius smiled. 'It *will* work for me.'

Then he slipped it beneath his own tunic, picked up the bowl, raised the thorn in his left hand high once more, walked up to Yeshua, and stabbed his right arm. Yeshua made no noise, but did wince heavily. Thin streams of blood trickled down his arm. Tavarius collected the blood in the bowl, then raised it to his lips.

'I ask, for your sakes, please, don't do this,' Yeshua said, his voice desperate.

Tavarius raised the bowl, as if to drink.

'*Listen to me,*' Yeshua said, his voice transformed. It was deep. Deeper and more powerful that Pilate's own. A transformation just like that which had taken place in the court room, when Yeshua had abandoned his wounded sheep act and granted the court the first glimpse of his divinity.

Pilate suddenly felt very conscious of the man's power. He was a God.

'The path you intend to take, it will not lead where you want it to lead. You will only condemn yourselves.'

Yeshua turned to Symeon first. His voice changed once more, soft, the voice of a true friend, or a brother.

'Symeon, I do not understand why you do this. But I do not believe that you are so given to venal thoughts that your motivations aren't merely misguided. I ask of you, I beg of you... *reflect.*'

Symeon looked to the ground. Yeshua turned next to Pilate.

'Pilate, I know that you are a fair man, corrupted by fear. But you are not yet so far gone. *Be* the authority you claim you are, make decisions based on the soul of Pontius Pilate, not the fear that all men share.'

Perhaps this is rash. Perhaps we overreach. Perhaps Yeshua, a God, is right...

'Eli,' Yeshua said to Tavarius, using his deep, god voice to speak Tavarius' abandoned name, 'Eli. Do not do this, I will make you regret it.'

Tavarius fell completely still, then he smiled. 'I have never feared a man who makes threats,' he said, 'only the man who does not need to.'

Tavarius raised the bowl to his lips, and gathered the blood with his tongue. 'I accept the Divine burden of Remembrance,' he said solemnly, and passed the bowl to Symeon.

'Symeon,' Yeshua pleaded, 'don't do this.'

Symeon turned away from Yeshua, lowered the bowl.

'You will do this Symeon Bar-Jonah,' Tavarius hissed, 'or I will have Maryam killed, only after she's been raped by an entire fucking legion.'

With trembling hands, Symeon raised the bowl to his lips, and drank. 'I... I accept the Divine burden... of Remembrance,' he said, then he passed the bowl to Pilate.

'Prefect,' Yeshua said, 'you will suffer. Please, don't do this.'

Pilate hesitated.

'He wants no rivals, Prefect,' Tavarius said, 'he wants to keep immortality for himself. We will be as gods, *as gods.*'

Immortality.

Pilate lifted the bowl to his lips, and reached for the liquid with his tongue. The blood was already starting to congeal, the taste was metallic and bitter. Pilate gagged, and fought the urge to vomit.

'I accept the Divine burden of Remembrance,' Pilate said, after the nausea settled. The words Symeon had given them. The words he knew he must say. The words that would make him as a God. But Pilate felt nothing. No rush of power, nor sense of doom. Just the coppery taste of blood on his tongue.

Yeshua wept then. And the weakness evoked Pilate's contempt, as it had in the Praetorium when Yeshua had first been dumped on his floor.

Some God.

'Princeps,' Pilate called out, 'our business with the prisoner is complete.'

The execution party marched back, and took guard of Yeshua once more. Soundlessly, but with tears still running down his face, Yeshua took up his burden.

'Come,' Pilate said, 'we will follow. I will see this business done.'

CHAPTER SEVENTEEN

Esquiline District, Rome
Month of June, 2024 AD

Churches are monuments to lies and slavery. Priests, whether or not they know it, are guardians of the greatest lie of all.

-BOOK OF YESHUA

Elliot pulled at the collar of his faded t-shirt. He wished to get away from the safe house, a red brick apartment that overlooked a cobblestone courtyard filled with badly parked scooters and dead leaves. They ate hurriedly, and in silence, Elliot, Judah and Andrea. The food was good, Elliot could tell, without truly appreciating or enjoying it. Centuries of memories taught a man much about food, and Andrea had been a good cook even two thousand years ago. They ate a pasta dish, the herbs and the tomato were fresh, and the Parmesan nutty. But it clumped in his throat, his mind on other things.

Elliot couldn't tell what galled him more, the idea that Andrea played them false, or the idea that he didn't. That his betrayal was simply... moot.

Not for me. Two thousand years I have paid for his treachery, I will not forget, and I cannot forgive.

'Come,' Andrea said, dabbing at the tomato sauce around his mouth delicately with a napkin, 'it is time.'

Elliot glanced at his watch, just one of the provisions he had picked up from the safehouse. *19.44.* They would be meeting the man sixteen minutes from now. They rose from the table, put on their freshly acquired jackets and headed for the door. The solemn procession wound down the stairwell, over cigarette butts, coke cans and smashed lager bottles, and out into the courtyard. The air was still warm, fumes and pulsations from the traffic adding to the sense of oppression Elliot felt.

Andrea led them through the incessant beeping of impatient cars and the high pitched whine of scooters darting between the narrow gaps left by trapped cars. They walked quickly, past the grey-white cuboid office blocks of Via Giovanni Gualberto, the quaint touristy cafes, bars and bakeries of Via Liberiana, and weaved their way around the groups of SS Lazio fans who had left the pubs and clubs to smoke and express their dismay to the football gods. Finally, they stood outside the unassuming facade of Santa Pressede.

A church, is this some kind of joke Andrea plays?

'He suggested the meeting place, not me,' Andrea said in response to Elliot's dismayed look. Elliot looked at Judah, who shrugged, as if to say, *what else is there to do?*

Santa Pressede was tall, made from washed out red stone that now carried only a pinkish tinge, and but for the large wooden door and sheer size, looked no different from many of the other buildings in the area. They walked inside, Elliot hesitating for just a moment before crossing the threshold.

The inside of Santa Pressede was every bit as remarkable as its outside was nondescript. The late evening sun coming through the stained glass windows was sending fractured shards of light across the marble tiled floor. Arches towered high above them, rich in ornament, unsmiling angels, frescoes with humble penitents grovelling before a Caucasian Yeshua, who looked stern, handsome and authoritarian.

Not a caricature. Not even a parody. Simply a lie.

For the first time as *Elliot*, he appreciated the sheer power and absurdity of the great lies of Christianity, and the Roman Catholic Church. Elliot had never been a believer, his parents

had never been religious, and belief always seemed something...
archaic. Theology had been easy enough to dismiss, a crutch of
the downtrodden and desperate.

But here he stood, more than two thousand years after
Yeshua's birth, and the lies about his death informed the world
around him. The lies of the Annunaki had become *foundational*,
the basis on which entire legal systems, belief systems, and even
languages were built. The lie of Yeshua's death was the most
powerful lie ever told.

Who could maintain such a lie?

Elliot felt overawed by the wealth and power of his
enemy, the architectural beauty and scale of their lies, a house
of cards solidified over millennia. The lingering scent of stale
incense tasted like evil in his throat. Despite his attempts to
shut out the thoughts that were pounding against his skull, de-
manding entrance, he could not block them. The memories of
the smell of incense mingled with the burning bodies of their
Knights Templar. Good men who wished only to serve the truth,
men who had suffered for fighting for a better world. Men whose
suffering had been largely in vain.

*And were those men conditioned to violence? Were their souls
rendered unstable? Are some of those men damned, because of the
path we put them on?*

'Where is he?' Judah asked.

'In the crypt, come,' Andrea replied.

The crypt was accessed through a small wooden door behind the altar, in the apse. Behind that door, stood a much stur-
dier, modern looking door of reinforced steel that required a six
digit pass code to be entered on the digital keypad. Andrea entered it, and the door popped open. Andrea held the door open,
and Judah and Elliot walked through.

Into the belly of the beast.

They walked carefully down the circular staircase of
crumbling stone, flaxen with the light from the halogen bulbs
embedded in the ceiling. At the bottom of the stairs, the crypt,
as long and wide as the church above them, opened into a path-

way of arches, so low that Elliot, Judah and Andrea, all tall men, were forced to stoop. The stone was so weathered that the frescoes down here were barely discernible, but Elliot could make out more angels, serpents, and at the apex of each arch, a lidless eye.

Towards the back of the crypt the halogen light bulbs became more infrequent, the shadows darker, the temperature colder, and the air staler. A row of sarcophagi stood at the back, and against one leaned a young, clean shaven, baby-faced man of middling height. He wore a long black cassock with some kind of piping. Elliot couldn't be sure in the almost darkness, but he would have guessed at fuchsia. The man looked too young, however, to be a monsignor, though Elliot would also have guessed at him being too young even for Priesthood, were it not for the dog collar. The man unwound with feminine fluidity, bringing a lit cigarette to his mouth. He took a long, provocative drag, and blew smoke into the darkness.

'Andrea, you came,' he said in English, then stepped forward. Elliot could see now that the sash around his waist was indeed fuchsia. A monsignor, a senior clergyman of the Roman Catholic Church.

'Fiero,' Andrea said, inclining his head slightly, 'this is Judah of Kerioth, and Yossef of Arimathea.'

Elliot twitched in irritation. Fiero the clergyman made no sign of surprise, or amusement. It was clear that Andrea had not only told Fiero of their ancient identities, but also convinced him of their authenticity. Not too difficult to believe, if he had truly spoken with Yeshua, as Andrea had said.

'Brothers, it is a great pleasure to meet you at long last. Andrea has promised me that this day would come, when the great names of history would walk into my church. But I must confess, there were days when I endured doubt.' Fiero took another long drag on his cigarette, and studied Elliot and Judah.

Elliot's dislike for this man extended beyond the clothes the man wore, though they represented the foundation of his distrust. They were the robes of the enemy, worn either by men who directly served the Annunaki, or who did so unwittingly, out of laziness, or a lack of moral agency.

What kind of man consults others, or a book, before consulting with his soul?

Elliot doubted that Fiero was *that* kind of priest. More likely he was the sort who knowingly peddled lies in pursuit of power.

But that was not all of it, Elliot felt a *personal* dislike for the man. He evidently enjoyed the sound of his own voice, and projected an arrogance as monumental as the church above.

'We resemble the men in your New Testament, *Monsignor*, in name only. You do not know us,' Elliot said.

Fiero did not seem put out by Elliot's angry retort. He dropped the cigarette to the floor, and stepped on it with an expensive looking, polished black shoe, then smiled.

'Perhaps. Andrea has told me something of you, however. And the Ophanim are well known enemies of those I used to serve. I have often found that we know, and understand, our enemies far better than we know our friends.'

'What is it that you think you know?' Judah asked with a calm that Elliot himself could not have mustered.

'Principally, your aims, gentlemen. Aims I admire, for they are mine also.'

'If that were true, Monsignor, you would not be wearing a cassock.'

'You would rather I were naked?'

Neither Elliot nor Judah smiled. Andrea lowered his head. It was evident that the meeting was not going how he had hoped.

'Forgive me my joke,' Fiero said, though there was no contrition to be read in his face, 'there is little joy in my life, I must take small pleasures where I can.'

'An ominous sentiment coming from a Priest,' Elliot said.

'True, too true,' Fiero said, folding his arms, 'but I wear the title of Monsignor much as I wear these garments, as a costume. Much as Andrea wears the red eye of the Igigi. In fact...'

Fiero rotated his dog's collar carefully, and from beneath the collar of his shirt was exposed a ruby red eye pinned to the collar.

'I wear it too. But know this,' Fiero added, raising a hand to forestall Elliot's stuttering objection, 'I am a man of God. Not the god of this place,' he said, stretching out his hands, 'a god of malice and deceit. The true god. Your god. The one who rots in captivity in the black heart of the Vatican. The one who wears the human form of Yeshua the Nazarene. I would see him freed.'

Silence filled the crypt.

'Why should we believe you?' Judah asked as last, 'wearing those robes, wearing that eye. If you help us free him, you are damned.'

'Because,' said Fiero, 'I am a man of God. And history will remember me as such. When I met Andrea, and he spoke to me with words of truth. When I navigated the Vatican Necropolis, the true Necropolis, not the false fraction they show to pilgrims and tourists, and saw the truth for myself, *heard* the truth for myself, I had already disfigured my soul. Climbing the ladder of this corrupt den of lies and sin, I had come to believe that there was no God. I lost my faith, and embraced the next best thing, the eternal reincarnation of the Annunaki, and worldly pleasure. I underwent the Initiation, gladly. Do you have any idea what that entails?'

'They do,' Andrea assured him.

'Then you know that I am damned, absolutely, and trusted for it, it is why only those who wear the eye are permitted to see Yeshua, even know of him. And when I saw Yeshua in his cell, I realised that I was the only true man of God in this entire world. And I could serve him. History will remember me as the man who made the ultimate sacrifice. I will be revered throughout the ages. And damnation is a small price to pay.'

The man is a narcissist, a perfect narcissist.

'You doubt me?' Fiero asked, when he received no response.

'Of course we doubt you,' Judah said.

'As you doubt Andrea?'

'A different type of doubt.'

'I see... I need to show you something. The reason I brought you to this place.'

Elliot turned to Judah, who shrugged.

What have we to lose?

Fiero obviously took the shrug for consent, and turned to the stone sarcophagus behind him. He pulled the lid, which Elliot had initially assumed immovable, open with surprising strength and gestured into the darkness.

'Come,' he said.

Inside the false sarcophagus, for there was no body, or skeleton, was a twenty foot drop into darkness, mitigated only by a rusty iron ladder anchored to the stone wall. Fiero climbed down first, followed by Andrea. Reluctantly, Judah and Elliot followed. As Elliot descended, he could smell death, a potent and familiar combination of piss, shit and rot. Once at the bottom, Fiero sparked up a metal lighter, then walked over to a wall, where he flicked a switch and brought dim light to the room. Elliot looked around in horror, the place was a medieval torture chamber, with dried blood on the floor and walls, iron cages some large enough to house a large group of people, some large enough only to house a dog, or child, and stone tables that looked like alters. Brackets on the wall housed knives and other implements of pain and death.

In one corner of this seeming dungeon was a large oven built into the wall. The retractable doors were open, exposing ash, and the remnant of bones.

Elliot gagged.

'What is this place?' Judah asked in disgust.

'A place of Initiation,' Fiero answered solemnly, 'one of many. A factory in which souls are shattered, and reassembled in the image of the Annunaki. My soul was shattered here, I do not deny it. But *I* have put myself back together. I chose the shape of my soul, even if the structural integrity is... compromised.'

'And who is that?' Judah asked.

Elliot had not seen the man in one of the larger cages until Judah pointed. Curled up in a ball, apparently asleep, the man was older, somewhere in his sixties, and plump. He wore an unflattering sweater vest and brown corduroy trousers.

'A solution,' Fiero said, 'allow me to introduce you.'

Fiero walked over to the cage, pulled out a key from the inside of his cassock, and unlocked the padlock holding the door to the cage in place. He pulled the door open, walked inside the cage, and prodded the man with his polished shoe. The man awoke in alarm, and pushed himself into the corner of the cage, trying put as much distance as possible between himself and Fiero.

'Professor Cove,' Fiero said, as though this were a dinner party, 'these are the gentlemen that you will be working with.'

The man turned to Judah.

'Help me,' he said desperately, 'please. Help me, don't let him hurt me.'

'He will not hurt you,' Judah said calmly.

'No,' Fiero said, 'not as long as you do as we agreed.'

'Yes,' the Professor said, 'yes, I've already agreed, haven't I?'

'Professor Cove,' Fiero explained, 'has been granted access in three days' time to the Vatican Apostolic Archive. More specifically, a closed section in the Necropolis where documents and Papal edicts from the latter years of the papacy of Pious XII are housed. Professor Cove has permission to take two research assistants with him. This represents the best possible route into the cell where Yeshua is held. Professor Cove has been persuaded of the virtues of my plan, and is prepared to work with us.'

'Impossible,' said Judah, 'there will be a small army of guards protecting the Annunaki's most valuable and dangerous secret, not to mention an entire security system. There is no way what you say is possible with one Professor, and who, myself and Yossef?'

'No. Not you Judah, your face is known to the Annunaki,'

Andrea answered for Fiero, 'Professor Cove is not the only individual who will be working with us. I have recruited another, a hacker for hire who will be able to shut down the security systems for us, at least for a time.'

'I thought,' Elliot said, 'that you needed us, because you did not trust in the help of mercenaries.'

'He will not be placing himself in any danger, and what other choice do we have?'

Dare I endanger Rock once more. He doesn't deserve this, but... do we have a choice?

'I may have someone better,' Elliot said.

Fiero laughed at that.

'Really? You do not even know the man we have hired.'

'I don't need to. The man I would bring aboard, his hacking skills are without peer, and his trust is without question.'

'Daniel...' whispered Judah, 'how would we get him here?'

'The same way you got here,' Andrea replied, 'cargo plane.'

'And what about his condition. The man was shot not a week ago,' Judah exclaimed.

'He need only walk and talk,' said Andrea.

'I don't like this, Judah,' said Elliot.

Judah pondered this.

'Nor I. But what other choice do we have? This is our best shot in two millennia.'

Elliot looked around the dungeon; the fear and terror that seemed part of the very fabric of this place were also his own.

CHAPTER EIGHTEEN

Golgotha, Jerusalem
Month of Nissan, 30 AD

I was there. I was in the crowd. I watched a friend suffer degradation, humiliation and pain. It is not a memory I cherish. Even within the framework of belief cultivated by the Great Lie, I cannot understand celebrating the image of a man being tortured.

-BOOK OF YESHUA

Despite death's conspicuous absence, Golgotha smelled of it. The fire pits were not alight, for there had been no corpses for three days, but ash filled the air nonetheless. The warm spring breeze was whipping the ash into the air, where it eventually settled on tunics and in hair and beards.

The sweet, pungent stink of rot filled Pilate's nose, and though he had been here for the better part of two days, he still had no appetite.

I must do something about the piles of rubbish dumped outside this city. Have it transported to some other place. I could get prisoners to do it. I'd need more prisoners, but that could be arranged.

Pilate stared up at Yeshua, who hung limply from the beam to which he was impaled. Behind him rose the cranial hill, bare rock that rose titanic above the ground and gave the place its name.

Golgotha, place of the skull.

Flies buzzed around Yeshua, like Pilate, eager for death's arrival. The man had shat himself, screamed, cursed, and most recently, laughed. But he would not die. He would not asphyxiate, as was normal for a crucified prisoner. He seemed no less alive than the first moments after being nailed to the beam. At the end of the first day, Pilate had had the execution party, Fretensis legionaries, ply Yeshua with wine, laced with poison. In the morning, when Pilate had returned, still Yeshua endured.

A few hours ago, Pilate had lost patience, and sent some of his soldiers to make an end of it. The legionaries had run him through with spears. Yeshua had screamed once more, blood had poured from his body like wine from a wineskin pierced with holes. He should have bled out and died in minutes, but still he endured.

He was sleeping, now.

He mocks us. Knew that we could never kill him, even without the Kishar Stone. I will have that fool Symeon suffer before I have him killed.

"Do not take me for dead," Yeshua had announced to the crowd that grew larger and larger, as news of the man who would not die spread, "I merely sleep."

I must make an end of this. But how? How do you kill a god?

Pilate had given commands to his personal guard that Tavarius, and the man who was called Symeon Bar-Jonah, be brought to him. He had sent Cornelius. He wanted Josephus, who he trusted implicitly, close by.

If Yeshua won't die, and my soul is forfeit, they will die in such agony that crucifixion will seem as a celebratory feast in comparison.

Tavarius arrived moments later, with Symeon and Cornelius. They had obviously not been far away. Tavarius' face was blank, even calm. Symeon looked horrified, eyes wide, lips apart.

He at least realises that we have wagered our very souls, and are losing.

'He will not die,' Pilate growled.

'Yes, I see that, Prefect,' Tavarius replied.

Pilate turned to Symeon.'You said that if he did not possess the Kishar Stone, then he could die. Do we not have the Kishar Stone in our possession?'

'We... do,' Symeon stammered.

'Then why in the name of Morta, goddess of death, won't he just fucking die?'

Tavarius had no answer, Symeon looked lost in horrified thought.

'What should we do?' Pilate asked, 'the crowd grows, they are witnesses to our deicide. Worse, our *failed* attempt at deicide.'

'Tell the crowd that he is dead,' Tavarius said calmly, 'that will send them home.'

Pilate scoffed. 'And when he wakes, and news travels that he is not?'

'Have him transported to a tomb. We will keep him there, while we figure out our next move.'

'There will be visitors to the tomb, what then? What then, *advisor*?'

Tavarius was silent. Pilate fumed, the command to have them both killed formed in his head, but then Symeon said something, quietly. Meekly.

'I... I might have a way.'

'Speak it, then,' Pilate said impatiently.

'I overheard Yeshua talking to Yohanan. The conversation was not meant for my ears, I think. At that point, he had started to distrust me.'

Pilate grunted. Half laugh, half disgust.

'Yeshua was explaining his aversion to vinegar. It was something we had all noticed, he avoided vinegar in all its forms, both as a preservative, and a condiment. I had always thought it a dislike, but in this conversation, Yeshua said something to Yohanan that suggested to me that it was something... more. For his immortality. I... believe... that with vinegar, and deprived of the Kishar Stone, he *can* be killed.'

'And you didn't think to mention this before?'

'I... believed that we would have no problems if Yeshua was separated from the Kishar Stone.'

'So what do you suggest we do?' Pilate asked.

'Lace the tips of spears with vinegar, and... run him through. That might get the job done.'

AΩ

Yeshua was awake again, and laughing maniacally. The crowd had swelled further, it seemed like half the city was now witness to this spectacle. The crowd buzzed.

Like a plague of locusts.

'They cannot kill me,' Yeshua shouted, 'witness the impotence of men who wilfully damage their souls.'

'Move the crowd back,' Pilate bellowed over the furore to the Fretensis legionaries who imposed what little order remained to proceedings. At spear point, the crowd backed up, none willing to be impaled, even those who had been kneeling, worshipping Yeshua as a god.

'Back. BACK!' Pilate screamed.

Not the voice of authority, the voice of desperation.

When the front of the crowd stood two hundred cubits from the impaled god, Pilate started across the barren expanse. He was followed by Tavarius, Symeon, Josephus and Cornelius. Eerie silence descended on Golgotha. Pilate shielded his eyes from the setting sun at Yeshua's back, casting the sands and the rubbish in a honey glow.

'Brother,' Yeshua shouted, as the group approached.

Yeshua was a ruin. It turned Pilate's stomach to witness. Yeshua's sides and stomach were a patchwork of crusty red scars. Dried rivers of blood snaked across his neck and torso. His feet were as bloody hooves, with toes barely discernible beneath caked blood. Nevertheless, Yeshua's eyes were bright with defiance.

'BROTHER,' Yeshua shouted again, louder.

He speaks to Symeon, but also to the crowd.

'Why? Why have you forsaken me?'

In reply, Symeon's voice was as quiet as Yeshua's had been loud. 'Damnation and salvation are a yoke that I would free humanity from.'

Yeshua spoke more calmly, and quietly then. 'It is how it must be, Symeon. Please, you must trust me, as you once did.'

'No, Yeshua. I see the way forward. With my actions... I have bought humanity eternal life.'

'You will bring *suffering*, and eventual damnation Symeon. Surely you know this?'

'Enough,' Pilate said sharply, 'enough. It is time to put an end to this farce.'

'And just how do you intend to do that, Pontius Pilate. I am a god, and I cannot die. Surely you know this now.'

Fear struck Pilate then, for there was great authority in Yeshua's voice.

Perhaps he speaks true. But I have waded so far into the river of sin...

'*Vinegar*, tradesman. Vinegar.'

The fear that flashed in Yeshua's eyes told Pilate that Symeon had spoken truly.

You should have guarded your words, Yeshua.

Pilate turned to his guards. Captain Josephus looked resolute, and nodded in reassurance at Pilate. The younger, shorter, Cornelius, his second, looked pale and concerned, but said nothing.

Is he with me?

'Cornelius. Do it.'

The younger soldier hesitated, took half a step forward, then stopped.

'I...'

'Do it,' Pilate commanded again.

The young man just stood there. Beads of sweat ran down

his face.

He is terrified.

Josephus yanked the vinegar tipped spear from Cornelius' grasp, then thrust it into Yeshua's stomach.

'NO!' Cornelius shouted.

Yeshua screamed.

'BE SILENT!' Pilate roared.

Blood gushed, Yeshua's head rolled, then flopped forward. Yeshua was still, and the world stood still with him.

It is left to me to take charge, it seems.

'Get him down,' Pilate ordered. Josephus and Tavarius obliged.

Behind Pilate the crowd hissed, jeered and shouted in a sizzling broth comprised of a thousand volatile emotions. Pilate could hear screaming, raw grief and agony, and high-pitched wailing. He dared not look back.

'Fetch the cart,' Pilate commanded Symeon, who set off, 'Josephus, check his pulse.'

Josephus obeyed, and Cornelius went to follow him.

'Not *you*. You stay with me.'

The man is a liability now.

'No pulse, Prefect,' Josephus shouted above the cacophony emanating from the crowd.

ΑΩ

The tomb was large, and ornate. Made from Meleke, it stood upon a hill, shimmering in crystalline brilliance, despite the gloom that was settling.

In the Lower City, entire families live in rooms smaller than this tomb. And Meleke is not cheap. This must have cost the Arimathean a fortune.

Only the top of the sun could be seen above the horizon now, and already Cornelius and Josephus had lit their torches and planted them in the sand.

'Put him in the tomb,' Pilate commanded.

Cornelius took Yeshua's body from the cart, then carried it tenderly into the tomb. Tears were in the young man's eyes.

I understand this man. But I cannot permit him to live. He is a liability. Like Josephus he knows too much, but Josephus, at least, I can trust. Josephus is a soldier, bred to instruction, not wayward thoughts, even concerning his soul. Would that I had more men like Josephus.

'Cornelius, your spear.'

Cornelius hesitated, but obedience ran deep within him. He had served in the Fretensis legion before joining Pilate's personal guard, discipline was more than habit, Pilate knew, it was part of his *nature*. Cornelius reluctantly passed Pilate his spear, and turned his head.

He knows, surely, what is to happen.

'Captain,' Pilate said to Josephus, 'kill this man. He is a traitor to the Empire.'

'Yes, Prefect.'

Josephus spun elegantly, and with skill and accuracy, thrust the spear underneath his jerkin, just above his groin, and out through the small of his back. Cornelius grunted, horror, a flash of panicked life filled his eyes. Josephus let the spear go, pulled his sword from his scabbard, then swung it in a graceful arc that left Cornelius' head barely attached, flopping to the side at angle that sickened, exposing sinew, muscle, blood and all that should be hidden. The shock was gone from Cornelius' face as quickly as it had appeared. His body fell to the floor.

'Put...put him in the tomb,' Pilate said, fighting back vomit.

Josephus pulled his spear from Cornelius' body, flecks of blood showering the sand. He wiped his sword on the sand, before replacing it in his scabbard. He then shouldered the corpse, and walked it into the tomb. He pulled the door to the tomb shut, then moved over to the large boulder that stood beside the door.

'I will need help, Prefect,' Josephus said matter-of-factly.

Pilate, Symeon, Tavarius, and Josephus all put their shoulders against the boulder, and with great effort, rolled it into the large ditch in front of the tomb door.

Now we must fill the absence we have created.

CHAPTER NINETEEN

Isle of Wight, England
Month of June, 2024 AD

A damned soul is beyond repair. A soul that knows it is damned has no incentive to try.

-BOOK OF YESHUA

Pilate was idling the time away on the balcony. He always enjoyed St Lawrence. Tavarius had purchased this place, formerly a hotel, a century ago, and the Annunaki still conducted business there on occasion. But Pilate often travelled to St Lawrence solely for pleasure.

His naked body filled the balcony chair, which was made from teak. He took a puff on his cigar and let the smoke roll around his mouth. Dominican, though less costly than Cuban, was kinder on the throat. He put the cigar down on the table, took a sip of freshly pressed orange juice from a heavy glass tumbler, and inhaled the view.

This. This is life.

The sun was at its zenith, and a wall-lizard scuttled along the edge of the balcony railings. Beyond the railings, the garden that stretched beneath him, once hotel grounds, had been designed and commissioned by Tavarius, some eighty years previous. The garden, Japanese in influence, was a reflection of Takeshi, the youth Tavarius had been before his soul-memories came flooding back.

A marble path which started underneath Pilate's balcony was flanked by acers. Closer to Pilate, the acers were a pale, washed out pink. As the path moved further away from the building, the colours became more vibrant, moving through salmon, cerise, lilac and mauve, and ending in a violent heliotrope that drew the eye to the large pond that dominated the centre of the garden.

The pond was spanned by a stone bridge without railings; an ideal place to watch the koi carp meander. Water, from a source hidden by lush, forest-green cloud trees, trickled over blue slag-glass rock high above, before tumbling towards the pond below. The water never disturbed the calm of the pond, transforming into a fine mist during its descent. How this was achieved Pilate had never found out, and did not care to. The aesthetics of the illusion were more important to him than mechanical reality.

Beauty, Pilate knew, was more important than joy. Joy was unsustainable, dependent on the qualities of being fleeting, or elusive. It was a relative concept. But beauty... beauty was permanent, sustainable. It had been many, many lives since he had experienced joy, at least beyond maturity and the remembrance that came with it. But beauty... he had found beauty in every single one of his lives. He was a connoisseur of beauty, had experienced more of it than any man alive, in all likelihood.

He closed his eyes, and inhaled deeply once more. He became aware of the burbling of the waterfall and the sharp tang in his nostrils from the lemon balm he kept on the balcony. The beauty of *this* place never ceased to amaze him. The garden was all the more astounding for being a product of the mind of Tavarius. Tavarius sowed, and reaped, the most unpleasant things that moulded a man's soul. That such beauty could come from such an ugly soul was oddly reassuring.

'What are you thinking about?' the girl asked in her lilting Estonian accent.

Irina was his favourite. Twenty-one, with shiny brown hair that fell around her narrow, ivory shoulders with careless elegance.

By Venus, goddess of sexuality, everything about Irina is sensual.

The thought filled Pilate with melancholy. How much simpler the world had been when his gods had been Roman, and had the decency never to show themselves, content with token sacrifice.

He opened his eyes, and turned his head to study Irina's naked form, starting with the plump lips she had a habit of biting, moving down past her small, pert breasts to her wide hips and narrow waist. His eyes scaled the length of her coltish, smooth legs and settled on the fuzz and promise in the hollow of her thighs.

She comes to my bed willingly, unlike Tavarius' girls.

Pilate was not so conceited as to believe that her eagerness was anything to do with his physical appearance, and everything to do with the six-figure sum deposited in her bank account in pound sterling each month. This didn't bruise Pilate's ego, he had been everything from strikingly handsome to grotesque and disfigured. His current face was bland, and his body lacked the athleticism and symmetry to make him physically attractive to women.

But Pilate didn't care, his wealth, power, and wisdom were aphrodisiacs to many beautiful women, and his needs were always met.

'You, my dear,' Pilate said in response when the girl raised her eyebrows quizzically.

She giggled.

There was a chill, despite the sun, though not a deep one, and her slender arms were covered in goose pimples, which Pilate found arousing.

'Good. Do we have time?' she asked, her voice oozing carnal promise.

Pilate's pager buzzed from the table.

'Not really,' he groaned. But Irina ignored him, and in one swift motion knelt, and took his cock in her mouth.

Yes, that's good. What is all this for, if not pleasure? And what else do I have left? Oh, she is good at this. What does she see, I wonder, when she looks at my cock? Five inches of taut, veined skin? Or does she see the source of her power. The control she has over me. Oh, who cares?

ΑΩ

Pilate was last in to the room. Symeon gave Pilate a nod and wink when he came in, a look that said *I know what you've been up to.* Pilate and Symeon were close, had been for many centuries.

As close to a friend as I will ever have.

They had even been lovers, on occasion, when they had both had young, attractive bodies and handsome faces, though it had been nearly two hundred years since everything had so aligned.

The room had once been a dining area, but Tavarius had converted it into a conference room of sorts, with a polished oak table in the middle of the room. Filippos was stood in one corner.

He pulled through then.

For a day and a half Filippos had hovered somewhere between life and death. Tavarius had put himself in opposition to death, and a team of doctors had been ordered to keep Filippos alive at any cost, save his memories. Despite the heart attack, despite Filippos willing himself to die from inside his medically induced coma, Tavarius had gotten his way.

But, clearly, there was something wrong with Filippos. He was swatting at the air, as though fighting off something invisible. He was murmuring too, a constant stream of nonsense. It wasn't glossolalia, more like the babble of a baby, with few distinct syllables. Suddenly, he went quiet, then pirouetted with surprising grace and speed for a man of his age, and starting scratching at the beige fleur-de-lis wallpaper.

Urday hovered nearby, on alert, as though this fragile old man posed a significant and viable flight risk, or even threat. The man was twitchy, twitchier than usual. Though successful in his mission to capture Filippos, mistakes had been made, there were escapees from Araboth, and apparently one of their number, one of the Igigi he had met briefly in Ekugnuna, had fled, and possibly even betrayed them.

'Good of you to join us,' Tavarius said from the back of the room with irritating pomposity.

The sarcasm rankled Pilate.

The man is my equal, not my better.

'What's wrong with him?' Pilate asked.

'Burandanga and LSD,' Symeon replied, with a trace of sadness.

Ah, compliance. All those millions invested in research look like they're going to pay off for Tavarius. For me too, I suppose.

'The compliance drug failed to work with Yeshua,' Pilate said 'what makes you think it will work with Filippos?'

'Filippos is not a god,' Tavarius said, 'we *know* that this works with everyone but Yeshua. Filippos is just a man, and we've been after this man's mind for two thousand years. We've tried every violent means to force it open. Every single one has failed. But now...' Tavarius beamed, exposing straight white teeth, 'now it's about to pop open for us, Pilate, I assure you.'

Pilate noticed that Symeon looked a little uneasy.

Symeon has never viewed the Ophanim as his true enemy. They were his friends and brothers once. They just happen to be on the wrong side.

'Two millennia we've been waiting for this,' Tavarius said, then he walked over to Filippos, who was still scratching at the wallpaper.

'Filippos,' Tavarius addressed the man with a gentleness that Pilate had never heard from his old advisor, as though Filippos was an infant.

Filippos stopped and turned to look at Tavarius. He stood still and silent, in anticipation.

'Filippos my old friend, won't you come and sit down with me?'

Filippos nodded, the bashful agreement of a toddler to something he did not quite understand. Tavarius took Filippos by the hand, and walked him slowly over to a chair. Continuing to clasp Filippos' hand in his own, Tavarius sat, pulling Filippos into a chair next to him.

'Don't you recognise your old friend, Filippos?'

Filippos shook his head sadly, as though he had let Tavarius down.

'Ah, but you wouldn't Filippos, I have a new body. We change our bodies, don't we? What do you think of this body, Filippos? Do you think it suits the most notorious villain in history, or so the Great Lie would have the world believe?'

The Great Lie. Pilate recognised the phrase, it was taken from the *Book of Yeshua*. The book had been written by Tau'ma, Pilate knew, and taken from a safe in the compound that Urday had stormed. Tavarius had now finished skimming the book, reading from the early hours of the morning. Pilate himself had only glanced at it, there had been too much truth for his liking. But even in the first few pages, that phrase, *The Great Lie* had been prevalent and powerful.

This version of Tavarius is a sharp mind welded to an already shrewd soul. He uses this Book of Yeshua *to our advantage, to convince the drug addled mind of Filippos that he is an ally.*

The silence dragged out, while Filippos sat, in apparent thought.

'Judah?' Filippos said finally.

'Indeed. How have you been Filippos? Your old friend wishes to know.'

Filippos screwed up his face, forehead furrowed in concentration, as though the question gave him great difficulty. 'Scared,' he said finally, 'and confused.'

'These are scary and confusing times, Filippos, and that is why I need your help.'

'Oh, I see,' said Filippos, who quite clearly, did not.

'Filippos, it's vital that you help me to see, so that we can defeat the enemy. Will you help me, old friend?'

'Yes,' Filippos said, after a pause, 'I will Judah. I will help.'

'Good, then I really need you to think. I need you to tell me everything that Yeshua told you about performing miracles. He told you, didn't he? He told you how to perform miracles.'

Filippos looked pained. 'You...you...you told me never to say, not even to you.'

Tavarius nodded, and placed his other hand under Filippos' so that the Ophanim's hand was enveloped. 'I did Filippos, I did. But the situation has changed. Can't you see that?'

Filippos nodded slowly.

'So you'll help me, Filippos? Tell your old friend what he needs to know?'

Filippos nodded, then began to speak, slowly, as if he were one child talking to another.

'Yeshua took me aside, just before Pilate's men caught up with us. Do you remember that, Judah?'

'I do,' Tavarius replied solemnly.

'He told me that to perform miracles, we would need the stone that he carried with him, it would have to be split so that we might each receive a portion of its power. Do you remember it Judah?'

Tavarius pulled something from underneath his shirt. A stone like an apricot on a chain he wore about his neck. He showed the stone to Filippos.

'*This* stone, Filippos? Is it this stone right here?'

'Yes. The Kishar Stone but... but I thought it was lost, I thought the Annunaki had it.'

'I retrieved it. So tell me, old friend, how does it work? There must be something else to it. Please think, this is important.'

Filippos frowned.

'Yes. There is, he said that the power that the Kishar Stone holds, the power that belonged to Yeshua, can only be transferred to another at a certain location, where the planet's own divinity is most directly accessible to us, where it can best be tapped in to. Marked by the ancients as a stone monument. On an island. Isn't in extraordinary, Judah, the planet has a soul!? That's what Yeshua was saying.'

'Extraordinary,' Tavarius agreed flatly, barely containing his impatience, 'this island, did he say where it was?'

'Yes, he told me. It is in what we would now call the British Isles.'

'So the monument, that would be Stonehenge?

"I... I believe so, Judah.'

Stonehenge. Tavarius has been there already. He has visited every major landmark this world has to offer. There must be more.

'There must be more, Filippos. There must be something else.'

Gone was Tavarius' gentle tone. The facade was stripped away exposing anger, impatience, and lust.

Filippos hesitated, opened his mouth, and then closed it, as though he waged a battle within.

'I need to know, Filippos, it is important. Yeshua would want you to tell me,' Tavarius said, more gently this time.

'You must say the words, Judah, the words he shared with me.'

'What words, Filippos? Please, tell me, what words?'

'... I accept the mother's gift, and will use it for her benefit.'

'Thank you, Filippos. Now, kindly lie on the floor.'

Filippos left his chair, then lay himself down on the floor, staring up, like an adoring puppy. Tavarius stood over Filippos, then stamped on his face. The blow was well aimed, and there was a sickening crunch as his nose broke, blood squirted dark across the navy-blue carpeted floor. Filippos screamed, a piercing noise that pained Pilate, who covered his ears.

Symeon ran at Tavarius, and grabbed him by the throat. Though by no means an imposing physical specimen himself, Symeon was able to lift the diminutive Tavarius from the ground. Tavarius began to splutter and choke.

'WHY?' Symeon shouted into Tavarius' face, 'we weren't

supposed to be like this.'

'Ur... Ur...day,' Tavarius managed to gasp.

Urday moved with terrible speed, and pulled Symeon roughly away. Tavarius slipped from Symeon's grasp and collapsed to the floor. Pilate was reminded of the way Yeshua had crumpled to the auditorium floor, the first time their paths had crossed.

Would that they hadn't. Perhaps I would have had many happy lives, instead of this one, interminable existence.

'Why?' Tavarius repeated between wheezy breaths, '*Why*? We should have learned this information two *millennia* ago. Two thousand years we've needed this. Denied, by this fucker.'

Tavarius turned to talk to Filippos directly.

'Was it that fucking difficult? That's all I needed. You fucking fuck.'

Tavarius spat into the crimson mess that was Filippos' face.

'Urday,' Tavarius said in a voice that was stronger, and sounding more like his old self, 'hold Symeon for me.'

With a skilled soldier's quickness and deliberateness, Urday whisked behind Symeon, and twisted his arm against his back. Symeon looked terrified.

'What are you doing, Tavarius?' Symeon asked in a voice several octaves above his normal pitch.

Tavarius pulled down his suit trousers and boxer shorts in one aggressive motion. Despite the circumstances, his flaccid penis did not look threatening. Pilate had a bizarre urge to laugh.

This is too much, I must play the diplomat once more, I was always good at that.

'Enough Tavarius,' Pilate said, in a voice that he hoped captured something of the authority he had once wielded over the man, 'this goes too far.'

Tavarius sneered, turned his back to Pilate, and began to urinate on Filippos' face.

'Understand this,' Tavarius said, and it was clear that he

was addressing both Pilate and Symeon, despite the fact that his back was turned to them, 'everything we've built, is because of me. I'm in charge. You two didn't want to get your hands dirty. You didn't want to be involved with the Initiations. Well I did, and I have built us an *army.* I control the Igigi. It was me that commissioned the greatest story tellers to plant the seeds, and I cultivated them, grew a belief system for half the fucking world for our benefit. I covered the truth with manure, and out of it I grew a lie far greater. I did that. *Me.*'

The stream of urine was spluttering now, and then came to a stop. There was an overpowering stench of urine, the thick smell of piss from a man who drank too much whisky, and too little water. Tavarius turned to face Symeon, who was held, helpless, by Urday. Tavarius didn't pull up his boxer shorts.

'So if I want to break this prick's nose, then I will.' Tavarius turned back to Filippos, and stamped on his face once more. Filippos, who had been whimpering, made no more noises.

Passed out from the pain, I expect.

'And if I want to fucking piss on him, then I will.' At last, Tavarius pulled up his trousers and boxer shorts. 'Urday, escort Symeon to somewhere where he can cool down and reflect.'

The Igigi took Symeon by the arm. Tavarius turned to Pilate.

'We're so close to achieving everything we wanted, no-one and nothing is going to fuck it up.'

Power, wealth, control, and soon the ability to work miracles. We're practically gods. So why do I feel so empty? Why do I always feel so empty?

CHAPTER TWENTY

Lower City, Jerusalem
Month of Nissan, 30 AD

Our actions are shaped by our souls, and our souls are shaped by our actions, Yeshua taught us. The longer we exist, it must follow, the more it is that our souls are entities of our own making.

-BOOK OF YESHUA

With Josephus following at a discrete distance, Pilate skirted the edge of the narrow alleyway. The moon was bright, and the night sky clear. Pilate longed for more darkness, for more cover. What happened tonight would cast a shadow over the world, but it must remain as a shadow on the wall of the cave, the true source of its origin hidden.

For only the second time in his life, and the first without a full complement of his personal guard, Pilate was in the Lower City. He was heading ever downward. Two drunkards in tattered tunics staggered up the middle of the stone path, their movements languid but unbalanced, as though in parody of elegance. They stopped, their faces suddenly alert like wild animals that had caught the scent of prey, their movements suddenly sharp and precise. Narrowed eyes, quarrelsome expressions. They stopped in the middle of the alleyway as though adopting a defensive position. They cast their eyes over him, but found something, perhaps his martial bearing, perhaps the rapid approach of Josephus behind him, that they did not like.

Josephus was as careful as he was observant, and indeed, the captain of his guard had almost seemed to grow in stature, seeming more dangerous, and walked towards the men with deliberation, but not concern. Drunkards, Pilate knew, for he was often one of their number, possessed a keen instinct for danger, and these two were no exception, relinquishing the middle of the path, skirting around Pilate and Josephus, their filthy, stained tunics brushing against the sandstone tenement walls.

Poverty, it turned out, had a stench, the fetid stink of unwashed armpits, the acrid sting of urine. From the overwhelming smell of it, animals such as those he had just encountered did most of their pissing on the street.

Do these creatures have no self-respect?

High above him, a prostitute dangled a bruised, veined leg, drawing the eye towards the shadow at the top of her thigh. Despite himself, Pilate looked into her face, and saw desperate eyes and missing teeth.

If I were to endure such a life, death would come as sweet relief, like wine after council. And if death was followed by rebirth...

Pilate lowered his gaze and quickened his pace.

After turning right at the potters, head down, until you come to The Sinkhole.

That was what Tavarius had told him. Their business tonight was not fit for the Praetorium, and its being conducted in *The Sinkhole* would result in far fewer unwanted questions.

It would seem that Tavarius has won this game, Yeshua is dead. We killed a god, and made ourselves immortal. I was the last in on Tavarius' plan, but at least now I am on his side. The power of this world, now, rests with us. We are immortals.

The place was better marked by the sounds of cruel revelry than by the name scratched carelessly into the wooden door: muffled drunken cheers, bitter laughs, and jeering. It was the muted sound of men unshackled by reputation, wives, or conscience. Men living according only to their base instincts.

Josephus walked up behind him, his hand resting on the

pommel of his sword, and Pilate pushed the door open. There was an explosion of noise, men chanting in Aramaic, cursing, and laughing. A large, pock-faced man stood before them, barring their entrance. If he recognised Pilate, the man did not let it show.

'We have business tonight with Hozai,' Pilate said firmly.

The man simply nodded, and began to escort them through what was evidently the common room. Cheap incense filled the densely packed and poorly lit space, masking much, but not all, of the stench of humanity. Men gambled, serving girls swerved and pirouetted to place drinks on tables while avoiding gropes and pinches. Men drank, and whores sat on laps, encouraging wandering hands with false rapture on their painted faces.

Pilate and Josephus were admitted through a door in the back, and then another, beyond the kitchens and store rooms. The pock-faced man knocked on the last door, which stood in the shadows.

'Yes?' someone that might have been Tavarius answered.

The pock-faced man opened the door, and walked inside. Pilate followed him. Josephus made to do likewise, but Pilate, seeing Tavarius, motioned for him to stay.

'I have nothing to fear inside, Captain, guard the door'.

The back room was nicer than Pilate had envisaged, logs and kindling crackled in the fireplace, the stone table seemed smooth, and expensive. Three wooden cups stood on the table, brimming with burgundy promise. There was a dagger too, that seemed to shimmer with the reflected, flickering light of the fire. The room might even have felt cosy, were it not for the dirt floor, and the naked man tied to the chair, his mouth stuffed with cloth. The man, who was of middling years, was pale and frail. A man meant for clothing, his nakedness seemed somehow even more obscene for the visible ribs, and the beard which seemed like it would have been more fitting covering his pitiful genitals.

'Thank you, Salem,' Tavarius said to the pock-faced man,

who gave a perfunctory bow, and left the room. If Salem thought it unusual, or indeed inappropriate, that a naked man was tied to a chair, there had been no reaction to betray such thoughts.

'Prefect,' Tavarius said reverently, bowing deeply.

'Prefect,' Symeon aped from the darkest corner of the room.

How far back does their scheming go?

Pilate turned his eyes to the naked man, whose limbs strained against his bonds, and whose voice fought against his gag.

'What is the meaning of this?'

'Before we proceed, I felt we needed a display of commitment from our newest associate here,' Tavarius said to Pilate, indicating Symeon with a slight nod of the head.

'I have sold my friend, knowing it will result in his execution,' Symeon said, 'I have forsaken my brothers. What more do you want from me?' His voice was pitched much higher than was natural for him.

'That, I think, should be obvious,' Tavarius replied, '*damnation*, I want your damnation.'

Symeon said nothing.

'Kill this man,' Tavarius insisted, 'his name is Nohra. He is, as far as I can tell, a good man. A man with a family that he provides for. Kill him, and damn your soul. Think of it as a right of... *Initiation*.'

'Mmm. Mmmmmm,' the man strained against his bonds with desperation and a ferocity that belied his physique. For a moment, Pilate wondered if they would hold, and that he hadn't been unwise in leaving Josephus outside the door.

'It... serves no purpose,' Symeon said quietly.

'But that is exactly the point,' Tavarius said, 'the cruelty and *sin* must be for its own sake. You are either with us, or against us. I must know that you will never regret what you have done, I must be assured that you are damned, and as such, will never turn against us, and our work.'

181

Symeon continued to look reluctant. Tavarius' voice took on a hard edge.

'If you do not do these things, then you will take Nohra's place. But your death will not be quick. It will be years in the making. Painful years, the sort of pain a soul such as yours could never conceive of... until experienced.'

'Is there no other way?' Symeon whimpered.

'No,' Tavarius insisted, 'and truly, what harm will it do, if everything you have told me has been truth? We are giving him a second chance, are we not? As many chances as he could ever want. He might come back a nobleman, a wealthy merchant, a chieftain of some faraway tribe, even a king,' Tavarius shrugged, 'or maybe he'll have the misfortune of being reborn in the Lower City, as a leper. *It does not matter*. He will get his turn. Show me that you are more than words, Symeon Bar-Jonah. If you do not do this, you will suffer. And everything you have done until now will count for nothing with me... with us. You will be nothing, just a man who carries the memories of his weakness, of his fail-ure, from one life to the next.'

Still, Symeon remained motionless.

'*Show* meeeee,' Tavarius hissed.

Symeon picked up the dagger from the table, then raised it high. The naked man's desperate protests intensified, becom-ing muffled shrieking.

'Ahhhhh,' Symeon yelled, and slashed with the dagger, a clumsy motion that nicked Nohra's neck. The man shrieked, a sound that was clear, despite his gag. Symeon stabbed at Nohra's throat, which seemed to explode. He thrust the dagger back into the crimson mess, then again. The attack became a frenzy, blood squirted from a dozen wounds to the neck and chest. The man was silent now, but still Symeon stabbed, the sound of skin being punctured, the stench of shit and death heavy in the air. Pilate closed his eyes to the horror, he may have been well edu-cated in military matters, but he had always had a sensitivity to the ugly reality of war and death.

What he saw in his soul's eye was worse. The wounds were

deeper, Symeon's face more crazed, and Tavarius was licking his lips in arousal. Pilate forced his eyes open, Symeon had ceased his frenzy, he lay crumpled on the floor, weeping, covered in blood that was not his own. But it was the corpse that Pilate studied, despite himself.

The skin on the man's torso, those bits that had escaped the dagger's frenzy at least, were paler than before, so that he seemed as a marble sarcophagus. But in patches, where the blood was staring to congeal around the stab wounds to his neck, throat and chest, his skin had gone black. More of his blood was splayed across Symeon's tunic and pooling on the floor, than remained in him, it seemed. Pilate was sickened by the sight, but it was still better to keep his eyes open. Even in blinking, he witnessed once again the man's murder at Symeon's crazed hands.

By Ultio, goddess of punishment, I was not made to witness such things.

'We are damned,' Tavarius said solemnly, as if he were the Flamen Dialis, the high priest of Jupiter presiding over a wedding ceremony, 'but this is *not* the end, it is only the beginning. We have given the world rebirth, and ourselves immortality. Take a cup from the table, my new brothers.'

Brothers? He no longer sees me as his superior. If ever he truly did.

Pilate was the third wheel in this conspiracy, he knew. It had been Symeon who made this possible with his betrayal of Yeshua, and Tavarius who had made it happen. Pilate had only been brought in when it was unavoidable, though of course, Tavarius claimed that it was entirely for Pilate's own good.

I should have taken the Kishar Stone, as insurance. Tavarius holds all the power.

Tavarius had already taken his cup, and was staring at Pilate, expectantly. Insolently. Symeon, rising from his misery on the floor, was the last to take his cup.

'Drink deep,' Tavarius said, 'the sweet taste of immortality.'

Pilate brought the cup to his lips. By some trick of the mind, the wine was Yeshua's blood again. A molten metal piquant that stung. The blood trickled over his tongue, bitter, thick, and unpleasantly warm. Against all instinct, he opened his throat to the cup and titled his head backwards. The wine did not so much pour down his throat, as *slide*, such was its viscosity. A macabre parody of honey. He fought the overwhelming desire to vomit, and swallowed hard.

Pilate turned to Tavarius. There was red about his lips, and the fire from the torches burning behind his narrow, angular features made him seem as a demon ascended from Tartarus. There was hunger in his eyes, and madness too. He wore the Kishar Stone about his neck, fastened with a golden chain.

He has gone insane already, and this is but a fraction of the power he might one day wield.

'The world will be rewritten by us, and it starts today. We are family now. The only immortals on earth, now that Yeshua is dead, his godhead abandoned. Are you with me, till the end?'

'There is no end, now,' Symeon said, eyes cast downward, 'only new beginnings. But, yes, I am with you.'

Pilate said nothing, he did not know what to think, he was a passenger now, tethered to a wild animal he had no control over.

'And you, Prefect. My old friend. Are you with me?'

Pilate sighed. 'I am.'

Would that I were not. Would that I had ordered him executed before laying eyes on this accursed man.

CHAPTER TWENTY-ONE

Salisbury Plain, England
Month of June, 2024 AD

To work what have been called miracles, is to reprogram the world, something I only truly began to understand with the dawn of computing. Within this context, the Kishar Stone was the backdoor to the divinity of Earth itself that Yeshua had built in to his program.

-BOOK OF YESHUA

Pilate looked down at the approaching fields, dark and still.

'Two minutes till landing,' the pilot informed them.

This was always the part of flying Pilate despised most, hurtling towards the Earth, the difference between safe landing and a fiery death completely outside of his control, a matter of *faith*.

The Chinook landed on the plain in near total darkness. Urday and one of his subordinate Igigi, Tavarius and his brace of bodyguards, Symeon, and Pilate all disembarked, while the pilot remained. A khaki coloured jeep was waiting for them.

'Come,' Tavarius said.

Who is he to give commands?

Pilate hesitated, but then caught sight of Urday, whose hand lingered near the holster which housed one of his visible pistols. Pilate followed Tavarius and the group towards the jeep.

Tavarius and his mute bodyguards, Symeon, and Pilate all squeezed into the back, Tavarius sat in the middle. At a nod from Tavarius, the Igigi, unknown to Pilate, turned the key in the ignition. The jeep rumbled in to life, and crawled off across the bumpy plain, leaving behind a trail of black exhaust fumes. Pilate started to feel nauseous.

'Tell me Urday,' Tavarius said conversationally, 'do you covet it?'

'Covet what?' the Colombian replied in that ludicrous squeaky voice of his.

'Of course you do. What man wouldn't covet such power?' Tavarius replied, pulling something from his jacket pocket.

'I...' Urday began, but he was interrupted when Tavarius thrust a Taser into the man's neck. Urday's body jerked as if in the throes of death. For thirty full seconds, he continued to spasm, fighting. After what seemed like an eternity of pain and suffering, Urday slumped back in his chair, in apparent paralysis.

'W... why?' Urday managed to croak.

'You know too much, and covet too much, Urday,' Tavarius said, 'perhaps even you don't yet see the treachery in your... mind. But you are a creature of lust, and you have witnessed the most potent arousal this world has to offer. How could you *not* covet it?'

But Urday said nothing, he had slipped out of consciousness.

'Cut his throat,' Tavarius ordered his body guards, who brought the jeep to a standstill.

'Careful!' Tavarius warned the Igigi as they moved towards Urday's lifeless body, 'he may be acting.'

The bodyguards took Tavarius' warning seriously, keeping their eyes firmly on Urday. One un-holstered his pistol, pulled the hammer to release the safety, and pressed the gun into Urday's gut. The other slowly unsheathed a brutal looking hunting knife, and with movements that were deliberate, practised, and would have been graceful but for the violence and brutality they portended, raised the knife, and slashed Urday's throat. Blood gushed from the perverse second mouth that opened beneath Urday's chin.

'Put the body in the back,' Tavarius commanded. One bodyguard opened the door, and dragged Urday's corpse out of the vehicle. With the help of the other, the body was dumped in the boot.

How long has Urday been Tavarius' man? Bought with the promise of extended life. Now he's discarded like so much trash. And over what, was there any evidence of betrayal? A mere hunch?

Pilate didn't waste any time feeling sorry for Urday, the man's mere presence had sent shivers down his spine. Being in the same room as Urday had always been a deeply unsettling experience, like being near a black mamba, capable of striking at any moment with terrifying speed and deadly effect. But Tavarius' treatment of his loyal servant was disconcerting to say the least, and when Pilate closed his eyes, he saw the blood gushing from Urday's throat.

'Drive on,' Tavarius said cheerfully when his bodyguards re-entered the vehicle. The ride was bumpy, and no-one talked. On occasion, Pilate tried to catch Symeon's eye, to gauge something of Symeon's reaction to the brutal events they had both witnessed, but Symeon would not meet his furtive looks, staring instead out of the jeep's tinted windows at the colourless, featureless expanse.

Over the horizon, the great trilithons came into view, as solid shadows. Pilate was reminded of a child's building blocks, some complete and erect,while others had been toppled by time.

'Park here, we walk the rest of the way,' Tavarius commanded, and the group exited the jeep to the rhythmic clicking and thudding of doors opening and closing.

Beyond the great stones, a full moon appeared between parting clouds, lending the great monument shimmering silver.

The Igigi, the man who had, until recently, looked to Urday for instruction, led, wielding a flashlight. The ground was bumpy and hard, evidently not having seen rain for many hot summer days, and treacherous with the threat of turned ankles. The group moved slowly, which suited Pilate, who felt great trepidation, but not Tavarius who seemed agitated at the slow pace. He was scowling, cracking knuckles and breathing heavily.

They walked as if drawn by the stones, the only landmarks on a barren plain. As they neared, the size of the monument started to impose itself on Pilate. The place was, Pilate realised in a dim, emotionally unaffected way, holy, and its construction had been worship.

Seemingly at the very base of the great stones, two circles of light bobbed up and down. The lights became brighter, larger, and, Pilate soon realised, closer. They swung up and down, shooting thin, pale shards of light into the growing night.

Torchlight.

Evidently their approach had been spotted, and was to be challenged. Tavarius had arrived at the same conclusion.

'Kill them on sight,' he said to the Igigi.

The Igigi stopped walking, and took the assault rifle from his back. The two security guards bobbed into view. The Igigi was unhurried, slowly affixing a silencer to the end of the rifle. He raised the gun, took careful aim, and with two muffled rounds of burst fire, left the distant guards as mounds on the floor, barely visible in the distance.

This is out of control.

'Tavarius...' Symeon began quietly, but he was silenced by a murderous look.

The group walked on, directly towards the motionless security guards. As they drew closer, no-one changed their pace, though Pilate couldn't help but stare at the corpses. The black sweaters, high visibility armbands, the ruined throat of one, the hole riddled chest of the other, and the pools of dark underneath and around them. They carried no weapons, only transceivers on their hips.

The Igigi stepped right over their bodies, and Tavarius

followed. Symeon stopped, but Tavarius, sensing this, turned to face Symeon. 'They will be reborn,' he said dispassionately, then turned back towards the stones.

Tavarius' pace quickened.

They will be reborn, but into what kind of world? We have already made the world as dark a place as it has ever seemed, and soon Tavarius will be wielding unprecedented, god-like power. No man should have such power, particularly not a man such as Tavarius.

The group came to a stop in front of a chain-link fence. The Igigi took a small bolt cutter from the inner pocket of his jacket and began cutting the wire. The fencing was not particularly robust, and had, in places, already been compromised with loose mesh. There were no signs of any more security guards, much to Pilate's relief.

'I would have thought they'd have had better security here,' Pilate said, not so much out of curiosity but as an attempt to dispel some of the toxic atmosphere that seemed to hover over the group.

'Why?' Tavarius replied happily, 'no-one's going to steal the stones. The security around the visitor centre is tighter, but could still be breached by a ten-year-old with a Glock. Those security guards didn't even have Tasers.'

The Igigi was pulling away sections of the fence now, and had peeled enough away to slip through. Tavarius followed with ease, as did Symeon, but Tavarius' body guards struggled with their extra bulk, and when it was Pilate's turn, he found himself stuck. With an undignified grunt, he managed to squeeze most of himself through, though loose mesh tore at his jacket, and caused rips in the Venetian wool. Eventually he forced himself all the way through, and took an undignified tumble on the hard earth. Pilate clutched his side, the breath knocked out of him as he rose unsteadily to his feet.

Fully vertical once again, Pilate studied Tavarius, who was beaming, expressing a joy Pilate had rarely seen in the man. There was something...manic in him. He was fiddling with his neck, undoing a top button and pulling out the Kishar Stone.

Tavarius clutched it reverently in a tight fist. His face resembled that of a man in the throes of sexual ecstasy.

If this works, he will never share this power.

Pilate was resigned to it. The ambition that had characterised his early life, his early lives, in fact, had faded now, into something too faint to leave an impression on his mind and his motivations. Would that he could drift gently through eternity. Instead, here he was, caught up in the whirlwind of chaos that Tavarius had unleashed on the world, a whirlwind that was about to intensify.

Tavarius strode confidently towards the stones. The air was still, and the night quiet. The first stars could now be seen. The colossal weathered stones stood with ominous dormancy, as though they themselves possessed an energy they were poised to unleash on an unsuspecting world.

Tavarius strode right into the middle of the great stone circle, his bodyguards, the Igigi, Pilate, and Symeon all hovered on the periphery, nursing private anxieties. Watching Tavarius, waiting for something... monumental. In the darkness Tavarius opened his fist, and let the Kishar Stone balance on his palm.

'I accept the mother's gift, and will use it for her benefit,' Pilate heard Tavarius say.

The Kishar Stone began to pulse, emitting a faint light at first, but growing so that it became a beacon in the darkness.

For a moment, nothing else happened, and Pilate began to feel relief, some of the tension that ran across his shoulders and neck started to dissipate. Then the silence and darkness exploded. Vast flames, twenty-foot-high, shot up out of the ground, a blood orange and scarlet vortex, a ringed wall of fire that completely obscured Tavarius from view. Pilate shielded his face from the blistering heat, and took several steps backwards. Plumes of smoke trailed into the night sky, and the smell of burned grass filled the air, an acrid taste in the back of his throat.

Perhaps Tavarius cannot control this.

Then Tavarius came *through* the wall of fire, unharmed.

He was laughing, and as he did, the flames grew larger, reaching the height of the tallest stones, though Pilate could detect no fuel. Above them, storm clouds gathered, and then with an explosion of noise and blinding white light, lightning struck the very centre of the ring of fire, where Tavarius had stood moments earlier.

The world itself seemed to blow apart. Everything was white, and for a span of terrifying heartbeats, Pilate could not tell if his eyes were opened or closed. Blinded to the world, the heat of the fire growing in his skin, the air itself dry as though set to burn, Pilate wondered if the fictional hell with which Tavarius had threatened the world through his greatest instrument, the Roman Catholic Church, had been made manifest. That his lie had become real, through him. But Pilate's sight returned, and he stumbled away from the fire.

'Back up, gentlemen, back up,' Tavarius said, his voice unusually high-pitched, almost unrecognisable. Pilate did not need to be told twice, nor, apparently, did Symeon, the bodyguards, or the Igigi, who had also retreated in haste.

'Further, further,' Tavarius chided, walking away from the stones. The rest of the group followed. When Pilate could no longer feel the heat from the fire, near the fence they had cut through, Tavarius turned back to the stone circle, which seemed now as a great lantern. The flames, Pilate realised, would be visible for miles over the mostly flat and featureless plain.

Tavarius gripped the Kishar Stone tightly in his fist again.

I nearly had him killed, back when he was my prisoner. I could have crushed him underneath the heavy boot of the power I wielded then, and instead I raised him high. What did I do?

There was a rumbling underneath Pilate's feet, his entire body vibrated, then the ground itself split, a great chasm opening right through the middle of the stone circle, sending the colossal stones tumbling to the ground. A series of tremors resounded, and Pilate struggled to keep his footing. In the time it took the stones to fall, a monument even more ancient than the beaten, exhausted, husk of a soul Pilate endured collapsed into ruin. The flames spluttered out. Swarms of ash were cast high into the night sky.

'And to think,' Tavarius said to Pilate, 'that you once called me a false prophet. I am a *god* that walks the earth. And if the Earth has now granted me its power, it now answers to me. Everyone, and everything answers to me.'

He is completely insane.

Pilate knew better than to ask if Tavarius intended to split the Kishar Stone into three and share its power, as he had always sworn he would. Pilate hadn't truly believed it when Tavarius had promised it two millennia ago, he knew it to be false now, and asking would simply anger a man who now held the power of life and death over every soul on the planet. What were Tavarius' promises worth? What had Tavarius promised Boaz Ben-Jada? Not, Pilate was sure, the death at the hands of Josephus that he was delivered. Ben-Jada's corpse had been fed to swine, Symeon had informed Pilate.

Pilate could hear sirens in the distance. Sirens that did not matter. Tavarius turned, his back to the ruin he had caused. A small whirlwind appeared in front of Tavarius, then moved forward at astonishing speed, and blew apart the wire-mesh fencing. Pilate and the others followed Tavarius.

All I can do now is follow the whirlwind. If I step in front of it, I will be destroyed.

CHAPTER TWENTY-TWO

**Praetorium of Pontius Pilate, Jerusalem
Month of Nissan, 30 AD**

*For all the hate within the Annunaki, it was the love of Andrea
which authored history's miserable course.*

-BOOK OF YESHUA

Wineskin in hand, head giddy with its former contents, Symeon
paced the garden. Pilate had forbidden him from leaving the
Praetorium, but he did at least have freedom of the grounds. He
might have been able to escape, if he had been so inclined, but
he saw no particular reason to. Maryam was gone, Yeshua was
gone, even Andrea lost to him. And the wine here was exquisite,
the taste unlike anything he had had before, and the smell of lav-
ender quite intoxicating.

I have killed a god.

Strangely, it wasn't Yeshua's death that haunted him in
the quiet corners of his soul, but the man he had killed.

Nohra, Tavarius has said his name was. Nohra.

Hours of clear thinking had not yet reconciled the horror
of what he had done with the more abstract promise of reincarnation. Perhaps befuddled with wine, he might stumble upon
some truth to ease his soul.

Do I lie even to myself now?

Symeon drank to forget.

He lay down on the moist grass and stared into the clear

night sky. A thousand thousand tiny suns. As many worlds as there were grains of sand in the Yeshimon, Judea's great desert wilderness, Yeshua had told them. He became lost in the stars, and the enormity of what they had done began to rescind.

Our world is but one of many. Yeshua is but one god of many. Is it so great a crime if he is dead? Men die, all the time. Fathers die. Shouldn't gods?

He took another swig from the wineskin, which was now near empty. The thick, sweet red was cool, and the liquid brought some relief to the tension that pressed in his head, from pulsing temple to pulsing temple.

It was this kind of worry, he realised, that he was fighting. It was why he had done what he did. Sold Yeshua to Caiaphas. Men worried, because of the consequences of their actions. With every action, they wagered their soul against an eternity of oblivion. What kind of perverse game was that? Symeon offered humanity an eternity of second chances. Didn't children, for that was what Yeshua had seen humanity as, deserve second chances?

The sky above began to spin, and Symeon felt the beginnings of nausea. He closed his eyes, brushed his fingers over the cool, wet grass. He slipped away from the world, and slept deeply and darkly.

AΩ

'Psssst, Sym. Sym. Sym!'

Where am I?

His tunic was wet, he was not in his bed. Recent events returned to him. He was in the outer garden of the Praetorium, and he had murdered a man, and killed a god.

'Sym! Wake up Sym.'

Andrea? Only he calls me Sym, at least since Mother died and Maryam left.

Symeon opened his eyes. His older brother was crouching

over him, clearly concerned. Andrea's tunic was torn, and his arms were scratched. He must have scaled the wall and landed in one of the bushes on the garden's perimeter. One of the thornier rose bushes, Symeon guessed, looking at the state of Andrea's tunic which looked as though it had been savaged by a ferocious pack of starving dogs.

'Andrea?' The wine had left his tongue clumsy. His head was thick, and his mind was slow.

'Yes, we don't have long Sym...' Andrea wrinkled his nose, as though in disgust, 'have you soiled yourself?'

He could smell it before he could see it, a rich stink. He had shat himself. Symeon started laughing.

'By all that is good, Andrea, look at me,' and Andrea shared his brother's laughter.

'I think I'll stick with the wine they serve down in the Lower City if this is what Upper City wine does to you.'

'What are you doing here, Andrea?'

At this, the laughter drained from Andrea's face.

'You've betrayed us, brother. What have you done?'

He won't understand yet, he never was a deep thinker.

'I don't expect you to understand brother, but what I did was *right*. I loved Yeshua. But his system, his governance, it was wrong. Every soul living under the threat of damnation. What kind of world is that? One mistake, and our souls are obliterated. But my way, our souls are protected. And yes, there will be evil, souls who do wrong, who will go unpunished, but everyone gets another chance.'

Symeon was becoming more animated, speaking more quickly.

I'm rambling. Focus, perhaps he can understand.

'Just think of it Andrea, the world I'm going to build! The world you can help me build. Every soul granted life, after life, after life. Suffering is temporary, and what I'm giving the world is immortality, and an infinity of joy, cushioned in blissful ignorance.'

Andrea looked stunned. 'Did you hear *nothing* of what

Yeshua taught us Sym? Don't be a fool! Suffering is temporary, you are right, but life *is* suffering. And without Yeshua, there is no divinity, no chance to return to the One Whole Consciousness. This isn't why I shared the secrets of soul-imprinting with you. I just wanted to be with you, for more lives than this.'

Symeon rolled his eyes.

'Life is suffering, is it?' he spat, 'what I had with Maryam, the nights we had drinking in the garden of Gethsemane, friendship, love, all of it means nothing?'

'Of course not. But we all suffer, in the end,' Andrea said with a despondency that cut right through the tension, 'there is joy in life, but life is a journey, and a journey must have a destination in order to be meaningful, or at least, to maintain the illusion of meaning.'

I never knew Andrea to have such depth of thought.

There was a long pause, as both men thought how to penetrate the wall of silence that now stood between them.

'So, why *are* you here?' Symeon said at last, sitting on the ground, easing the feeling that he was squaring up to his brother.

'To help you.'

'Why, if you think me a fool?'

'Because you are my *brother*. And I made our mother a promise, while she lay on her deathbed. I swore that I would *always* be there to look after you. To protect you, my younger brother. I swore, and no words I have ever spoken have been more important to me. I was not sure, exactly, what it was you needed of me. But I knew that I could not head into the desert with my other brothers, without seeing you. Besides, you are not yet damned.'

Symeon laughed. A laugh filled with bitterness and spite. 'Oh, but I am, Dre, I truly am. Tavarius made quite sure of that.'

Andrea looked as though he was going to be sick, and slumped to the ground beside Symeon. 'What have you done?' he asked in horror.

Symeon looked away. 'There's no need to talk about it, it

is done now.'

Andrea let the silence hang about them, and despite himself, Symeon felt compelled to break it.

'Tavarius questioned my commitment. He wanted to see that I meant what I said. So he had me do something... unspeakable. Make no mistake Andrea, what I did... my soul is now damaged beyond repair. But it does not matter, for I am reshaping the very order of things, creating a better world.'

Symeon put his arm around Andrea. 'I don't need your help brother. I just want you to understand.'

He starts to see. It horrifies him, but he does begin to see.

'If....' Andrea began, then paused. The night was still and calm. There was nothing in the world outside of the pair of them. Andrea turned away.

'If you are damned, then I have no choice,' Andrea said eventually, as much to himself as to Symeon, 'I cannot see you damned, brother. There is something you must know.'

'What?'

'Yeshua, he is not yet dead.'

Horror held Symeon captive as truth crept up on him. 'What do you mean? I saw him die. *I saw him die.* There was no pulse.'

'You saw what he wanted you to see brother. And as for his pulse. You have seen what he is capable of? How difficult do you think it would be for Yeshua, a *god* to suspend his pulse?'

'But..' Symeon said

'Yossef, the Arimathean,' Andrea said over the top of his brother, 'he and Yeshua have been plotting more than you know, ever since you... sold him to Caiaphas and the Sanhedrin. Yeshua wanted to win the trial, believed that he could win with a display of divinity, but *he did not count on it.* They believed, Yeshua and the Arimathean, that should Yeshua make a display of defiance and immortality, tales of his divinity, and following that, his *message,* would spread like wildfire. And tales of Yeshua are on the tongue of every single citizen of Jerusalem this night, and for many nights to come I am sure.'

Smart souls plan against their hopes, and the Arimathean is a deep well of cunning, and Yeshua it would seem, despite his poor showings in Ka'ab, is not without the capacity for deceit.

'Yeshua faked his death, Symeon. He staged a conversation with Yohanan... about vinegar. Does that sound familiar to you?'

Truth hit Symeon. Looking back, the whole situation felt so contrived.

How could I have missed it.

Symeon studied recent events from the perspective granted by this new information. 'Perhaps... perhaps Yeshua is not dead, but we have him trapped, and we have the Kishar Stone, Tavarius took it. So long as he cannot escape, he cannot resume Godhead.'

Andrea shook his head, sadly.

'The tomb, Sym, it has an escape tunnel built right into it. The tunnel leads through the hill on which the tomb stands, its exit point concealed by a thicket next to a distinctive purple-flowered tree. Yeshua has already met with Judah, Yohanan and the rest. All but me. They travel into Yeshimon now.'

Fear coursed through Symeon. The fear of damnation. The fear of having gambled everything and lost. It was too much for his soul, but not his mind, which remained, bizarrely, very clear.

'Where then will they go?'

'Yeshua intends to resume his godhead, but not before passing on the ability to perform miracles.'

'Miracles... but, we have the Kishar Stone, brother, I told you. Tavarius took it from him.'

'Brother, I thought you were the smart one,' Andrea said with a rueful smile, 'did you not think it odd that Yeshua gave up the source of his divine power without so much as a fight?'

'I... I did not, he was threatened.'

'How did you think he stilled his pulse?'

Symeon had no answer.

'Yossef anticipated that after your... defection, you would

inform others about the Kishar Stone. Your new friend took an imitation only, a worthless lump of stone.'

The understanding of his gullibility was almost as painful to Symeon as the truth of his imperilled soul.

'Shit. Where are they going?'

'Eventually? The Great Pyramids of Egypt, where he unearthed the Kishar Stone. From there, he can resume his godhead, he says. But they will head somewhere before that.'

'Where?' Desperate hands suddenly clamped his brother's shoulders. 'Where? Andrea, I must know.'

'I do not know. Yeshua simply told us that he would lead us there so that the power of the Kishar Stone might be shared.. Filippos has been given more details, and was charged in advance with the task of booking passage from Caesarea, but I know nothing more than that.'

'Shit, shit, shit. I must alert Pilate.' Symeon started back towards the building, but then turned to his brother.

'You might not see it, Andrea, but you have done the right thing.'

Symeon turned, preparing to run, but Andrea caught his arm.

'Symeon, you must understand. I have forsaken Yeshua now, just as you have. I cannot return to him, or our former brethren. He has already imprinted my soul, I was the first, but no-one can know. Yeshua did it before the trial. The very night he... suggested an alternative path for you. I do not know his reasons for imprinting me first. If anyone asks, any... co-conspirators you have, you *must not tell them*. You must do this for me.'

Symeon's heart was beating hard. There was... joy. They would be brothers through the ages. It was the first time in many days that his heart felt anything other than heavy.

'I... of course, brother.'

Then Symeon did run, his bare feet pounding scratchy grass, leaving his brother behind.

CHAPTER TWENTY-THREE

Vatican City, Rome
Month of June, 2024 AD

*The Holy Roman Empire is a great parasite that feeds on fear.
Its greatest trick is to convince humanity that the relationship
is symbiotic.*

-BOOK OF YESHUA

At Porta Sant'anna, two unmoving bronze eagles watched Elliot
from atop their column perches astride the cast iron gate which
opened into Vatican City, and the entrance to the Vatican archives.

'I came here once,' Rock said to Elliot in a hushed voice,
'Vatican City I mean. I was thirteen, Dad joked that I wasn't to
wander, in case I got captured, turned into an altar boy, and
"buggered straight to hell."'

Elliot laughed, partly at Rock, partly at the sheer absurdity of the situation. He stood at the very gates of his enemy, with
a man he did not know, a man he did not trust, and a man who
had betrayed him. Despite the guilt he felt, he could not say that
he was not glad of Rock's presence. The only man here he could
truly trust. Not that he had a choice in the matter, Rock had insisted on coming, and after all that Elliot had dragged him into,
how could he refuse him?

'He never seemed like a religions man, your Dad,' Elliot
said, 'remember when I stayed at yours for a few days the sum-

mer before we went to Oxford, and when he was driving me back to the station he swore at those nuns because they were crossing the road, at a pedestrian crossing no less, "too slowly"?'

Rock laughed. 'Funnily enough I *do* remember that. I also remember him taking a piss against a church wall at cousin Barry's wedding.'

'Is that the cousin with the weirdly shaped head?'

'Bald Barry, yeah. The one who looks like a dinosaur egg. We came here for Nanna, she was Catholic.'

It feels good to be speaking in the old way, as innocent, naive souls, even if it is pretence.

'We ought to get moving,' Andrea said.

They walked through the gate and passed into Vatican City. Monsignor Fiero in his black cassock with fuchsia piping and sash, looking pale, sweaty, ill at ease, and ill-suited to the sunshine and heat. Lurking in the darkness of crypts was an aesthetic to which the clergyman was far better suited.

Behind Monsignor Fiero walked Andrea, who wore a plain black cassock with a dog's collar. He was dressed as a simple Priest, and would, if asked, pass as a guest of Fiero's, a priest visiting from Nigeria. His ID card, procured and doctored by Fiero, would say the same thing. Fiero and Andrea both concealed the ruby red eye, attached to the part of their dog's collar that remained hidden. They could display the eye, if required, by rotating the dog's collar.

Behind them walked Professor Cove, who had said nothing since his release from the room of Initiations, and Rock and Elliot, who wore sweater vests and jeans, looking for all the world like the research assistants they masqueraded as.

'We're inside,' Elliot informed Judah through the small communications device in his ear when they had all passed through the gate. Judah was sat, about a mile away in a small apartment, ready to remotely implement the hacking software that Rock had designed.

The idea behind Rock's software was simple. Having been provided surveillance access by Fiero, Rock was able to create a program that captured all data from the video feeds inside the Vatican necropolis, which were monitored both on site, and remotely, by a rotation of Swiss Guardsman and Igigi, and loop them back one hour, but with an overwritten time stamp. The watchers would be seeing what had happened one hour ago, thinking it to be the present. Given that shifts lasted four hours, so the same guardsmen would be wandering the labyrinthine necropolis, the watchers would, it was hoped, fail to spot any discrepancies, and place the entire Vatican City in lock-down.

At least, that was the plan.

'Good luck, brother,' Elliot heard Judah reply with alarming immediacy and clarity, as though Judah had taken up residence inside his head.

They were approaching the entrance to the archives now, squeezing their way past large groups of the faithful, who looked indistinguishable from tourists, sporting cameras, baseball caps and merchandise. Elliot could see that Rock was becoming agitated and nervous, and put an arm on his shoulder.

'It's not too late to back out, Rock,' Elliot said.

In front of him, Fiero turned to scowl, but Elliot ignored him.

'I appreciate your loyalty, Rock, but this has been my fight for longer than you can conceive...'

'No,' Rock said firmly, 'I am a part of this now. I will see it through.' Elliot could see his jaw jutted in that stubborn way of his, and he realised that there would be no turning his friend away.

I'm not giving Professor Cove the same choice.

Elliot tried to swallow his guilt, but some of it stuck in his throat. Professor Cove had not chosen this. He had been bullied and threatened into this, held in the worst kind of hell imaginable until his will and spirit were broken. And Elliot was simply going along with it, for what other choice did he have? They needed the access Professor Cove provided to the third level. Were he and Judah as bad as Fiero for utilising his ruthlessness? He couldn't think about that now. He had to focus.

The stakes were now too high. If they failed, even on the basis of a morality that might once have hampered him, the Annunaki would do as Andrea said, encase Yeshua in concrete and drop him into the greatest depths of the ocean. They would never find him, and the planet and One Whole Consciousness would both be fatally undermined by the imbalance.

The entrance to the Vatican archives was unassuming, the building lacked the grandiose ornamentation and immense scale of those around it. The group passed through simple wooden doors into a lobby that reminded Elliot of the hall-way of St Peter's in Oxford that housed the college's adminis-trative offices. Near the end of the lobby, as they had known there would be, stood two security guards, and a body scanner. Behind that, was the reception desk, and another set of tinted glass double doors.

Andrea scratched his nose. This pre-arranged signal in-formed the group that the two security guards were, as Fiero had relayed, Enzo and Giampaolo and that they were to con-tinue with the plan.

'Now,' Elliot said quietly, trusting the ear-piece to pick up what he said. Affecting a scratch behind his ear, he removed the communications device and slid it into his phone case. Andrea had provided the entire group with new phones, though they would serve little purpose beyond this point.

After a prompt from the security guards, the group placed their phones into the tray next to the body scanner. The tray was pulled along a conveyor belt into an X-ray machine, whose scan was barely glanced at by the second security guard. One by one, Fiero in the lead, Elliot at the back, the group passed through the body scanner without triggering it.

'Your phones will remain with us,' the security guard who had barely watched the X-ray of the phones said in the listless, bored manner of one who had repeated that phrase countless times. 'No photography is permitted in the Archives. I will pro-vide you with tickets.'

'Ah wait,' Elliot said, feigning something remembered urgently, 'can I send a text quickly first?'

The guard shrugged, which Elliot took for assent. He grabbed his phone from the tray, and with his left hand, slid the minute ear-piece out from the pocket of his phone case. He kept the ear-piece concealed between his thumb and index finger, then made a show of sending a text, and handed the phone back to the guard.

The guard pulled a sticker sheet from his jacket pocket, and marked each phone. The corresponding ticket was handed to the member of the group who identified the phone as his.

Theatre and deception. We'll never see those phones again.

'Sign in at reception,' the guard said without looking at anybody. The guard, Giampaolo, Fiero had informed them, had one of those long faces that seemed permanently entrenched in boredom, the ends of his mouth turned ever so slightly downward, a lack of interest behind hazel eyes. Giampaolo leaned back against the wall, arms folded, sighing deeply, exhausted and exasperated by his work.

The reception desk was manned by someone surprisingly young and athletic, given his desk-bound profession. 'Hello', he said in English, with only the faintest trace of his Italian accent. 'Welcome to the Vatican Apostolic Archive. How can I help you today?'

'Monisgnor Fiero Mazzanti,' Fiero said in an accent as flamboyantly Latinate as the receptionist's had been reserved. Fiero handed his ID card to the receptionist.

'I need one guest pass for my friend here, Father Bako. First level only.'

The receptionist studied the ID card for a moment, then returned it to Fiero, evidently satisfied with whatever evidence of authenticity he had managed to source.

'Very good Monsignor.'

The receptionist printed out a guest pass for "Father Bako", and slipped the pass into a laminated lanyard, which he passed to Andrea, who slipped it over his head and around his neck. The receptionist pressed a button, there was a loud buzzing noise, and the tinted glass doors parted. Fiero and Andrea walked off confidently.

Professor Cove walked up to the desk hesitantly.

'Um. Professor James Cove, UC Irvine,' he said haltingly in a soft California accent, 'I have an appointment for the third level of the archives, these are my research assistants.'

'Ah yes, Professor Cove, we have been expecting you,' the receptionist said brightly. 'Can I see your IDs please.'

Cove, Rock and Elliot handed over their UC Irvine IDs, which the receptionist made such a show of checking that Elliot became convinced that he had no idea what he was looking for. The receptionist nodded to himself, as if quite satisfied, then turned to his computer and printed out three passes, before slipping them into lanyards.

'You will need to present these at both the second, and third level,' the receptionist informed them. Once again, the loud buzzing noise filled the corridor, and Cove, Elliot and Rock walked through the tinted glass doors that had parted for them.

When the doors slid back together behind them, Elliot felt the noise of the world disappear. It was quiet, and still, and ancient. The books that were packed tightly into the ceiling-high bookshelves were old, with crumbling spines. There was a stale quality to the room, which felt preserved, but badly, with slow disintegration.

Centuries of lies and control buried out of sight. This was the greatest reserve of human knowledge once. It remains the greatest collection of lies ever told, I suspect. Well, unless you count the internet. But there was much truth here too. The kind of truths people thought important enough to bury.

'First level accessed,' Elliot whispered.

'Acknowledged,' Judah said, 'any problems?'

'None so far,' and though Elliot had never been superstitious, he touched one of the wooden book shelves.

Andrea and Fiero were huddled over a book in one of the cubicles around the edge of the room. A few cubicles to the right, a wizened scholar stood turning the pages of a book reverentially with a gloved hand, then scribbling notes furiously. Elliot wandered over, and Rock and Cove followed.

'Proceed to level two,' Andrea said quietly, without turning around, 'you know what to do.'

Elliot did, and it was that knowledge that was causing his heart to pound and the thunderstorm in his head to rage. He wound through the bookshelves, encountering a pristine white-gloved librarian who carried an ancient looking book with a level of care appropriate to a new-born baby. The librarian said nothing, but Elliot could feel his stare boring into the back of his skull.

Eventually, Elliot came to the next set of glass doors, which would lead, he knew, to the second level. A Swiss guardsman, a young man, not far removed from his teenage years with lingering acne, though not so pronounced as Rock's, stood to attention in navy blue service dress with a black beret and white gloves.

'May I see your passes, please?' he said, as Elliot approached. Elliot gave Cove a covert nudge, and the Professor walked up to the guardsman and presented his pass. The guardsman removed a small, handheld scanner from a bracket on the wall, and pulled the trigger while holding it over the Professor's pass. The small LED on the scanner turned green, and the guardsman nodded to himself. When Elliot handed over his pass, he felt very aware of the fact that the guardsman held the pass in the lanyard which was attached to his neck.

The guardsman pulled out a card from a pocket in his service dress, and pressed it to a black receiver on the door. The LED on this too went green, and the glass doors opened. The guardsman said nothing, so Elliot walked through, followed by Cove and Rock.

Beyond the door were marble stairs which seemed to go on and on. With each step, Elliot felt his stomach lurch, as though he were falling, and could do nothing but wait to hit the ground. He felt sick. He looked at Cove and Rock, who were both pale and clammy.

Pull yourself together Elliot.

At the bottom of the marble stairs, a corridor led into a room that was three or four times the size of the first level. Everywhere was dim, dusty, and packed with ancient books. All of the libraries in all of the colleges of the University of Oxford combined would struggle to put together a collection of literature as voluminous as was present in this room.

'Level two entered successfully,' Elliot said.

'Understood,' Judah replied.

'Christ, this place is creepy,' Rock said quietly 'can you feel it?'

He hadn't noticed it at first, but Elliot *could* feel it. A sense of dread creeping through the place. Perhaps it was the total silence, a library of secrets that hoarded, rather than shared knowledge, perhaps it was the sense of stagnation. Most of all, Elliot could feel the evil manifest from the Papal edicts and lies hosted in this room. How many lives had been ruined or ended, how many souls cowed, how many atrocities committed stemming from the words contained in this room?

'Professor Cove...' Elliot began to whisper as they walked, before silencing himself as he passed a librarian with a withered face and crumpled posture shuffling between the book shelves.

'Professor I am so sorry for... for whatever it was Monsignor Fiero did to you. I just hope that one day you will realise that even if what he did was wrong, what you are doing is right.'

'A man can do neither right, nor wrong,' Cove said, after a long pause, 'if there is no choice to make. He threatened my family.'

'You have my word, Professor, that your family will come to no harm.'

'Oh, so you're in charge, are you?'

'Well...'

'You are not, and you should not be making promises, so let's just get this nonsense over and done with. Now, what is it we're supposed to be looking for here?'

'A Papal Edict from 1533 known as *Sempiterno Regi.*'

'Ah yes,' Cove said, suddenly a Professor and not a hostage, 'Pope Clement VII's condemnation of the forced baptism of Jews in certain parts of Portugal.'

'I'm glad you know of it,' Elliot said, 'do you know where it is though?'

'It won't take me long to find,' Cove said, with a degree of pride.

The professor did not bother to explain his methodology as he worked, muttering incomprehensibly as he checked reference cards and book spines.

'Do you trust him?' Rock whispered in Elliot's ear.

'More than I trust Fiero,' Elliot said.

CHAPTER TWENTY-FOUR

Yeshimon, Judea
Month of Nissan, 30 AD

During the quietest, darkest moments, I sometimes wonder if anyone ever found my bones in the desert.

-BOOK OF YESHUA

Josephus was pushing them hard now. The horses flecked spit, their breathing desperate. The dogs that had picked up the scent of their quarry were far behind, at the mercy of a strangling death at the cruel, dry hands of the Judean desert.

We must *catch them.*

Sweat fell from his forehead in buckets. Symeon was no rider, and it was hot, even though it was still early morning. They chased footprints now, where earlier they had followed the dogs who had caught their scent, and before that, his brother's word. The men he had called brothers once had partaken of Yeshua's blood, as Symeon, Pilate and Tavarius had. They had set off into the desert, heading north, intending to board a ship at Caesarea. Or so Symeon, and in turn Tavarius, had trusted, and his brother had spoken true.

The party thundered on. Josephus, captain of Pilate's personal guard, flanked by his most loyal men, six on each side. Pilate rode just behind, and just as competently, on a magnificent palomino, who remained composed, where all other horses showed their desperation. Tavarius, who rode well, but had the

Arimathean trussed on the back of his Andalusian, and Symeon, were starting to lag.

Symeon began to panic, what if they had come too far into the desert? Yeshimon was merciless, an enemy that would not relinquish its grip on them. What if the horses died? They had only a few skins of water, such had been their haste in departing. Symeon held his hand in front of him, protection against the clouds of sand swept up by the pack in front of him, but could see nothing.

Though he moved at terrifying speed, only rocks, and small withered looking cacti being thrown backwards gave any visual sense that he was moving at all. Sweat stung his eyes, his thighs chafed, and his mind was a vice, pressed between two diametric terrors, those of catching Yeshua, and those of not.

I do this for the world, for those I love, and those I do not know.

Suddenly a great sandstorm rose above the horizon, against which, the rest of his party were mere specks. Hundreds of cubits high, possibly thousands. So massive that it blocked out the sun, and seemed to cast the entire desert into unnatural diurnal shade. Shortly after, the sound of the storm hit Symeon, a howling that pounded his eardrums.

Yeshua?

Symeon pushed his horse hard, galloping, pulling up when he reached the rest of his party, who had all come to a stop. The hunters and the hunted faced each other. Yeshua stood in front of his friends, his arms outstretched, as though shielding them from any harm. Above Yeshua, sand swirled in a vortex with unnaturally perfect geometry.

Facing Yeshua and Symeon's former brothers, Josephus stood furthest forward. The men of his guard stood in a row behind him, but they seemed to exude an anxiety lacking in Josephus, who stood like a statue, unintimidated by the whirlwind above. Symeon didn't know whether to be impressed by the man's loyalty and bravery, or concerned by the man's stupidity.

Abruptly, part of the whirlwind above unfurled into a tentacle of sand so dense as to appear solid, and lashed downward at Josephus' feet, covering him in sand. Josephus stumbled backwards.

The sand storm above resolved itself into an image, a depiction of Yeshua himself, but stern, and terrible. The sand Yeshua, at least a hundred times the size of the real Yeshua, lent forward, as if about to puke, and indeed, its lips parted, spewing sand all over the hunting party.

And then, in an instant, sand Yeshua was no more. Sand cascaded down from the sky, and a heaped dune stood between the parties

'What do we...?' Pilate began, but Tavarius held his hand up for silence, never taking his eyes from the crest of the dune. Then Yeshua appeared, a silhouette above them, his arms outstretched. He spoke then, with a voice, that though mundane, nevertheless seemed to fill the entire desert.

'Come no further, Tavarius. Return, and do not follow, or I will leave you as corpses for the vultures, your skin shredded for a thousand thousand cuts.'

Symeon bowed his head. In his periphery, he could see that Pilate had actually knelt, a supplicant, begging for mercy.

It is over, I am damned.

But Tavarius stood still, keeping his gaze on Yeshua. Then, absurdly, he laughed.

'You have threatened me before, and did nothing. Do it then, tradesman, have us killed.'

The ground itself moved, sand whipped up, a roaring filled the desert as the sandstorm loomed large above Yeshua's head once again.

'DO IT!' Tavarius screamed, the sound barely perceptible over the roar of the sandstorm. Two of Pilate's guard bolted then, jumping on their horses, and thundering away.

Oppius and Quintus, Pilate had named them.

Two more guards broke and mounted their horses, fleeing into the endless desert. The others looked like they wished to join their comrades, but were held firm by Josephus, whose stare was like a tether, stronger than fear.

Symeon sobbed, threw up his hands, braced himself against the death he knew was coming.

But it did not. The whirlwind remained. Tavarius laughed again, and began to walk *towards* the whirlwind. Towards Yeshua.

'You cannot kill us, tradesman,' he shouted over the whirlwind, 'I have the Arimathean.'

The whirlwind stopped promptly, this time the sand blown far behind them, temporarily blotting out the sun again, casting the shadow of darkness over the desert for a fleeting moment.

Tavarius continued up the dune, stopping only a few cubits short of Yeshua.

'I have the Arimathean,' Tavarius said again, this time quietly.

'What of it?' Yeshua replied and though the tone was firm, Symeon could sense the trepidation beneath it.

Not so adept at deceit after all.

'I will cause him to suffer as no soul has ever suffered.' Tavarius turned, and nodded at Josephus, who walked over to the horse to which Yossef was trussed.

'He bluffs Yeshi,' Yossef shouted in a muffled voice, for his bonds were tight, and his face was pressed against the Andalusian's hindquarters.

Josephus pulled a dagger from his belt, raised it, and sliced through Yossef's left thumb. Blood dripped on the sand, where it was swallowed, and the Arimathean screamed, a sound that rent the air and sent a chill down Symeon's spine.

Storm clouds gathered above.

'Yossef!' Yeshua shouted, and the god was suddenly nothing but human, running down the dune, the Kishar Stone temporarily forgotten.

Then Oppius and Quintus, the first two guards who had bolted, or at least pretended to, appeared at the crest of the dune. In the commotion, Yeshua did not hear the hooves on the soft sand, and as Yeshua stumbled towards Yossef, a sandstorm whipping up in front of him and speeding ahead towards Josephus, one of the fled guards brought his sword down from on high, in a swift, violent arc. Yeshua's hand fell from his arm, which spurted blood. The Kishar Stone fell from the disembodied hand, which lay open on the desert floor. The sandstorm simply stopped, and the sand fell to the ground. Josephus wasted no time, and sprinted across the freshly fallen sand, pounced on the hand, while the remaining guards set about Yeshua with swords. Blood squirted like red paint flicked carelessly across the still, desert canvas.

Symeon watched in horror as Yeshua was dismembered, and then, worse *regrew his limbs.* It was all the more miraculous, and horrifying, for seeming *natural.*

Truly, he cannot be killed.

'Leave him, the others are coming.'

Tavarius was right. Symeon's unarmed brothers were running down the dune. What happened next was slaughter.

Yohanan was the first down the dune, and the first to die, almost cut in half by the great sweep of Josephus' broadsword, but he *continued running,* stopping to die only when he reached Yeshua's feet. Little Yacob died next with one guard's ear between blood stained teeth, and his guts hanging like blue sausages from his open stomach.

Filippos also made a beeline for Yeshua, and managed to reach him just as a soldier stepped behind him and slit his throat. Taddai was cut to pieces, his screams piercing the entire scene. Levi managed to hit Josephus with a rock he had picked up from somewhere, but it clanged harmless from his helmet, and, enraged, Josephus charged Levi down, stabbing him in the gut, then making a ruin of his throat.

Judah had managed to get a sword from one of the guards, and used it to stab the disarmed man through the chest. But the remaining guards were quick to the threat, and Judah was cut to pieces beneath the onslaught of steel.

At first, only Symeon saw Yossef fall from the horse, his arm bent at a sickening angle, then crawl to Yeshua, and lick

blood from a gash in his neck. Yossef began to mutter something, words Symeon could not hear, but could guess.

I accept the Divine burden of Remembrance.

Tavarius, who had been watching the slaughter with
gleaming eyes, suddenly spotted Yossef, pulled out his own dagger, strode over to the Arimathean, and opened his throat. More
blood was added to the saturated sand.

Symeon watched Netanel executed. His old friend knelt,
all fight drained from him, his head parted from his torso. His
arm had been lopped off at the elbow at some point during the
fight. Symeon the Zealot and Yacob Bar-Zebedee tried to run.
But they did not run far. Their headless bodies lay next to each
other.

When Tau'ma's neck was snapped, and Josephus' sword
thrust through the back of his neck for good measure, the sand
of the desert was darkened with the blood of twelve corpses:
the guard Judah had killed, ten of Symeon's former brothers,
Yossef of Arimathea. Scattered around Yeshua were his superflu-
ous dead limbs. The only sound was Yeshua's weeping.

Tavarius spat on the ground. 'Tie up the Nazarene.'

Symeon returned to his horse, all emotion drained, there
was no horror, no disgust, no relief. He had been broken and he
felt nothing.

'The guards who ran...' Tavarius said ominously once the
party was mounted.

Josephus nodded.

Tavarius opened his palm, and stared with undiluted lust
at the Kishar Stone clutched there.

*If he should learn the secret of the Kishar Stone, the world
should tremble.*

CHAPTER TWENTY-FIVE

Vatican City, Rome
Month of June, 2024 AD

Yeshua was not a serious man, his greatest joy was in making others laugh, others feel comfortable. I hope I see him again, but more than that, I hope that captivity has not rendered him entirely serious.

-BOOK OF YESHUA

Professor Cove pulled out *Sempiterno Regi*, the papal edict for which he had been searching. Elliot glanced nervously over his shoulder.

We are alone.

Elliot put his hand on Rock's shoulder. 'Are you ready to do this?'

Surprisingly, Rock smiled. 'Do you remember Oblivion, at Alton Towers, when I refused to go down. I was too scared.'

'I... yeah?'

'Well that was way worse.' Rock's smile widened further.

'Lunatic,' said Elliot, whose heart swelled with love.

Elliot reached in to the gap on the bookshelf that Cove had made by removing the Papal Edict. His fingers caught cloth.

Fiero spoke true. It's here.

Elliot cleared a few more books, then yanked at the cloth. It was a large sack. The sack had been planted, Andrea had told them, many years ago, when surveillance had been less sophisticated.

Elliot put the bag on the floor carefully, grunting with the weight of it, then opened it, and began to remove the contents. A large gas canister, five gas masks that looked like relics of the second world war, three original Beretta 950 pistols, Semtex with a fuse, a lighter, and a tungsten-tipped saw blade.

Only five masks, shit. But... perhaps it's for the best.

With the contents inventoried, Elliot stuffed all but the canister and two gas masks back into the cloth sack.

'Judah?' Elliot said.

'Yes?'

'Is the looped security feed running?'

'It is.'

'Good, then we're doing this. See you on the other side, old friend.'

'See you on the other side. Daniel too.'

I hope so. With everything in this dense, crippled soul, I hope so.

Elliot turned to Professor Cove. 'Professor,' he said, 'I am so, so sorry for what has happened to you, that you were co-erced into... this. And if the situation were different, had we any choice in the matter, this would not have happened to you. Please, believe me when I say that you are changing the world, for the better. Your part in this is over. This gas is nitrous oxide; it will knock you out. Everyone on this floor in fact. When you come to, leave this place, leave and do not come back.'

The Professor said nothing, and for a moment, Elliot was concerned that he had not understood.

'Professor...'

'You are insane,' Cove interrupted in a harsh, self-assured tone Elliot had not heard from the man before, 'insane, and criminals.'

Elliot couldn't disagree on either count, and so he said nothing. Instead, he passed one of the gas masks to Rock, who fumbled with it, until he had a tight seal around his mouth.

'Breathing okay?' Elliot asked.

Rock gave a thumbs up.

Elliot put his own mask on, then turned to the Professor. 'Move away from here, please, Professor. I don't want you getting the full blast of this.' His voice was tinny, but clear, through the mask.

To Elliot's relief, the Professor did as he was told.

We need this to work. I must put my faith in the non-degradation of a gas canister that must be forty years old.

Elliot turned the nozzle on the gas canister, which begin to hiss, and gas, invisible but for a small vapour trail, oozed out, reaching into the abandoned alleys of this corrupt city of knowledge. Elliot dropped the canister on the floor. The room was tightly sealed, Fiero had informed them, in order to preserve the books and scrolls. As such, the gas would work quickly, and effectively.

Elliot heard Professor Cove coughing first, behind them. He was curled up on the floor, beneath an endless stack of ancient scrolls.

'We must head back, we must meet with Andrea, and Fiero.'

Elliot pointed his Beretta, and set off the way they had come. The entire floor seemed to erupt into a cacophony of coughing, and spluttering. They were running now, Elliot hurdled one librarian, who lay, completely still, on the floor.

'Nearly there,' he shouted back over his shoulder at Rock.

The soft carpet was replaced by hard marble, and suddenly their feet hammered noise into their surroundings. They slowed, and started up the staircase, back up to the first level. The doors were already open. Andrea and Fiero had evidently overcome the guard, who was sprawled, unconscious or dead, Elliot didn't dare question which, on the floor.

Elliot dropped the cloth sack on one of the steps, half way down, pulled out two gas masks, then hurled them up the stairs. Andrea picked them up, passed one to Fiero, and the pair affixed them to their heads. They walked through the open door, which closed behind them, and started down the stairs.

'Everything go as planned?' Andrea asked.

'Yeah,' Rock answered.

Andrea nodded, and Elliot could sense, but not see, the smile within Fiero's gas mask. With his cassock and mask, the sight of Fiero was deeply unsettling, and Elliot was reminded, unpleasantly, of the bird masks worn by physicians during the time of the plague.

What a shit life that was.

Elliot remembered being in Tournai, watching families, entire streets, succumbing to the plague. The world had never seemed darker than it had then, save, perhaps, for recently. And of course, as he had awaited death in the desert, the coppery taste of Yeshua's blood on his lips.

'Elliot!' Rock shouted, snapping Elliot from his reverie.

'Yeah?'

'The guns.'

'The Berettas. Yeah.' Elliot passed the two remaining pistols to Andrea and Fiero.

'Follow me,' said Fiero, and walking briskly, led the party back down the marble stairs. It was too quiet at the bottom. Elliot knew something was wrong. The bodies of two researchers lay stretched across the floor, the accusatory finger of one pointing at Elliot. Their faces were black.

Corpses.

Horror engulfed Elliot. He turned, angrily, to Fiero, and disregarding the Beretta the monsignor held, put his hands around his throat, and held him against the wall.

'What the fuck did you do?' Elliot snarled, 'what was in that canister?'

'What's going on?' Judah asked Elliot in his ear. Elliot ignored him

Fiero began to splutter.

'Let him go, Yossef,' Andrea said calmly, 'the deception was mine.'

Elliot let Fiero go, and the man slid down the wall. Elliot turned, and pointed his pistol at Andrea, disengaging the safety.

'It was hydrogen sulfide,' Andrea said calmly, 'fatal, in about three minutes, if the concentration is above 500 parts per million. I am sorry Yossef, but we couldn't take the chance.'

'It wasn't your decision to make,' Elliot snarled.

'Yossef, we both know you're not going to kill me. And we are wasting time, do you want the sacrifice to be for nothing?'

'There's... nothing we can do for them, except continue,' Rock said, with surprising calm.

Elliot had no counterargument. Instead, he pushed the hatred down, into his gut.

'Let's fucking get on with it then.'

Elliot picked up the cloth sack, and followed. Andrea, took the lead, followed by Fiero. Every hurried step Elliot took in Fiero's wake was horror and misery. Askew limbs, blackened faces. Elliot counted eleven corpses, a few librarians, mostly researchers, and of course Professor Cove. There may have been others, the group had made a direct line for the centre of the floor, and had not explored every nook and cranny. Elliot remembered his last moments as Qara, as life had been choked from him.

Suffocation is the worst way to go, save fire.

In the depths of the second level, Fiero led the group down a narrow space between two tall bookshelves, stacked with faded red leather tomes. There was single file room only.

'We breach here,' Fiero informed them, 'pass Andrea the explosives, and back up.'

Reluctantly, Elliot reached into the cloth sack, and pulled out the Semtex, and the lighter, and passed them to the man masquerading as a Nigerian priest. Andrea planted the Semtex on the flimsy looking wall, lit the fuse, then retreated, motioning the group still further back, until they were all around the corner, outside of the blast radius. The explosion was more muted than Elliot had expected, but sent shock-waves through him nonetheless. Little remained of the wall, and there was a singed opening into an unlit sandstone hallway.

'The *true* Vatican Necropolis,' Fiero announced, as if he

were a tour guide. Andrea went through first, his Beretta pointing into the darkness. Fiero and Rock followed.

It wasn't supposed to happen like this.

Heavy with guilt and regret, Elliot followed.

'Daniel, get behind us. There will be armed guards' Andrea said quietly.

'Won't the hydrogen sulfide have got them?' Rock whispered.

'Probably not, too much space in here, too little gas. But keep your mask on anyway. Come.'

Andrea moved smoothly down the hallway, with the confidence and practised movements of a combat-tested soldier. Fiero and Elliot were twitchier. They could barely see, and they were moving further away from the only light: the opening in the wall they had blasted. Until, ahead, a small neon light hung in the darkness.

'We are close,' Andrea said. Then there was an explosion of noise, and burning pain in Elliot's cheek. Pain such as he had rarely felt in his many lives.

Rifle fire.

Elliot touched his cheek, and the pain nearly caused him to pass out, but there was no bullet hole, he had only been grazed. Fiero and Andrea returned fire. A hail of bullets from their pistols disappeared into darkness, and then the rifle fire was no more.

'Got him,' Fiero said happily, lowering his gun. Andrea held up his hand, indicating that the group should stay, and edge down the passageway, towards the light, but out of sight.

An eternity passed.

'Come,' Andrea said eventually, his voice booming through the necropolis. And they did.

Elliot stepped over the bullet-riddled body of the dropped Igigi, but this time felt no remorse. Thinking of Professor Cove, and the room of Initiation underneath Santa Pressede, he mourned still only the victims of Andrea's gaseous lie.

On the left, underneath the neon light, was a passage that

took them left, and slightly down. Elliot could see the brick-work, illuminated by the cold neon light. Intertwined serpents, and eyes that never blinked.

'It's... so quiet down here,' Rock said.

It *was* quiet. An ominous quiet, not a peaceful one. A complete absence of life. A void.

'We must move quickly,' Fiero hissed, and set off down the passage.

The passage soon became a labyrinth, but it was clear that both Fiero and Andrea knew the way. They passed rooms, some with sealed doors, concealing dark purposes, others with no door at all. They made no noise. Andrea raised a hand sharply, and the group stood still. There was a shuffling noise.

Footsteps. More than one set.

Andrea hurriedly ushered the group into one of the dark rooms they had just walked past. Elliot and Rock moved further into the room. There was the shadow of a table, with manacles. Nothing else could be seen, in the darkness, save the grey of the passage from which they had come. Fiero and Andrea were poised, each side of the doorway. Rock was breathing heavily through the gas mask.

A pair of rifle-bearing men walked past the door. Andrea and Fiero shot out behind them. There was grunting and struggling, and then a clattering noise. But no gunfire. Rock made as if to walk out, but Elliot caught his arm.

'Wait,' he said firmly.

'Judah?' Yossef whispered, 'can you hear me?'

There was no response.

'They've probably got some kind of frequency blocker down here,' said Rock.

A minute passed in heavy breathing and fear. Elliot clutched the sack-cloth tightly. Andrea came back into the room, and beckoned Elliot and Rock out. Two men lay dead at Fiero's feet, their heads at sickening angles, their rifles cast aside.

'Igigi,' Andrea said, his voice clear despite the gas-mask,

'we need to get the bodies into the room.'

Elliot took the feet of one of the corpses, while Fiero grabbed the other end. Andrea and Rock did likewise with the remaining body. Elliot's Igigi was a great weight, even shared with Fiero. Despite himself, Elliot caught a glimpse of the man's face, pale, even in the limited grey light. Peaceful, and youthful.

How did he end up an Igigi? How did he end up damned?

With the corpses stashed in the corner of the open room, Fiero walked over to the rifles, and carried them back over to the corpses, and dropped them.

'Shouldn't we take them?' Rock asked, his high-pitched voice sounding almost like a whistle through the gas-mask.

'They have biometric data. Only registered users can fire them,' Andrea replied.

'We should take *that* though,' Elliot said, pointing at what looked like a security pass on a lanyard around the neck of the older corpse that Andrea and Rock had carried.

'Good thinking, they may have disabled Fiero's.'

Andrea grabbed the lanyard, and yanked it, so that it snapped, and came loose, then stuffed it in his pocket. Fiero motioned for silence, and carried on, the group following tentatively. He led them down a passageway on their left hand side.

'This is it,' Fiero whispered.

Past another neon light was a steel door. Andrea tried the handle, it was locked. He pulled out the security pass he had taken from the fallen Igigi from his pocket, and pressed the pass against the black box above the handle. The light switched from scarlet to green, and the handle clicked as Andrea pushed it down.

The room was cold and hard, a place of despair. Elliot felt chills as he stepped through, then warmth coursed through his blood when he saw *Yeshua.*

Two thousand years.

His friend and god was unconscious, shackled to a table. He looked pitiful, much as he had done in his trial, but so much smaller. Yeshua had been a man of middling height when Yossef had known him last. Although his height had not changed, the world had, and now he seemed almost laughably tiny, standing no higher than five feet.

He has suffered so much, is he still the same man? Am I?

'Yeshua, you must wake, now,' Andrea said loudly, then slapped the living god across the face.

Yeshua moaned, and stirred.

'Yeshua, my Lord, I...we have come to free you,' Fiero said.

'Yes... thank you,' Yeshua said with uncharacteristic coldness.

'We must work quickly,' Andrea said.

Elliot pulled out the saw blade from the cloth-sack.

'Cut his manacles!' Andrea barked.

Yeshua's eyes opened. Elliot started with the manacle around his left wrist. It was surprisingly easy to cut, and he was through it in about a minute.

'Andrea...' Elliot heard Yeshua croak beside him as he started on the manacle on his other wrist, 'you came, as you promised.'

'I did,' Elliot heard Andrea reply.

'Yossef...' Yeshua said, turning to Elliot, who paused. Then Yeshua smiled at him, a smile that cut through all the guilt and fear.

'What have I missed?' he said, in perfect English.

Elliot laughed. 'Who taught you English?'

'Symeon.'

The traitor.

The second manacle came loose.

'We must move quickly,' Andrea warned.

Elliot started on the manacles on his feet.

Fiero, who was stood in the doorway, fired his pistol twice. Elliot heard the sound of two bodies hitting the floor.

'More will come,' said Fiero.

And then, Elliot was through the final manacle. Yeshua sat up.

'Rock, grab the clothes from one of the dead Igigi' Andrea

shouted.

Rock jumped to the task, darting past Fiero. Yeshua was now sat upright. He extended his limbs, cracking them in the process.

'Ah, that feels good.' he said, then he studied Elliot's face.

'How many died for this?' he asked solemnly.

'Too many.'

Yeshua nodded, sorrowfully. Then he pointed at the gun Elliot was clutching. 'I have seen many of the men who guard me carrying such things, what are they?'

'Weapons. Powerful weapons,' Elliot replied.

Rock returned with a jumper and trousers. 'I couldn't get his boots,' he squeaked, tossing the clothes to Yeshua, who hastily pulled them on.

'No matter,' Andrea said, 'give him the gas mask.'

Elliot passed Yeshua the gas-mask, then discarded the now empty cloth sack.

'Thank you,' Yeshua said, with the sincerity that only he was capable of. 'What now?'

Yeshua looked so absurd, with his, oversized clothes, gas mask and bare feet, that Elliot wanted to laugh.

'Now?' Andrea said, 'now we run.'

The group ran back up the passageway, there were no guards to block their path.

'They *will* be looking for us,' Fiero shouted over the pounding of their feet.

The monsignor lead the way, moving with feline grace, and speed. Rock and Yeshua were barely able to keep up, and were nearly lost to the labyrinth, forcing Elliot to shout to Andrea and Fiero ahead.

'Wait!'

'For fuck's sake,' Andrea growled, but he stopped.

They passed back through the opening made by the Semtex, back into the Archives. They hurdled corpses, sprinted across carpet, and bounded up marble stairs. Andrea used one of his acquired security passes, to open the glass doors at the top of the stairs.

Still no guards.

They flew past shelves of history and lies. Then, the sound of bullet fire exploded around them, pages of books flew into the air, and began to drift slowly downward, like snow. The group took cover behind one of the shelves. More bullets tore through wood.

'Fiero!' Andrea shouted, 'how many bullets have you got left?'

'Five,' the Monsignor replied nonchalantly. Each Beretta held nine bullets, Elliot knew, and there were no spares.

'Hold them off with me Fiero,' Andrea said, 'Elliot, lead Yeshua and Rock through that vent down there. It comes out in the reception area.'

Andrea spun round the corner, got off a single shot, then ducked back. Elliot made to pass his, as yet unused, Beretta to Andrea.

'No. You may need it. Go, for fuck's sake. Go.'

'Your name will live on,' Andrea said, now addressing Fiero, and his hesitation, 'in history.'

Fiero turned to Yeshua, as though awaiting divine confirmation of Andrea's words.

'He speaks truly,' Yeshua said then, sounding to Elliot more stern, and less human than was usual, or natural. 'When I resume my godhead, you will not be forgotten.'

This seemed to harden Fiero's resolve. The Monsignor darted across the corridor, narrowly avoiding the flurry of bullets that were a response to his sudden movement. Then he spun back gracefully, and fired two shots.

'*Go*,' Andrea said, pointing to the covered vent where the wall met the ground. Elliot didn't need telling again, with all his strength, he pulled the vent cover free. He beckoned for Rock and Yeshua to follow him.

'Thank you, Andrea,' Yeshua said, with divine sincerity, and human pain.

Yeshua looked back at Andrea, then crawled into the

vent. Andrea replied by sending another two bullets at those that wanted them dead. Rock followed Yeshua, and Elliot crawled through.

Just get out of here, and make for the safehouse on Via Aurelia, where Judah awaits us.

They crawled through the vent, so narrow that had Elliot, Rock or Yeshua carried any extra weight, they would not have been able to proceed. With every burst of gunfire Elliot winced. They moved as quickly as Yeshua could.

'Those... *things*,' Yeshua said, almost to himself, but Elliot knew he spoke of the guns. He knew that Yeshua's gentle soul would struggle to deal with technology that made death so easy, so impersonal.

Guns sanitise the act of killing, disguise the damage that killing does to your own soul.

Finally, they reached the end of the vent. Yeshua pulled off the plastic vent cover, and crawled out beneath the reception desk. The startled receptionist froze, then made to run. Elliot aimed the Beretta, and shot him in the leg.

'Run,' Elliot said to his friends, as Rock stood up, 'run, and don't look back'.

The gunfire had stopped.

CHAPTER TWENTY-SIX

Isle of Wight, England
Month of June, 2024 AD

I have been hunted for so long, that I forget sometimes that those who hunt us are, or at least were, human.

-BOOK OF YESHUA

Tavarius sat at the head of the conference table. Behind him, his twin, mute bodyguards, Jiri and Josef stood either side of a large white-screen, on to which was projected a world map. To Tavarius' right sat the Chief Adviser to the Prime Minister of the United Kingdom, a small, wiry man with old-fashioned round glasses who was gaping in astonishment. To his left sat the Secretary-General of the European Commission, a stern looking Belgian woman with cropped, dyed-black hair, and the only visitor to have kept anything akin to composure. Pilate was sat in amongst the rest of the men and woman of power around the table: the CEO of Freiheit Bank, the Italian minister of Economy and Finance, and high ranking politicians and civil servants from the United States, Canada, Russia, Australia, and Nigeria.

All the visitors were members of Semu, the secret society tasked with bringing about greater centralised control. Control that belonged to the Annunaki. Control that belonged to Tavarius. For decades, they had worked under the direction of Tavarius' *Sustainability Agenda.*

They come to him, these men and women of power. Tavarius is at the very centre of the web.

All eyes at the table were trained on the water-likeness of Tavarius, a small Asian figure of perfect transparency, and stillness, that hovered three feet above the table, without a drop of water falling. Tavarius had conjured it from the jug of water directly underneath.

'Does anybody here doubt me, now?'

The silence that followed was intense, as though daring someone to break it. The hum from the air-conditioning seemed unusually quiet.

'Good... good... excellent,' Tavarius said as he studied the open mouthed astonishment and wide-eyed incredulity of the assembled.

'The world is changed,' he said, standing. The water-likeness of Tavarius fell to the table, splashing the shirt and tie of the CEO of Freiheit Bank, and the lap of the Clerk of the Privy Council of Canada, who had pushed his chair back in shock after seeing the water rise.

'You have all worked tirelessly, I know, to implement the principles of the *Sustainability Agenda.* I am not ungrateful for your efforts. But the *Sustainability Agenda* is now redundant. I now possess the power to accelerate the change we have all worked to achieve. Before we have had to work carefully, from the shadows, unable to draw attention to ourselves, working for the complicity and compliance of others. But we need do this no longer.'

The wildness had returned to Tavarius' eyes. The madness that Pilate had witnessed at Stonehenge.

He will happily burn the people of this world, as a child with a magnifying glass burns ants. Out of boredom, and with ease.

'I have, now, the power destroy the crops of entire countries, to send a tidal wave, to bring drought, or storms. There is no political force, no military, no man or woman who can blunt my power. The new world, the one you will help me build, my friends, is one of diktat. I will demand a single, unified world currency. I will demand the abolition of the independent nation state. All will answer to me. I will be an Emperor. Quentin,' Tavarius said, pointing at Pilate, for such was the name Pilate was known by in Semu, 'will be my right hand man. And you,' he said, looking around the table, 'will be my court.'

'Today, ladies and gentlemen, is the day that we move out of the shadows. But how to proceed?'

He paused, as if it were a genuine question, but no-one moved to answer.

'Well my suggestion, is that we proceed with an understanding, a global understanding, of the extent of my power. So I think that we should pick a country, and wipe it off the fucking map. What do you think?'

'You're... you're insane,' said the CEO of Freiheit Bank in that camp German accent of his.

'Oh don't worry,' Tavarius said, 'obviously I'm not going to pick Germany. Nowhere important. Somewhere small, I'm only making a point. Any suggestions?'

There was a deep unease around the table, as people looked nervously at each other, or their shoes.

'No suggestions?' Tavarius said cheerfully, 'ok, fine, well I was thinking Iceland. Any objections?'

The CEO of Freiheit stood, forcefully.

'You are insane. You do not wield such power, you cannot.'

Fire burst into existence around the man's head. The man screamed, a terrible sound that intensified until it seemed to fill the entire room. Men and women backed away from the burning man, terror and panic taking hold. Then as suddenly as it had appeared, the fire was gone. The CEO's face was blackened, his blistered skin wept blood. His eyebrows had burned off. He collapsed in a heap, making a horrible rasping noise, as though breathing were the greatest agony.

'Oh you'll be fine, fool,' Tavarius said calmly.

There was a knock at the conference room door. Violence flashed in Tavarius' eyes. He turned to Jiri and nodded. Jiri walked over to the door, opened it, and moved outside.

'You have proved my point,' Tavarius said to the room at large, 'power must be demonstrated. Accept the new order of things, or burn.'

Jiri came back in through the door. Though as expressionless as usual, there was... something... an almost imperceptible and uncharacteristic tension in the man's bearing.

Jiri hovered by the door. Clearly Tavarius had picked up that something was wrong, because he walked over to the door. As though it were an afterthought, he turned to Pilate, and beckoned him to follow.

AΩ

Pilate wondered how the job had fallen to the nervous looking young Igigi who towered over Tavarius, and still quailed beneath his glare.

Someone had to give him the news.

'Say it again,' Tavarius said.

The young Igigi swallowed.

'Yeshua... the prisoner... he escaped.'

Tavarius fiddled with the Kishar Stone in his hand. The Igigi winced.

'When?'

'We received word twenty minutes ago, I'm not sure when exactly it happened, within the past hour though.'

'How?' Tavarius hissed, 'how is it possible?'

'I... do not know. He had help though, it was a break-in. They had weapons.'

Tavarius turned to Pilate. 'The Ophanim. Who else could it be? I will make those fucking bastards pay. Why can't they just fucking disappear. Why do they fight us? Ready every Igigi we have at Ekugnuna, and have them ready to depart as soon as possible. How many Chinooks do we have there?'

'Six, at the moment.'

'And just the one here?'

'I believe so, Tavarius.'

'Have it readied. In the meantime, I want all Igigi that we have in the middle east setting up checkpoints at the great pyramids. Not one individual passes through. Make that understood.'

'You think they'll make directly for Egypt?'

'Yes. They'll want to catch us off-guard. But even if they don't, they'll have to head there eventually. He clearly intends to resume his godhead. But there is only room for one god on this shitty, fucking planet. Where is Symeon?'

'No idea. You didn't invite him to the Seru conference.'

'Fuck him. It's just us now, you understand. You are my right hand, the second most powerful man in the entire world, as once I was your right hand man in Judea.'

'Yes, Tavarius,' Pilate said obsequiously.

And how did that work out?

Tavarius smiled. There was no joy, only threat, like a baboon bearing its teeth.

'Perhaps this is for the best. A chance to put an end to our greatest enemy. I have the Kishar Stone, old friend. And we're going hunting.'

CHAPTER TWENTY-SEVEN

Prati District, Rome
Month of June, 2024 AD

I have become so used to the imbalance of the world, the wrong, the injustice, that when it is righted at last, I cannot imagine what that will look like.

-BOOK OF YESHUA

'There's a roadblock ahead,' Judah said through the communications device in Elliot's ear when they reached Via Fabio Massimo. 'Take the next alley on your right.'

This part of the Prati district was a network, narrow alleyways and tall buildings. More and more resources were being thrown into the search for the three of them, but according to Judah, they were still spread around the Prati district, and were not yet concentrated on any one particular area.

'This way,' Elliot said, beckoning Yeshua and Rock from behind one of the golden maidenhair trees that lined the streets.

They moved at a jog, Elliot was more concerned now about time, than discretion, and besides, with his diminutive stature, middle-eastern features, and bare feet, Yeshua could hardly help but stand out. But that was the least of it. Judah had told them that Yeshua was now the focus point of a city-wide hunt for an Islamic State terrorist, who had attacked Vatican City. The name Yussuf Haddad, coupled with an artist's impression of Yeshua' profile, was circulating on phones, tablets and laptops around the city. Yussuf Haddad was, Judah had informed them, the number one world-wide trend on twitter. They needed to meet Judah, and get out of the city before it became inescapable, as the Carabinieri mobilised more officers, more vehicles, and more roadblocks.

'Interesting start to your second coming, Yeshi,' Elliot said, picking up the pace.

Behind him, Yeshua was breathing too heavily to respond. His dirty bare feet slapping against scorching concrete that even Elliot could feel through his boat shoes.

'Okay, second alley on your left,' said Judah, 'then up the fire escape, and through the window, I will open a window on the fourth floor. Try not to be spotted.'

Elliot led them according to Judah's instructions. Rock and Yeshua struggled behind, climbing the fire escape. Clearly two thousand years of incarceration had done nothing for Yeshua's fitness levels, and Rock was adamantly opposed to all forms of exercise.

This... is real. Two thousand years of futility, and now, Yeshua is returned.

It was beautiful, and it was... wrong. That Levi, who had been so diligent, and careful with their finances, that Yohanan and Yacob and Symeon the Zealot, whose lives were characterised by sacrifice and suffering should simply... miss Yeshua's return. That Tau'ma would return with the Book of Yeshua complete, if not written. That all his brothers would return to...

Where? Yamaloka is compromised.

That they should return and the journey of their souls would be ended. But Filippos...

I cannot think of Filippos. What he suffers, again. This must be the last time. Yeshua cannot be recaptured.

One floor above them, a window opened. Elliot sprinted up, the fire escape creaking ominously beneath him, then pulled himself through the open window, and into Judah's open arms. Elliot patted his old friend on the back, then disengaged from the hug, as Rock's face appeared, rosy, sweaty, and fearful at the window.

'It is good to see you again, my friend,' Judah said to Rock, as Elliot's friend, and now brother, tumbled clumsily into the room, barely staying on his feet. Yeshua's face appeared at the window.

'Yeshua,' Judah said, his voice breaking, the depths of his emotions, usually hidden, temporarily exposed. Judah hurried back to the window to assist the man he had last seen nearly two millennia ago.

'You look like shit,' Judah said, as he lifted Yeshua into the room as if he were a child. Yeshua and Judah embraced tightly.

The room was barely furnished, just a couple of chairs with clean clothes stacked neatly on top, a desk with a laptop sat on it where Judah had been tracking Elliot's GPS equipped communications device, and a fridge.

'We've got to move, get changed, all of you, and quickly.'

Elliot, Rock, and Yeshua walked over to the chairs, and began pulling on clothes. Elliot's were easy to identify, being a good deal longer than those meant for Rock and Yeshua. Judah walked over to the fridge, and pulled out cold bottles of water, and tossed one to each of them. Elliot drank quickly, and splashed some of the remaining water on his face.

'Have you got anything to eat?' Rock asked, 'I think my blood sugar is running low.'

Judah grunted, and walked over to the desk, opened the top drawer, and pulled out a pack of biscotti, which he threw to Rock. Rock filled his cheeks, so that he looked like an overgrown hamster, then passed the packet on to Yeshua, who took one biscuit, and nibbled at it suspiciously. He spat water biscuit paste on the floor.

'That's so disgustingly sweet,' Yeshua said, gasping, 'how can anybody eat that?'

'We must hurry,' Judah chided, 'there is a net around this city, and it's closing in on us, we must slip out while we can.'

As Elliot was zipping up his hoody, Judah walked over to

the drawer, and pulled out four Glock pistols, two of which he passed to Yeshua and Rock.

More death. How much has this cost already?

Yeshua held the gun at arm's length, as though it gave off a bad odour. Rock was refusing to look directly at his.

'I have no need of this,' Yeshua said eventually.

'I wouldn't be so certain,' Judah said, 'we are in a war that we cannot afford to lose. We have already done things that run contrary to the essence of our souls...'

'All violence runs contrary to the essence of any soul,' Yeshua interjected.

'Yes, but more than just *our* souls are at stake here Yeshua. The whole world of souls is in jeopardy, you know this. You *taught* us this.'

Judah turned to Elliot. 'My brother, we cannot hesitate, there is nothing you must not do to get out of this city, to get to Egypt.'

'I understand this Judah, we have come this far, and there is no turning back.'

'Good. Will you stick with the Beretta, or switch to the Glock?'

The Glock, Elliot knew from their planning, was lighter, more durable, had greater bullet capacity and a reduced chance of misfiring, even though it didn't boast a traditional hammer safety.

'The Glock.'

'Good, show Yeshua how to operate them, then we move.'

Elliot turned to his god, and demonstrated how to apply pressure on the trigger safety to fire the weapon. Yeshua pointed the gun.

For two thousand years, I have missed him. This feels... surreal.

'Who needs the Kishar Stone when you've got one of these?' Yeshua said, his joking tone laced with sorrow. 'They make killing, murder, damnation, so easy. One movement of the index finger. These *should not be*.'

'Come on, we need to go,' Judah said, starting to lead them down the building's staircase and out into a courtyard below, where a maroon Land Rover Discovery awaited them. Judah activated the key fob, opened the left hand door, and hopped into the driver's seat.

'Daniel,' Judah said, 'up front with me. Yossef, Yeshua, get into the back, the seats lift up, and there's a compartment for you to hide in.'

Elliot hopped through the door, then offered his hand out to Yeshua, to help him in. Just as Judah had said, the back seats lifted away entirely, and revealed a space into which he and Yeshua could just about squeeze themselves, so long as Elliot remained in the foetal position, laying on his side, his knees tucked into his chest.

The Discovery was boiling hot, the black faux-leather seats above having absorbed the afternoon sun. When Elliot pulled the false seats above them back into place, he felt as though he couldn't breathe, and though not claustrophobic by nature, felt trapped, and on the edge of a panic attack. The vehicle roared into life, and Elliot's head felt like it was going to split with the noise. They moved off. The air was stifling hot, and it felt as though there was no oxygen.

I... can't... breathe.

Then Elliot felt Yeshua's arm touch his knee cap, and he immediately felt a little calmer. 'Remember your meditations, old friend,' Yeshua said in Aramaic. Elliot started to shut out his environment, focusing on his heart beat. The rhythm soothed him, and the beating gave him strength. Slowly, Elliot started to feel peace, the peace that came from connecting with the One Whole Consciousness.

I am one drop in the great ocean. I am one drop in the great ocean. I am one...

Suddenly the Discovery had stopped, and Judah was conversing in Italian with someone outside of the Land Rover.

'Is there a problem, Signor?'

Elliot couldn't hear the muffled response. There were two

explosions of gunfire in quick succession, and the Discovery sped off.

'How fast do these things go?' Yeshua asked, with a calmness that soothed Elliot's now frantically beating heart.

'Fast,' Elliot said.

The car started to slow rapidly, and suddenly was stopped. Judah and Rock were opening the back doors, and pulling up the false seats above them. Light dazzled, and then Judah's face was there, flecked with droplets of blood.

'Up, quickly, they will chase us now, we will have need of the guns.'

Elliot and Yeshua pulled themselves out, with difficulty.

'Rock, you drive!' Judah shouted. Rock jumped into the driver's seat, looking terrified.

He only passed his test last year.

Judah hurried to the boot, opened it, grabbed something, and when he sat in the passenger seat, Elliot realised he was holding the assault rifle he had been training with two days previously.

Judah hoped he'd never have to use it.

'GO!' Judah yelled, 'and open the windows.'

The Discovery moved off from the side of the road. Elliot could hear sirens in the distance. The electronic windows were lowered, and Elliot put his torso out of the window on the passenger side. Beside him, Yeshua did the same on the opposite side. Elliot pulled the Glock out of his back pocket.

'LOWER,' Judah shouted over the rush of wind.

Elliot lowered his head, and pointed the gun down the road. He could see the sirens coming up on them now, red and blue twinkles on top of two police cars, flying down the badly paved road, three hundred or so metres behind them. They were obviously on the very outskirts of the city now.

Behind Elliot, there was a burst of gunfire from Judah's assault rifle.

'Aim for the tyres!' Judah shouted, 'and drive faster Daniel!'

The police cars were closer now, no more than two hundred metres behind.

To Elliot's right, he heard two pistol shots from Yeshua's Glock.

'Aim at the tyres!' Elliot shouted to Yeshua.

'The what?'

'THE WHEELS!'

The wind, which had seemed non-existent when they had navigated the alleyways on foot, whipped through Elliot's hair.

Elliot aimed his pistol at the cars tearing up the broken road behind them, and with the ruthless accuracy that had made him a prolific wicket taker for the University of Oxford firsts, squeezed the trigger. The police car in the lead slowed, and turned, pulling into the dirt at the side of the road, allowing the other to overtake. A hail of bullets flew over Elliot's head, and thudded into the remaining police car. From Elliot's right, there was another brace of shots from Yeshua's Glock, and then the police car spun suddenly, and flipped onto its side, and then over onto its roof. Sirens continued to whine pathetically, and wheels span in futility.

'Good shot, Yeshi!' Elliot shouted, as the car disappeared into the distance behind.

'Next turning on the right, then follow the dirt path up to the farm,' Judah said, pulling himself in from the window.

As the Discovery juddered over the bumpy dirt path, Yeshua asked what it was he could hear. Something ominous.

Elliot put his head out of the window, and listened for a moment.

'I don't...'

And then he heard it. A police helicopter, the mechanical sound of death. A speck in the distance, but unmistakable, a tiny solid chassis, and blurry rotor blades.

'Look up Yeshi,' Elliot shouted, and he watched his god look up, and saw the awe on his face, something almost approaching terror.

'Shit,' Rock said, and put his foot to the floor. Elliot's head banged the vehicle's roof when they went over a bump. There was blinding pain, and for a moment he thought his head had split open. He put his hand to his scalp, and it came away wet, and red.

The helicopter Andrea had arranged was waiting for them in the field closest to the farmhouse. They jumped out.

'I'll talk to the pilot,' Judah shouted.

Judah sprinted over to the helicopter, and as he approached, the rotor-blades whirred into life. Then Judah was heading back.

'Quick, to the garage.'

As they were running up the path that lead to the farmhouse, they heard the decoy helicopter, Rock's idea, take off.

'Will he be ok, the pilot? Rock asked, between breaths.

Judah shrugged as he ran. 'He should be. Andrea chose a pre-initiate Igigi, a particularly nasty piece of work who kills for pleasure. Served as a mercenary in Syria.'

They reached the garage attached to the side of the old, dilapidated farmhouse. Elliot and Judah pulled the garage door open. They all jumped into the small red Fiat Panda that awaited them, a tight squeeze for Elliot and his long legs. Judah was in the driver's seat once again and he started the engine of the car that would take them on ten kilometres or so to Bracciano, where their true helicopter awaited.

CHAPTER TWENTY-EIGHT

Isle of Wight, England
Month of June, 2024 AD

Symeon was my brother once. If I cannot let go of my hatred, I may remain trapped in a cycle of reincarnation, even if Yeshua resumes his godhead. But my hatred runs deep, and burns bright.

-BOOK OF YESHUA

Symeon walked up to the Igigi who guarded the underground basement where Filippos was being kept. His name was Ivan, and he was a young man, whose taut, muscled body promised violence. The tattoos on his inner arm, a story of his bloody years as a young adult spent in a maximum security prison in Orenburg, Russia.

'I need to talk to the prisoner,' Symeon said, with as much confidence as he could muster.

The man appraised him, with barely disguised contempt. He seemed to be weighing up whether it was even worth his while answering Symeon.

'I have orders from Tavarius that none but he can enter,' the man said eventually, as though the words cost him energy and dignity.

'You also work for me,' Symeon said, in a voice that he hoped was forceful.

The Igigi scoffed.

A different tact then.

'I have a letter, from Tavarius.'

Symeon reached into his jacket pocket, and pulled out a handgun. He aimed at the man's panicked face, and pulled the trigger. Brains and blood splattered out of the back of Ivan's head, on to the door he had been guarding so diligently.

How many Igigi has Andrea killed? The large man I saw at Ekugnuna, the one who fled at Araboth, that must have been him. He was Annunaki, he went through Initiation. And then he betrayed the Annunaki, betrayed me. But... I understand.

Everything Andrea had ever done, Symeon reflected, had been for love. Though superficially this might have seemed like betrayal, just as it must have seemed to the Ophanim that Andrea had betrayed them two thousand years ago, Andrea always did what he thought was best for Symeon. Undergoing Initiation, damning his soul, Andrea was trying to release Symeon, and correct the mistake he had made. A mistake he had made out of love. And *that* was what was wrong with Yeshua's system. A man could be motivated by love, and damned for it. Still, what the Annunaki did, what Symeon himself had done, was merely postpone damnation. Humanity could not endure indefinitely, and to endure indefinitely was a punishment all of its own.

Symeon looked down at Ivan's corpse. He searched Ivan's clothing, and pulled out three keys. The door itself was unlocked. Symeon walked in. Though the lighting was poor, the little sunlight that permeated the small, high, barred window fell directly on Filippos' face, so there seemed something angelic about the man who was shackled to the wall, covered in blood. Symeon was reminded of images of Jesus on the cross on the stained glass windows at St Thomas', the Catholic church he had attended as a child. Back then, ironically, he had believed nothing of Christian doctrine. Thought it irrelevant, and false.

Well, I was half right.

How Symeon missed the days of David, the uncomplicated boy he had been.

'Which are you?' Filippos snarled.

'Symeon,' Symeon replied, and Filippos studied him intently.

'*Traitor,*' he said eventually, and spat bloody phlegm onto the floor, far short of Symeon's feet.

'A long time ago. Yeshua told me that he did not mean for me to be soul-imprinted, to be given powers. Did you know this?'

Filippos nodded, warily. 'What of it?'

'He told me, then, that my greatest strengths were also my greatest weaknesses. I was solid, and strong, and resolute. But I was also unbending, stubborn, wilful. "Cephas... Rock" he named me, as a *joke.* As if I would find amusement in this humiliation. I saw only the insult, and did not hear the words. But he was right then, and I see it only now. Like a rock, I do not live. I merely exist, and endure.'

Filippos said nothing, but some of the contempt in his hard face had melted, just a little.

'I never meant to cause you pain, or suffering,' Symeon said.

Filippos scoffed, just as Ivan had, moments ago.

There is no place in this world for Symeon Bar-Jonah. I have little credibility, and there is nothing left of my soul.

'I came to let you go, Filippos,' Symeon said.

'Why?' Filippos asked, warily.

'I... am tired. And Yeshua was right, this existence is worse than damnation. I cannot continue as Symeon. That man is dead.'

'Not dead enough,' Filippos said, studying Symeon's expression. 'What is it you have come here for? Do you expect... *pity*?'

'Yes,' said Symeon, matter of factly, 'from you, Filippos, I do.'

'From me?' Filippos hissed, 'after all that I have suffered...'

'Yes,' Symeon interjected, 'I know of your suffering. I know of what happened to you in Toledo, though I did not condone it. It was Tavarius' doing. But I did not stop it either. And therein lies *my* misery, my suffering. *You* live with the suffering that was imposed upon you. It must come down on you, like an avalanche, every time you reach maturity. And you walk away, again, and again. But... you have something to walk *towards*. I do not. I have the misery that I imposed on you. On your brothers. On most of the entire fucking world. I must live with the suffering that I chose. And I can do that no longer.'

Symeon began to use Ivan's keys to unshackle Filippos from the wall. He was free now, but he stood there.

'You made your choices Symeon,' Filippos said.

'I did. And I cannot unmake them. I cannot fix them. All I can do now, is *cease*.'

'Did Tavarius activate the Kishar Stone?' Filippos asked.

'Yes.'

'You have created a living hell, you know this?'

'Yes. But... there is something you should know. Yeshua... has been freed.'

There was a fire in Filippos' blood shot eyes then. Such a fire as Symeon could never again manage to stoke in his own, shattered soul.

'Tavarius hunts him. Perhaps he will be recaptured... perhaps not. I hope not. Go, now. There is a boat on the shore, waiting to take you to Southampton. I hope you can find some peace Filippos.'

'I have peace.'

'Then... I am glad. You must go now. Here.' Symeon handed Filippos a large, padded envelope. 'Money, to get you to wherever it is you need to go. And... the Book of Yeshua is in there. I read it, you know. It was Tau'ma who wrote it, I can almost hear him talking from the pages.'

Filippos inclined his head every so slightly.

'Tell him, when you can, tell him that it is... beautiful. That the truth is beautiful. And tell the others... tell them that I am sorry, and that I am nothing now. Do not let them be consumed by hatred of me, for their sakes, not mine.

Filippos gave another small, almost imperceptible nod of his head, and then walked away. At the doorway, he stopped, and turned. 'And what will you do?'

Symeon glanced up at the high window, and pulled a noose from underneath his jacket.

'I will hang myself. And hope that Yeshua resumes godhead. If he does not. I shall kill myself again when I reach maturity in the next life. Symeon Bar-Jonah is dead.'

Filippos merely grunted. But Symeon could see something in his eyes, even through the fire that burned there. Perhaps it was pity. Didn't he deserve some pity?

Filippos walked out of the door then, and did not turn back.

Symeon grabbed the interrogator's stool, and stood on it. He tied a strong knot around the bars of the cell's tiny window, and stood there for a minute, then placed the noose around his neck.

Damnation beckoned, he hoped. He kicked the stool out from underneath him. The noose tightened. There was panic, and there was pain. His body betrayed his mind, his legs kicking, desperately, in searching of something, salvation perhaps. His hands tore at the noose around his neck. Pain was all he felt. Life was choked from him, and then, he felt nothing at all.

CHAPTER TWENTY-NINE

Matrouh, Egypt
Month of June, 2024 AD

Symeon the Zealot likes to speculate on the state of the world to come when Yeshua resumes his godhead. His pictures are always idyllic. He forgets, I think, that Yeshua makes mistakes, even in godhead. He forgets too, that the world is populated by people, little gods. As for me, I think only of the escape from this world that Yeshua in godhead promises.

-BOOK OF YESHUA

They were in Egyptian airspace now, dark desert below them, clear night around them. The lack of landmarks seemed to make the journey slower. Sorrow tipped the balance, outweighing the fear of being caught, the closer they got.

We have liberated him. With Andrea and Fiero and their Annunaki ruthlessness.

It didn't seem real. The enduring nature and immensity of his millennial task was such a part of him now, that its completion might leave him feeling completely hollow.

They had talked, on the flight. Yeshua and Judah first. Experiences were compared, not to measure scars, but to help them heal. Yeshua had been Elliot's next, and Elliot had spoken of his grief. Of Qara's suffering, Chide's sacrifices, and of Miguel. Of the tiredness he felt now, and as long as he could remember. He had shown no tact, paid no heed to Yeshua's suffering, because after Judah, Elliot knew that Yeshua did not need it. Yeshua wanted to heal, not to be healed.

Soon, though, Yeshua would be gone, and it was tough to look past that. It was right, it was what the world needed. The world and One Whole Consciousness both were precariously imbalanced, and both could be destroyed as a result. But to be reunited so briefly with his friend *hurt*. And there was one question he had not asked. That Judah, too, had not asked.

Judah was piloting the craft, having learned the skill in his previous life. The SAR he flew now wasn't so different from the Kamov he had used to pilot.

'How far?' Elliot asked Judah, who was piloting.

'Fifty miles. We're close, old friend.'

So close.

Rock was getting to know Yeshua now, and the pair of them... chatted. It was strange, and made Elliot feel nostalgic, to watch Yeshua establish a relationship that was simultaneously superficial and profoundly deep. But it was also *odd*, seeing Yeshua and Rock interacting so. It felt like his nineteenth birthday party, when he watched his friends from Harrow who hadn't gone on to Oxford interacting with his law classmates, a jarring collision of worlds.

'How did you come to be known by "Rock"?' Yeshua asked, genuinely curious.

'My second name is Rockett,' Rock answered, 'it's a Huguenot name originally, it used to be *Rocquett* generations back. Evidently somewhere along the line my ancestors wanted to sound more British. But also, they call me Rock because I am Hard. As. Fuck.'

Rock flexed his puny muscles, and grinned. He seemed to take a particular pleasure in swearing in front of a living god.

'Yossef, I think your friend *likes* me,' Yeshua said mischievously.

'Ewww, gross,' Rock replied, with mock indignation, 'he's not my type at all.'

'So, who is your type?' Yeshua asked, clearly savouring the

conversation, savouring what remained of his humanity.

'Well, not you, if that's what you're asking,' Rock said

'Oh, that *is* a shame,' Yeshua replied, rolling his eyes.

'Yeshua?' Elliot asked with trepidation. He did not want to ask, but he had to, for Judah had not, and they might not have another chance.

Yeshua was silent, he looked thoughtful.

'Yeshua, we know of what they did to Filippos, for the short time they had him... what... how did you... are you okay?'

'You mean their attempts to extract understanding of how the Kishar Stone is activated?' Yeshua said matter-of-factly. 'Only the knowledge of what they did to others hurt me, Yossef. Whenever they tortured me, I receded fully into the One Whole Consciousness. Whenever they hurt, or killed, others, in my presence, I did the same. I only let the sorrow, and hurt, affect me later. I could not make the same mistakes I made before. I am hardened now. On the outside, at least. At one point, I was with the One Whole Consciousness for an entire century, while they plied my body with the worst imaginable tortures. And do you know what was extraordinary?'

'No...' said Elliot.

'I felt... lonely. I was with the One Whole Consciousness, and I felt lonely.' A long pause followed Yeshua's pronouncement.

'Why don't you look older?' Rock asked, 'you look no older than fifty.'

Oh shut up Rock.

But Elliot smiled, even a god wasn't immune to Rock's curiosity and impertinence.

'Being immersed in the One Whole Consciousness prevented my body from ageing unduly. I knew that a time might come when I needed to prove physically adept at tasks. Anyway, why don't *you* look any older? You said you were twenty-one, you look about fourteen.'

'Oh shut up,' Rock said.

'Shit,' Judah said suddenly.

His radar was bleeping.

'We're being followed. Six craft.'

'Fuck,' Elliot replied, 'can you tell what they are? What speed? Will we get there in time. Any chance this isn't the Annunaki?'

Judah studied the radar for a minute. 'They're not jets, based on their speed, but they are significantly quicker than us'.

They were flying in a civilian helicopter. The Annunaki, they knew, boasted Chinook and Puma attack helicopters in their arsenal.

'At present, they'll catch us about five miles short of Khufu.'

The pyramid where Yeshua can resume his Godhead. Our salvation.

They flew in silence, each plotting in their head.

'Have we got a parachute?' Rock asked at last.

'Yes,' Judah answered, 'why, what is your plan?'

'We send Yeshua down in a parachute, before they catch up to us. We distract them as long as we can. Yeshua can walk to Khufu.'

'Walk, across the desert, being hunted by helicopters? What chance would he have?' Elliot replied.

'Well he can't die, so a better chance than us. And we'll give him the blanket to avoid infrared detection.'

'We must act quickly.' Judah said, from the cockpit, 'Yeshua, what do you say?'

'I... see no other way,' Yeshua replied, tears in his eyes, 'but what is a parachute?'

'A large piece of material to slow your descent to a safe speed,' Elliot replied, 'it works a little bit like dandelion seed. You would float gently back to the Earth.'

'Then I have no need of it,' Yeshua replied, 'I will survive the fall, and this parachute would only make me easier to spot, easier to track.'

'Won't that hurt?' Rock asked.

'I am no stranger to pain,' Yeshua said.

Judah laughed. 'That, my old friend, is something of an understatement.'

'If we are shot down,' Rock said, his voice several octaves higher than usual, 'we'll be reincarnated right?'

'Your soul will,' Elliot replied, 'but Daniel Rockett, he'll be dead.'

'Unless we use the parachute?' Rock asked hopefully.

'Death is far preferable to being captured by the Annunaki,' Judah replied, 'we cannot risk it.'

'I could...' Yeshua interjected, 'I could imprint your soul, Daniel, so that you carry the memories of this life with you in the next.'

Rock paused. 'I... I would like that.'

'Be certain,' Yeshua replied, 'it is a burden, as much as it is a blessing. Judah and Yossef can attest to that.'

'I was forced to make the same decision with little time, as death closed in,' Elliot said. 'I would do it again, but the burden is great. Even death cannot part you from your regrets, your worst memories, and your mistakes. If all goes well, this will be for just one lifetime, Daniel, but even then, it can be hard.'

'If you are going to do it, do it quickly!' Judah shouted.

'I am sure. I want it,' Rock said.

'When I give you my blood, drink it, and say these words "I accept the Divine burden of remembrance."'

Yeshua pulled up his sleeve, and bit hard into his arm. Blood oozed where his teeth had broken the skin. He gathered the flowing blood in his hand, then poured it into Rock's open, cupped hands. Rock drank the blood, and said the words.

'I accept the Divine burden of remembrance.'

We are brothers now, not just in this life, but until we return to the One Whole Consciousness.

They flew on.

'Jump when I say,' Judah said, studying his radar intently. Yeshua moved to the door, and opened it. He turned, first, to Judah.

'For all the sorrow and pain I have caused you, I am so

sorry, Judah of Kerioth. If I could take it all back, I would. I will miss your friendship more than you could possibly fathom.'

'And I yours,' Judah said.

'Daniel,' Yeshua said, to his new friend, 'the divine burns brightly in your soul, may your next life bring you peace, and joy.'

Rock said nothing, but he leaned over from his seat to give Yeshua a tight hug.

'Yossef,' Yeshua said next, when at long last, Rock had relinquished his grip, 'you must let go of any guilt that you feel. The fault is all mine. You are one who has healed the world, not damaged it. What you have done for me, what you have *given* is truly remarkable. I will miss you, old friend. I *have* missed you. To lose the immediacy of your friendship... I have experienced no greater loss.'

'I... I will miss you too, old friend.' Elliot said, not bothering to hide the tears that poured down his cheeks, 'I wish you didn't have to go.'

'Me too,' said Yeshua, and then he jumped.

ΑΩ

The Annunaki caught up with them slightly sooner than Judah had estimated. Seven Chinook attack helicopters. Suddenly, a great sandstorm whipped up in front of them, assembling itself into a terrible image of Tavarius, as he had been, two thousand years ago.

'When our soul memories return,' Judah shouted, 'we shall meet at the Louvre, by Venus de Milo at midday on the first day the museum opens in the new year.'

The terrible sand Tavarius took a deep breath, then lashed out with a serpent's tongue, which wrapped itself around their helicopter. The craft was cast downward. During the descent to fiery death, Elliot, Rock, and Judah managed to find each other's hands.

CHAPTER THIRTY

I hit the desert sand with a thud, and my body crumples. The pain is immense. I am lucky, the breaks are severe, my spinal chord has been snapped, and my legs are shattered. I feel my body heal. Only superficial bruises and sprains remain. I stand, warily, my body is shocked by the immediate healing. I feel cleansing, sharp pain.

Behind me, I hear the threatening sound of the air-ships that have come to destroy. "Helicopters" Elliot had called them. *Spiral Wings*. I lay down in the sand, and cover myself with the blanket, the one that hides me from their sky-eyes. The night is still, but cold.

I forgot how cold the desert can get.

I feel that my body is ravaged by hunger and thirst. How I will miss this. The helicopters fly over, and past. Nothing happens.

They did not see me.

I reflect, savouring the humanity of such an act, on my hope. The Annunaki have directed their resources, their guns, their traps to the Great Pyramids. Misdirection and misinformation, two human skills in which I have proved to be largely deficient, have served their purpose. I can see the pyramids in the distance. I walk, and as I walk, I connect with the One Whole Consciousness.

I am one with everything, and I am walking through the sand. The hunger, the pain, the fear, are all there, but I do not feel them. I acknowledge them, and they recede.

Above, and in front of me, in the distance, I see a great

sandstorm form.

The Kishar Stone.

An image of Tavarius, as he was when I knew him first, comprised of sand, large enough to be seen even from this great distance, appears. I feel disgust, and hatred. The man who disfigured his soul beyond recognition, all in pursuit of... what? A lizard-like tongue of sand lashes out from the sand Tavarius' gaping mouth, and sends the helicopter in which my friends travel hurtling towards the ground, and death.

The pain in my soul threatens to stop me in my tracks.

I love all three of them. Yet more death and suffering caused by my failures.

And then, as I knew it would, the sand Tavarius turns on its instigator. The Kishar Stone was never to be used to kill, that was not the deal struck with Ki, the consciousness of the Earth. The sand tongue lashes out once more, and knocks one of the gunships out of the sky.

Tavarius' gunship.

I force myself to take one step, then another. I retreat into the One Whole Consciousness. Only there, and in the company of loved ones, can I find any relief from the suffering I have caused. I must walk on.

I walk. I walk. I walk. I am with the One Whole Consciousness, and I feel no pain. The sun creeps over the horizon, a sacral orange glow bringing extraordinary colour to this lifeless plain. It is a thing of dazzling beauty. I stare directly at it, until my eyes begin to water.

I walk. I walk. I walk.

I reach the Gaza plateau. I see a man and a woman, staring at me. I have just walked out of the desert. I am from a different world to them. I smile.

The great Sphinx rears up in front of me. The monument that marks the portal.

Salvation lies in my deception. That I did not trust even my closest friends with the exact location of the portal to my godhead.

The Annunaki, I hope, are concentrating their resources on the Great Pyramids.

There is no-one here. I am relieved, and I am terrified. To relinquish my humanity, to condemn millions to oblivion. I walk around the back of the great Sphinx, and I face the shaft that leads down to the portal.

Andrea, who shattered his soul to save me, will be damned.

But what other choice do I have? Souls must be able to settle. The system must be restored. Balance must be restored.

I cannot do this, I must find another way, some way of resetting.

I enter the shaft, and walk down.

I walk. I walk. I walk.

A few more paces, and I will relinquish my humanity, resume my godhead.

I step forward once more, and I am no more.

AΩ

I see everything, and feel less. But this is not like before. I am not entirely objective. I feel *something*. Something of my humanity has ingrained itself into my divinity. Traces of regret, of love, of compassion, of *hope*, have remained.

I see, what has become of humanity. The disregard for life, the brutality. There was always war, and suffering, but the *scale* of it. I would scowl, had I a face. How I miss having a face.

I see the souls of Rock, Yossef, and Judah growing in the womb. And I would smile.

I see the corpse of Tavarius, his dark soul fled to the unwitting, innocent womb of a gentle soul I recognise. Too long has this woman been settled, and captive here in the relentless whirlwind of reincarnation.

I see Filippos. A free man, the immediacy of his suffering gone, but the weight remaining.

I think of Andrea. The man who hastened his damnation for others. I would weep for his fate.

And then, as if proof that my humanity has carried with me, I receive an *idea*. Something outside of me, and I am *compelled* by it.

I must relinquish my godhead, once more. Temporarily. I must find a way of reclaiming lost souls from damnation. Souls damned, because they spent too long trapped. Souls damned because violence was done *to* them, and it put them on the wrong path. I must speak with the gods who minister to other worlds. I must find a way of forestalling damnation, without preventing settled souls from rejoining the One Whole Consciousness. I must try.

My compulsion will come at a cost. The neglect I have unwittingly bestowed on this world, the neglect that has so nearly destroyed it, I must now choose. I must relinquish my godhead and travel, visit the gods who minister to other, conscious planets. Gods who have done a better job than I, or so I must hope.

But first, I must leave some token, a message for those who took on the greatest burdens so that I might resume godhead. Some proof that I have not forsaken them, that their sacrifices were not in vain.

Another idea hits me. Something that Judah will understand, something Elliot, and Filippos, and perhaps the others, will understand too. I do it. And then there is no delaying. I can lose no more souls to damnation.

Had I a face, I would weep. I am uncertain, but I am compelled nonetheless. I am, it would seem, still human. I depart.

BOOK OF SOULS

Book of Souls, the sequel to Book of Yeshua and the second in the Alpha and Omega trilogy, will be published in 2021. Follow @thefranchapman on Twitter, or join the francis-chapman.com mailing list for updates and sneak previews.

FIND OUT MORE

If you have enjoyed Book of Yeshua, please consider visiting my website. You'll be able to read my blog and find out about progress on forthcoming works, get in touch with me with any questions you have, and sign up to the mailing list for exclusive access to free short stories featuring characters from Book of Yeshua, and offers on future novels. I hope to see you there!

ACKNOWLEDGEMENTS

Book of Yeshua would not have been possible without Leah, my partner and editor. Leah, I am hugely grateful for your ideas, scrutiny, meticulous editing, and total support. You are a fantastic editor, a wonderful partner, and my best friend. Thank you.

I am also hugely grateful for the invaluable help and input of Ian and Catherine.

Finally, I also want to thank you, the reader, for your support in buying and reading Book of Yeshua.

Printed in Great Britain
by Amazon